EX LIBRIS

The Girls from Corona del Mar

Rufi Thorpe

HUTCHINSON
LONDON

Published by Hutchinson 2014

2 4 6 8 10 9 7 5 3 1

First published in the United States in 2014 by Alfred A. Knopf, a division of
Random House LLC, New York, and in Canada by Random House of Canada Limited,
Toronto, Penguin Random House companies.

First published in Great Britain in 2014 by
Hutchinson
Random House, 20 Vauxhall Bridge Road,
London SW1V 2SA

www.randomhouse.co.uk

Addresses for companies within The Random House Group Limited can be found at:
www.randomhouse.co.uk/offices.htm

The Random House Group Limited Reg. No. 954009

A CIP catalogue record for this book
is available from the British Library

ISBN 9780091954192 (Hardback)
ISBN 9780091954208 (Trade paperback)

The Random House Group Limited supports the Forest Stewardship
Council® (FSC®), the leading international forest-certification organisation.
Our books carrying the FSC label are printed on FSC®-certified paper.
FSC is the only forest-certification scheme supported by the leading environmental
organisations, including Greenpeace. Our paper procurement policy can be found at:
www.randomhouse.co.uk/environment

Printed and bound by CPI Group (UK) Ltd, Croydon, CR0 4YY

For Simone

The Girls
from
Corona del Mar

CHAPTER ONE

The Best Tea in the World

"You're going to have to break one of my toes," I explained. Lorrie Ann and I were sunning ourselves in the tiny, fenced-in patio of my mother's house on thin towels laid directly over the hot, cracked pavement. We had each squeezed a plastic lemon from the supermarket into our hair and were praying to be blonder, always blonder, our eyes closed against the sun. There was jasmine on the wind.

In the narrow cove of our nineties California neighborhood, there was no girl more perfect than Lorrie Ann Swift, not so much because she was extraordinary, but because she was ordinary in a way that surpassed us. Her parents loved her, and she loved them. In fact, it was difficult to even get an invitation to their house, so much did they prefer one another's company to the company of outsiders. Even her older brother, instead of cruelly taunting her or running her over with his bike, shared his CD collection and advised her on her breaststroke.

Most of our parents had wound up in the sleepy ocean hamlet of Corona del Mar through a series of increasingly devastating mistakes. The Southern California real estate market, which had seemed throughout the eighties to have no ceiling, had suddenly crashed, and many fathers were now stay-at-home dads whose time was divided equally between the bottle and the couch, an ice pack over their eyes, as their wives scrambled to become certified dental hygienists. One girl, Miranda, had a mother who worked at Disneyland during the day and then worked all night from home as a telephone hotline psychic. "It pays better even than phone sex," Miranda reported one afternoon as we licked sugar-free orange Jell-O powder from tiny saucers. I remember too that they had four extremely aged rottweilers, two of whom had lost control of their bowels.

Mostly, our parents had assumed that life would be self-explanatory and that, bright and eager as they were, they ought to be able to handle it just fine. This faith, a faith in their own capableness, was gradually leaving them and being replaced, at least in the case of my own mother, with an interest in the occult and a steady red wine habit. Some have characterized the boomers as optimistic, but to my view they were simply soft and rather unprepared. They didn't know how to cook or sew or balance their own checkbooks. They were bad at opening the mail. They got headaches while trying to lead Girl Scout meetings, and they sat down in folding chairs with their fingers pinching the bridges of their noses, trying not to cry over how boring and hard life had turned out to be, as around them feverish little girls screamed with laughter over the fact that one of them had stepped in poop.

Lorrie Ann's parents were not losing faith, though. They were living in some other, better world. They went to church every Sunday. They rented classic horror movies every Friday night, and even Lorrie Ann's older brother, then sixteen, stayed in to watch, as they ordered Domino's and made popcorn in the tiny one-bedroom apartment all four of them shared. Her father, Terry, had an earring (a big golden hoop like a pirate's) and wore a black silk top hat to parent-teacher night. He was a Christian rock musician, and Lorrie Ann's mother, Dana, was a preschool teacher who collected gnomes: ceramic and wooden gnomes of all sizes and styles, standing on the floor and on tables and shelves, their backs to the wall, their dull eyes turned on the center of the room.

Certainly, it seemed to me, Lorrie Ann would never have been stupid enough to get pregnant in tenth grade by a boy she didn't even like, which was precisely what I had done. And yet, the spring I was fifteen, it was Lorrie Ann who came with me to get the abortion, who helped me to plan it all out. She had already turned sixteen and gotten her license, but I didn't just need her as my driver. I needed her, in all her goodness and her primness, to forgive me, to give her consent by participating in my scheme.

"Can't you just say you're having your period? Why do I have to break your toe?" Lorrie Ann asked, her eyes hidden behind the dusty lenses of my mother's borrowed sunglasses.

"Who misses a championship game because they have cramps?" I argued. Trying to get an appointment at Planned Parenthood had been a nightmare. There wasn't any way I could reschedule, and I doubted I could play softball the very next day. I wanted Lorrie Ann to break my toe so that I could show my coach a real and visceral damage. Also, in some strange way I viewed the breaking of my toe as the price of the abortion itself, a way of reassuring myself that I was still a decent person—it was the punishment that makes the wicked good again. Though raised entirely without religion, I was somehow Catholic through temperament alone.

"Just say you're sick!" she insisted.

"I don't like lying, and this is as close as I can get to making everything true."

Lorrie Ann looked at me dolefully. "You're nuts," she said. "You lie all the time."

"Yes, and I hate it. It'll be fine. We'll get drunk and you'll just do it."

It made a lot of intuitive symbolic sense to force the beautiful, pure, and good Lorrie Ann to break my toe and punish me for my abortion. To us, Lorrie Ann's family was magic, and this magic transferred to Lorrie Ann herself. It honeyed her golden hair and deepened the oceanic blue of her eyes. It made her upturned nose seem elegant, instead of Irish. It was what made it sweet, not dorky, that Lorrie Ann was the last girl in sixth grade to start shaving her legs. I think we all were jealous of those fine golden leg hairs, like a shimmer of fairy dust along Lorrie Ann's calves. Why did it look so beautiful on her and so ugly and shameful on our own stolid little shins? Why did Lorrie Ann look graceful in beat-up

Keds and shorts a bit too small for her? Why was it charming when she snorted from laughing too hard?

Yes, we were jealous of her, and yet we did not hate her. She was never so much as teased by us, we roaming and bratty girls of Corona del Mar, thieves of corn nuts and orange soda, abusers of lip gloss and foul language, daughters to sham psychics and newly certified phlebotomists.

And so, just after high school, when terrible things began to happen to Lorrie Ann, we were all shocked. It was like some bizarre postmodern rendition of Job. We were transfixed, struck dumb, without access even to the traditional gestures of delivered casseroles and decent silences. The story of Lorrie Ann became the thing stuck in our throats, keeping us quiet as we nervously chose careers and, with many doubts and superstitions, consented to marry the men we were in love with. (All of our parents had gotten divorced—how could we fail to be afraid? All of our parents except, of course, Lorrie Ann's.)

In a way, Lorrie Ann made me everything I am, for my personality took shape as an equal and opposite reaction to who she was, just as, I am sure, her personality formed as a result of mine. People do that kind of thing. They divvy up qualities, as though reality, in order to be manageable at all, should be sorted, labeled, pinned down. To this day, my mother considers herself the smart one and her sister the pretty one, even though her sister went on to get a PhD in marine biology and my mother became a makeup artist. For me, my friend Lorrie Ann was the good one, and I was the bad one. She was beautiful (shockingly so, like a painting by Vermeer), but I was sexy (at thirteen, an excess of cherry ChapStick was all that was required). We were both smart, but Lorrie Ann was contemplative where I was wily, she earnest and I shrewd. Where she was sentimental, I became sarcastic. Normally, friendships between girls are stowed away in boxes of postcards and ticket stubs, but whatever was between me and Lorrie Ann was not so easy to set aside.

———

And so, the following weekend, we had gone to the Planned Parent-hood on Nineteenth Street in Costa Mesa, I had gotten the abortion, and then we had eaten In-N-Out afterward. I felt ill enough that proba-bly I should have just gone home and curled up on the couch like it was a sick day in elementary school. A heating pad and a handful of Advil would have been heavenly. But I didn't want to admit that I needed cod-dling. I wanted to be tough, even violently blasé, about what had just happened, because maybe if I acted like it didn't matter, then it would actually matter less. When I requested In-N-Out, Lorrie Ann had no choice but to drive me there. "Are you sure?" she asked. "How do you feel?"

"I'm fucking aces," I said, and Lorrie Ann laughed nervously.

But after we ordered and were sitting on the scalding stone picnic bench with food that neither of us wanted, we didn't seem to be able to talk, and I knew that in order for us to be friends completely once more, I would need to find a way to let her in, to give her access to those cold and brightly lit minutes I had just spent without her.

"The nurse had kind of a mustache," I said finally. I was thinking about her face, hovering over me during the procedure—that was what they had kept calling it, "the procedure." The expression in her eyes was hard to parse; it was not pity, but it was not judgment either. There was no overt emotion, and yet her face was honest and open. Finally it struck me: the nurse was looking down at me in the same casual way one looks at one's own face in the mirror—studying it without any sense that the face belongs to another.

"I think she hated me," I said. "Or else she hated all of it: abor-tions and young girls getting them on Saturdays. Or maybe she was just bored. Maybe she was just bored during my abortion. That's weird, isn't it? That it can be the biggest, scariest, worst thing that's ever hap-pened to me, and for her it's just another day at work?"

"I'm so sorry," Lorrie Ann said, setting down a fry. She flicked her fingers to get rid of the salt. "I just keep thinking that I wish it were me, that I could have done it for you so that you didn't have to do it your-self." She was on the verge of tears, which was helpful. If she was going to cry, then I couldn't, and it was easier to comfort her than to comfort myself.

"It really wasn't that terrible," I told her. "They kind of keep it from all the way happening to you. They hide it from you. Maybe it would be better if they didn't, if you got to see, if you knew. But really, I've had trips to the dentist that were worse on a pain and ickiness scale."

Lorrie Ann looked at me, then laughed softly. "Fucking liar."

Afterward, we went back to my house, where my mother was annoyingly home and annoyingly drunk. What was most upsetting about my drunken mother was how sentimental she became. "I love you girls so much," she whispered as she tweezed our eyebrows for us, her own eyes filling with tears. "You're so beautiful."

I remember I was bleeding like a Romanov, going through Kotex after Kotex all afternoon, as she gave us facials, the one fan making a clicking sound every time it feebly rotated around the living room. I had to lie and say I had the runs to explain my frequent bathroom breaks and glassy-eyed distraction. I could feel Lorrie Ann worrying about me, and I kept trying to smile and shrug at her, mouth that I was fine, whenever my mother's back was turned. But the finer I claimed to be, the more frantic I became inside, which resulted in a peculiar, languorous anxiety.

My brothers, struck dead by the heat, lounged on the leather sofas. Really, they were my half brothers, progeny to my new stepfather, Paddy. My real father was off living some kind of glamorous car-salesman life in San Francisco, where I visited him annually, usually for two or three days, though we were often exhausted from trying to be nice to each other by the end of the very first day. My father never felt like family, not like my brothers. They were five and six then, naked except for their Superman briefs, their satiny tan skin seeming to glow against the black leather.

"This is an exfoliating serum," my mother informed us, slurring only slightly. She was a makeup artist for Chanel, and my whole life was a series of sample-size beauty products: tiny tubes of cream pressed into my palm as talismans against danger.

All afternoon and evening, Lorrie Ann and I waited: for our new faces to be revealed, for my mother to finally pass out, for my little brothers to go to bed (they still loved *Goodnight Moon* then—God, what a boring book! Good night this, good night that, over and over again). Finally, past midnight, Lorrie Ann and I snuck out to the small patio with the claw hammer.

I remember Lorrie Ann was chewing on her fingernails. Her mother, Dana, to discourage this habit, had painted them with a product disturbingly called Hoof Hands. But Lorrie Ann confessed to me that she liked the bitter taste and positively gnawed the polish off in flakes that melted on her tongue like battery acid, only to beg her mother to please paint them again.

"I can't, Mia," Lorrie Ann said, setting down the hammer and immediately beginning to chew on her nails again.

"Bitch, do it!" I shouted. We were both very, very drunk. My mother had been buying jugs of Carlo Rossi ever since my stepfather had been fired from the Italian restaurant where he worked. Supposedly, now he was going to become a hair stylist.

"I just can't," Lorrie Ann had said, starting to cry.

"Fine," I said, "you fucking baby." I remember that the night sky was clear, simply swimming with stars. And I grabbed the hammer and brought it down as hard as I could on my toe.

As to how I had gotten pregnant in the first place, I was one of what must be a magnificently small percentage of girls who become pregnant at the loss of their virginity. In my case, his name was Ryan Almquist, and he had insisted that the condom, when I asked for one, went on at the end. We were in his van, which smelled of surfboard wax and mildew, a combination that was not entirely unpleasant.

"At the end?"

"Yeah, dummy," he said, kissing my neck.

Since I knew that the condom's purpose was to catch all the sperm and that this definitely happened at the end, and was, in fact, The End of sex, it did not seem so improbable to me. Afterward, and especially after I realized I was pregnant, I was mortified by my naïveté.

I would have been angrier if I believed Ryan had intentionally deceived me, but I felt fairly sure he really was just an idiot. That was, after all, part of why I had chosen him to lose my virginity to. Lorrie Ann had been patient with me as I explained my reasoning to her, though I could tell she was not convinced: one of us had to go first, I argued, and it might as well be me. Ryan was (a) harmless, (b) hot, and (c) in possession of a van. Besides, he went to a different high school and so resulting gossip would be minimal.

"Don't you want to love the person you do that with?" Lorrie Ann had asked.

"No," I said. "Because what if it hurts and it's awful and you wind up embarrassing yourself and crying or bleeding or farting or something? It's better to do it with someone you don't care about at all."

"I think I'd rather do it with someone I loved," Lorrie Ann said softly.

"Well, that's an option for you," I said, "but who am I going to love with this black heart of mine?"

Lorrie Ann and I often joked that my heart was nothing but a small, dark stone, lodged painfully in my chest, glittering dully like graphite or charcoal.

"I don't even love my own mother!" I would cry out as Lorrie Ann collapsed in peals of laughter.

"You do too," she would say.

"No," I would say, breathless, laughing, "I really don't."

Years and years later, in Istanbul, I would still worry that my heart was a stone. It was Franklin, a visiting scholar at UMich, who introduced me to cuneiform, the very first system of writing ever invented, which was his subject, and it was also he who first made me wish my heart were made of something else: bunny rabbit essence, perhaps, or pixie dust and nougat, or just whatever tender flesh a regular girl might have.

I had not studied cuneiform before; my subject was classics, in particular Latin. But in the spring of 2005, we decided to try to do a translation together of the full Inanna cycle, a series of ancient songs that tell the story of the Sumerian goddess Inanna. As a classics scholar, I had come across my share of goddesses. In fact, I credit my mother's midlife crisis purchase of *Goddesses in Everywoman* for my later decision to study Greek and Roman literature and culture. I can still remember reading that peeling paperback in the bathtub as my brother Alex pounded and pounded to get in so he could use the toilet. I was fascinated by the gods: their amorality, their capriciousness, their bloodlust. But even in all my reading, discarded books littering my apartment like the carapaces of beetles, even in graduate school, those seven strenuous years of tugging myself slowly toward excellence, I had never come across a goddess like Inanna. She was a fucking rock star. She tricked her father into giving her all his wisdom while he was drunk and then gave it as a gift to her people. She married a mortal man and made him a king. And then, when she had it all, when the entire world was hers, she developed a hunger for death and insisted on traveling by herself to the underworld, where she was killed and then reborn.

No one had ever published the full Inanna cycle before. Her story was still unsung, waiting inside those clay tablets simply covered in peculiar wedge-marked script, the writing without punctuation or spaces between words so that it reminded me of the lacy designs on Ukrainian Easter eggs. Only small pieces of it had been published in papers all through the last hundred years, so in the fall of 2006, we received the grants and the funding and we moved to Istanbul together to begin the first cohesive translation of the entire Inanna cycle.

Before Franklin, I hadn't even heard of Inanna. Franklin explained there was a reason for this. When the fragments, which had lain undiscovered for some four thousand years in the ruins of Nippur, were discovered in 1889, the spoils had been divided evenly between the University of Pennsylvania, which was funding the excavation, and the Istanbul Museum of the Ancient Orient, which was allowing the excavation to take place. But no one was reading the tablets as they were being sorted, so they were simply divided equally and shipped off to their separate destinations. And so it came to be that half the tablets containing the story were in Istanbul and half were in Philadelphia, and no one alive had read the entire story.

So that's what I was doing in Istanbul: turning Franklin's rough translation into something Americans would actually want to read and falling in love with a goddess no one had worshipped in thousands of years. In our apartment building, there was a little girl named Bensu, which means "I am water." She lived in the apartment below us and was perhaps five, with a pursed plum of a mouth and huge, rolling green eyes that seemed fashioned out of lab-synthesized emerald, and a tongue that curled out neat little phrases of English or Turkish, as though she were a toy designed by a multicultural idealist. And because of the innocence I projected onto her, I was time and again surprised by the perversity of Bensu's whimsy.

"Just for a minute," Bensu said to me. "Just for ten seconds," she said.

What Bensu wanted was for me to stop in the stairwell, set down my grocery bags, and pretend to drink tea out of a plastic doll shoe. She did not have a tea set, and so she made do with the shoes of her biggest doll. She poured the tea into these shoes by artfully tilting a pincushion that must have belonged to her mother.

Some days I gave in, and some days I did not. But when I did, Bensu raised her doll shoe and smiled at me, her eyes twinkling. "My tea is very good, isn't it?"

"Yes, Bensu," I said. "What do you put in it that makes it so tasty?"

Bensu sipped slowly at the air inside the doll shoe. "That's a secret," she said.

"No fair!"

"Even if I told you the secret"—Bensu sighed, tired and patient—

"you would not be able to make it taste as good as I can make it because I make better tea than anyone in the world."

"In the whole world?" I asked. "Wow. That's incredible."

Bensu nodded modestly and sipped once more from her doll shoe. Suddenly and with great passion, she reached out for my knee. "Don't worry," she said, those huge emerald eyes glittering as though lit from within, "I'm sure someone will still marry you. Even though your tea is not very good."

"My tea isn't very good?" I asked.

Bensu shook her head sadly. My tea was so bad that it made her sad.

"It will be very difficult, but we will find you a husband," Bensu said.

"What about Franklin?"

Bensu knew Franklin, my boyfriend, who lived with me upstairs.

"I'm afraid he's been being paid off."

"Paid off?!"

"Yes, your mother has been paying him to pretend to be in love with you."

"Why would she do that?" I asked.

"Because she felt sorry for you because of your tea."

I never knew this kind of canny cruelty that lurks in even very little girls when I was growing up, half raising my little brothers, who were more like animals than children at times: perfect, golden little animals. Lion cubs. But even five-year-old Bensu was able to detect that there was something wrong with me that would keep me from finding a mate.

Was Lorrie Ann ever this cruel? I don't know anymore. I cannot say. I can only answer for myself, the girl who once literally spat in her mother's face, the girl who chose a boy to fuck because he was dumb, the girl who once, shamefully, kissed her two-year-old brother full on the mouth just to see what it would be like: yes, yes, yes. I was and am awful and terrible. I am sure I said treacherous things when I was five. In fact, I seem to remember informing a babysitter that our dog liked to hump everyone but her, and that it was probably because she was ugly.

And yet it was not me but Lorrie Ann whom the vultures of bad luck kept on visiting, darkening the yard of her house, tapping on the panes of her windows with their musty, blood-crusted beaks. "Wake up, little girl!" they cried. "We've got something else for you!"

CHAPTER TWO

Lost Worlds, Both Invisible and Physical

To be perfectly precise, I suppose I would have to say that tragedy began to nibble at Lorrie Ann as early as junior year of high school, though at the time it all seemed so glamorous that we were not able to be suitably sympathetic, but were, instead, almost jealous of her. A full year after my de-virginization debacle and ensuing abortion, Lorrie Ann's father, Terry, was killed in a motorcycle accident.

Because her father didn't survive the crash, and because the other driver (of a bright blue 1984 Toyota pickup) was drunk, it was never entirely clear what happened. "I didn't see him. I didn't even fucking see him!" the pickup truck driver insisted. He had turned left directly in front of Terry's bike, which was going about forty miles an hour—five miles under the speed limit. It was mid-afternoon. No one was clear on why the pickup truck driver was simply unable to see Terry, who was a large man on a large Harley. Even dead drunk, the driver should have been able to see him—the only vehicle in those lanes of oncoming traffic.

"I didn't even fucking see him," the man repeated to Dana in the hospital waiting room, as though these words could do anything for her. I was waiting with Lorrie Ann in that room, the two of us perched on chairs like nervous birds, ready to take flight. We did not yet know that Terry "hadn't made it." We were waiting for the doctor to come out, to let us know what was going on.

"Didn't even fucking see him." I remember the look on Dana's face as she regarded the man, still slightly drunk, presumably under arrest, but present at the ER for his own injuries. His attendant police officer, a chubby woman with dolorous eyes, wearing sharp perfume, shifted her feet as though to lead him away. But Dana only looked at him with the same sad patience as if he had been a child asking her to take a snotty Kleenex.

"I know you didn't," she said, with a kind of grace I knew my own mother would never have been capable of. My mother would have said something snide and then begun crying.

The whole family, of course, was devastated and mourned in the beautiful way that only perfectly happy families can. When Tori Stephenson's little brother Graham died of leukemia when we were in eighth grade, her mother had gotten drunk at the funeral reception and barfed in a plant. On the way to the car, Tori's stepfather, Rex, had slapped her, leaving a huge red handprint on her cheek.

Dana and Lorrie Ann and her brother, Bobby, did not barf in any plants, nor did they cry too loudly, nor fail to cry enough, nor slap one another, nor do anything except do everything just right. Lorrie Ann looked miraculously beautiful in her black dress—a simple cotton thing that managed to make her look almost freakishly long waisted, as though she spent summers performing in Cirque du Soleil. Her bitten fingernails, crimson and bloody, served only to show off her long-fingered, elegant hands. The black eyeliner my mother put on her made her look like a dwarf hotot rabbit, the pure white kind with black rings around their eyes that they sold at the mall, so shy they simply froze when you lowered your hand into their pen, their tiny hearts hammering with the fury of a kamikaze pilot's. Lorrie Ann was full of this same ferocious vulnerability after her father's death, which made it almost painful to look at her.

To be honest, I was insulted that her sadness seemed to somehow exclude me. I had imagined us weeping together, imagined myself comforting her. We had always shared even our smallest and most ridiculous tragedies with each other. Instead she was behind layers and layers of glass. It made me furious. I was sixteen; I had a little black stone for a heart; what more can I say? But Lorrie Ann had suffered a profound loss.

Terry had been, to a large extent, the raison d'être of the entire Swift family. It was for him, and out of love for him and his dream of being a musician, that they all scrimped and saved and shared the tiny one-bedroom apartment. (Lorrie Ann had annexed a portion of the living room behind some bookcases; Bobby had moved onto the balcony and slept in a tent out there even when it rained.) Dana faithfully taught pre-school, which paid badly, but was work she enjoyed, and Terry played as a set musician sporadically, but lucratively, and pursued his own musical projects full-time. They believed they were blessed to be so lucky as to do work that they believed in.

His band, called Sons of Eden, despite the name, did not sound particularly Christian. None of their songs even mentioned Jesus. Then again, they didn't mention sex, drugs, or alcohol either, which was remarkable in and of itself in a rock band. Terry didn't want to shove his religion down anybody's throat. He just wanted to be a decent man who was also a musician. It bothered him that so many rock stars were such revolting ethical specimens. Why on earth did people take a musician more seriously if he was loaded? How did that make his music more authentic? And yet it seemed to. Terry experienced every day this peculiar kind of discrimination. "Even if you're not loaded, try singing like you're loaded," a record exec had once advised him.

But Terry would not, and his crisp vocal annunciation and technically brilliant guitar playing allowed him to get small record contracts that rarely made any money at all, but did provide a creative outlet and some tangible proof for the family that all their sacrifices had been worth it.

I remember that I found it particularly maddening that he wrote songs for Lorrie Ann. We went once to a summer festival where his band was playing. It was a glorious day, filled with cotton candy and sunburn and corn dogs. Bobby's friend Tio was there, and I was convinced that somehow Tio might fall in love with me and decide that our six-year age difference was of no consequence. Both boys were indulgent of us and let us follow them around without making us feel like hangers-on. It was wonderful. And just as the sun was setting, Sons of Eden took the stage, and they started the set like this: "This song is for my angel, my little girl, my Lorrie Ann."

And then Terry proceeded to sing the most beautiful song I think I'd ever heard, with strange surreal lyrics I could barely follow wherein Lorrie Ann seemed to be conceived as some kind of barefoot angel that went around Southern California on the bus system, giving comfort to homeless schizophrenics and fat little kids and women who were afraid their husbands no longer loved them. The chorus went: "Get back into the bus, Lo-Lola / Get back into the bus, Lo-Lola!"

I had never been so jealous in my life.

And so when Terry died, an era ended for the Swifts. They went on living in the one-bedroom apartment. Lorrie Ann kept on going to high school. Bobby kept on going to community college, though what his ultimate plans were became vaguer and vaguer. But now they were all living in an untenable situation surrounded by far, far too many gnomes for no good reason. In a very literal sense, their lives had lost their music, their rhythm. Without Terry, they slowly stopped gathering for Friday-night horror movies or family trips to the world's oldest McDonald's, in Downey.

Perhaps the worst part of all this was that Lorrie Ann stopped singing. She had always been a talented singer with a sweet and natural soprano like one of those Appalachian folksingers. Her voice had a crystal-clear quality that made your heart shiver, as though the notes were all wineglasses falling but never hitting the floor. She had loved to sing complex harmonies with her father, and he had been teaching her both the six-string and the twelve-string guitar, at which she had shown tremendous promise. She stopped practicing entirely, as far as I knew, though perhaps she began again after I went off to college.

Everything was changing so fast. And Terry's death was just the first thing, the first *tap-tap* on Lorrie Ann's windowpane by those bad luck vultures. Over the next few years, more and more of them would come, bobbing their burned-looking heads, the skin of their faces red and raw and peeling.

In fact, the Corona del Mar in which Lorrie Ann and I grew up actually ceased to exist almost at the exact moment we left it. You can, of course, still go there now, but you will find only young women pushing Bugaboo strollers in Lululemon yoga pants, flaunting their postpartum tummy tucks. The playgrounds are swollen with little Jaydens and Skylers. The old bungalows have been ripped down and replaced with minimansions with two-car garages. More and more expensive restaurants serving "American cuisine" have opened along the highway, and boutiques have replaced most of the mysterious Oriental rug emporiums that once dominated that stretch of Pacific Coast Highway.

But when Lorrie Ann and I were girls, Corona del Mar was half empty, somewhat decayed, beautifully perfumed. Always there was jasmine on the wind, or the subtler, greener scent of potato vine, or the almost hostile peppery scent of bougainvillea. In every median and useless ditch, ice plant grew with frightening tenacity, and you could break off sprigs of it and write with water on the sidewalks, secret messages that the sun would dry to invisibility like disappearing ink. There were tufts of some kind of sour yellow flower you could chew as you marched along the highway, swinging your backpack on your shoulders so that it whacked you in a satisfying rhythm, on your way to the Chevron, where you intended to buy Dr Pepper but steal gum. There were hardly any cars, hardly any people. You walked around on sidewalks as blank and shining as drafting paper!

It was a distinctly unreal place, and I don't think any of us had any intention of staying. There were no jobs in the area; the houses were too small and too expensive. We couldn't picture ourselves making actual lives there. Even our parents planned on leaving, on moving somewhere more reasonable, eventually.

Still, back in the spring of Terry's death, we had no idea how quickly we would lose Corona del Mar. We thought, or at least I thought, that Terry's death was just another of the exciting things that was happening to us, a plot event planned out by the writers in advance to provide occasions for good dialogue and new romantic entanglements. I thought we were just a few digits off from being 90210, and, frankly, I resented the Terry Death Plot because it seemed to cast Lorrie Ann in the lead, and she was always cast in the lead!

When would it be my turn? When, when, when?

If my thoughts during this period were both predictable and disappointing, Lorrie Ann's were doubtless more interesting. I was given only fleeting glimpses into the labyrinth of her mind, and so was forced to piece together her inner world through inference and observation.

I already knew that Lorrie Ann had a peculiar predilection for the ethical. As a simple example, when we read *Little Women,* her favorite character was Beth. It so happened that I had read ahead and knew what happened in the book. (We often read books together, and I often read further and faster than she did, so that it became our practice to buy only one paperback copy, which I would then tear in half once I had reached the nadir of the novel, giving her the beginning and reserving for myself the end.)

"You can't like Beth best," I told her. "Pick someone else."

"But Beth's my favorite!" Lorrie Ann had insisted.

"You should like Jo," I said. "Beth's stupid."

"She is not. She's the only one who really cares about the soldiers and the war. She's always knitting socks and things. All the other girls are just kind of selfish."

I craned my head to look up at her. Lorrie Ann was sprawled on her narrow twin bed, which was canopied in a waterfall of fluffy mosquito netting and pink ribbons, her mother's budget version of every little girl's dream, and I was sitting with my back braced against the side of the mattress, facing away from her, so it hurt to crane my head to look at her. Her face was upside down to me, which made her mouth look like the mouth of a frightening monster, even though her teeth were nice and straight. (My teeth were not. They suffered from "crowding." I had had braces at one time, but then something catastrophic happened, and we were no longer able to afford it, and so I was given a retainer instead, which I promptly lost.)

"Beth dies," I said.

"No, she doesn't," Lorrie Ann insisted, sure that I was just messing with her.

"She does. Skip ahead. She dies." I was still craning my head awkwardly to look up at her upside-down face. Lorrie Ann bit her lip, and then—and this was such a Lorrie Ann thing to do, it almost made me sick—she said nothing.

"You don't believe me?" I asked.

"So she dies," Lorrie Ann said. "She's still my favorite."

You simply couldn't disabuse her of this kind of nonsense.

It was similar regarding the death of her father. Because she believed a number of untrue and contradictory things, her inner world began to have strange, Escher-like spatial contradictions that kept her going in unending and insoluble logic loops.

If there was a God, then life was meaningful.

And if life was meaningful, then things happened for a reason.

And if things happened for a reason, then her father was meant to die.

And if her father was meant to die, then there must be something she was supposed to learn from it.

But there was nothing to learn. There was nothing to fucking learn! Except maybe that the guy driving the pickup truck was a fucking idiot, loser, no-good piece of shit, who deserved to die for taking out one of the best men I have ever known and the father of a girl who deserved to have her daddy one day walk her down the aisle. I had fantasies almost constantly of finding the driver of that pickup and poisoning him or loosing bees inside his apartment or hammering an ice pick through his eye socket and into his brain.

I may have been jealous of Lorrie Ann at times, but she was mine. The Swifts were mine. He had no right to interfere with their lives so stupidly, so wastefully, so tastelessly.

Anyway, Lorrie Ann, during this period, began to worry that perhaps her father had been taken from them as some kind of punishment. If there was a reason for his death, maybe she was the reason. All of this is almost classically textbook, I know, but at the time I had read no such textbooks and neither had Lorrie Ann.

And so she became a vegetarian. She made a conscious effort to no longer gossip and refused to laugh at any of my jokes about poor Brittany Slane, whose downy, thin baby hair had never filled in and who would eagerly announce at the slightest provocation that she was a direct descendant of Abraham Lincoln. Weirdly, Lorrie Ann's new desire to be virtuous, however, did not extend to things like cigarettes, which she still smoked with me, Camels filched from my mother that we puffed behind the handball court at Grant Howald Park as we shredded yellow dandelion flowers between our fingers. In fact, I came to understand, the cigarettes were a form of self-abuse, much like a hair shirt.

It wasn't that Lorrie Ann was becoming a Goody Two-shoes. It wasn't that she wanted to be perfect or loved or approved of. No.

She wanted something much more dangerous. She wanted meaning. And she thought it could be gotten by following the rules.

For the rest of her life, Lorrie Ann would regret not breaking my toe for me. She would remember forever the way I brought the hammer down, too hard and too wildly, so that my baby toe did not just break, but became a pulp, its tender bulb split and flattened like a squashed grape, the concrete of the patio beneath it cracked and slick with blood. She would think: I could have broken her toe so much better. She would think: What failing is it in me that masquerades as pure-heartedness? And what was one to do if goodness was so duplicitous as to require you to wield a claw hammer at fifteen on a patio, serenaded by the barking of sea lions and the pounding of surf, just outside a bedroom where two little boys slept in a tangle on an air mattress, their golden limbs unblemished and soft as suede, their sleeping eyelids trembling with unknowable dreams, their very cells thrumming with the futurity of all that would happen to them, the men they would become, the things that they would want and do and fuck and know and taste?

These questions would become even more pressing for Lorrie Ann when two years later, just after our graduation, she discovered that she too was pregnant.

CHAPTER THREE

Decisions, Decisions

Really, what are the chances? Two high school friends, both getting pregnant within two years of each other. Both faced with the same difficult decision. And yet, I'm not sure I know a single girl from our hometown who did not, at some point in high school or college, go through this. No, we were not some statistical anomaly, but a disturbingly median norm.

Our health counselors had demonstrated to us how to put on a condom, and we used them. Except for me—I'm an exception here. But Lorrie Ann did. And the condom broke.

They never told us how often that happens. Or that sometimes the condom will get lost up there, like a snake's shedded skin, and you will have to get your partner, whose fingers are longer than yours and who has a better angle, to fish it out from where it has become trapped behind a corner of your cervix. We didn't even know our cervixes had corners! We certainly didn't know how to evaluate whether the men were telling us the truth when they said that "nothing felt any different," they hadn't known, they wouldn't have finished if they'd known.

And of course, Plan B did not yet exist. Our whole plan had been Plan A, and Plan A was condoms because the pill was retro and couldn't protect you from AIDS, which we were secretly sure absolutely everybody unknowingly had. We wouldn't have had sex with even a nun without a condom. It had been that firmly drilled into us.

And so it was that Lorrie Ann came to be impregnated, just at the tail end of senior year, by a young man named Jim Swanson, who was twenty-two years old and who had been her boyfriend all that year.

———

"Do you love him?" Dana asked with characteristic frankness, squinting through her navy mascara. Dana was one of those women who had begun wearing navy eyeliner and mascara in the sixties, found it suited her, and simply never stopped. Weirdly, we never judged her for it, just as none of us ever questioned the gnomes. These days, I am sure the sheer number of gnomes in their home would have occasioned some kind of reality TV show intervention, but at the time everyone thought it was perfectly normal.

Dana and Lorrie Ann were sitting on the wooden stairs that led up to their tiny one-bedroom apartment, eating Popsicles. This conversation and countless others were reported to me as we sifted through her various options that summer, like detectives trying to solve an unsolvable crime, scrutinizing blurry close-ups of unknown suspects taken from security tapes, analyzing again the word choice of our few witnesses.

"I'm not really sure," Lorrie Ann admitted. "But is that really the question?"

"What other question could there be?" Dana asked, nipping off the tip of her cherry Popsicle with her front teeth.

Lorrie Ann considered Jim. He had many admirable qualities. When he was younger, he had had terrible acne, so now, even though he was strong and handsome and well liked by everyone, he wasn't cocky and he never presumed. He loved his mother. He had an okay job as sous chef at a restaurant in Costa Mesa. He drank, but not so badly as to do anything stupid. He hadn't gone to college, but he was smart: able to make the fast joke, to read people, to train dogs, to fix cars. He was a good dancer. He knew how to give a compliment. He had an unfortunate tattoo: the name Celia in cursive script on his left biceps. She had been his girlfriend in high school. But he had plans to cover it up with a tattoo of a crescent moon, or else a line drawing of a turtle. He really liked turtles. There was a small sandstone statue of one on the windowsill in his apartment right next to his futon, which is where the impregnating had taken place.

The problem for Lorrie Ann, as she and I went over, and over, and over it, was not with Jim, but with the baby itself. In my estimation, Lorrie Ann was not in love with Jim. In her estimation, this did not particularly matter. No one, including Dana, was able to completely follow her on that one.

"But don't you learn to love someone?" Lorrie Ann asked. "I mean, what about arranged marriages?"

"Well, this isn't an arranged marriage, and it's your choice, and you're going to feel bad later if you choose wrong," Dana said. Her tone was not cruel. For a week now, they'd been having this same conversation every evening, and each time her mother had arrived at a different conclusion. One night, Lorrie Ann should keep the baby and marry Jim. Another night, Lorrie Ann should get rid of the baby and go to Berkeley. It was all terribly unclear. Part of what was making it unclear was Berkeley: the scholarship, the lure of San Francisco, the feeling of escape from Corona del Mar.

"I guess I'm just saying: he's a good guy, he loves me, he's willing to marry me. And that's a very different situation than if it were some one-night stand." Lorrie Ann scraped her teeth along her orange Popsicle, making infinitesimal amounts of shaved ice in her mouth.

"That's true," her mother said.

"And when Mia got her abortion," I imagine her saying, though of course she would not report this part of the conversation to me, and perhaps it never even happened, "I don't know. I always felt like she regretted it. I don't want to have any regrets."

Did I have any regrets?

I dislike talking about this, and I lied even to Franklin when he asked me about it. I lied right to his face as we lay in bed, glutted and woozy from too many banana pancakes on a Sunday morning in our apartment in Istanbul: "It was the best decision I ever made."

"No regrets?" he asked.

"None," I said, running a finger over the skin of Franklin's upper arm, marveling at the intricate mesh of his orange freckles, which covered his skin from head to toe. From across a room, he just looked faintly orange, but up close, the freckles were a world of pixelated detail that made me dizzy. I thought of the freckles as some kind of armor, fortifying him, protecting him from the world, a weightless and shimmering barrier, an enchantment.

But I lied to him all the same.

Did I feel the wrongness, the terrible violation of an ancient edict, when I lost that quickening inside me? Did I cry over the death of the child, whom I imagined would have been a girl, a daughter of the moon, like me, like Inanna? Of course I did.

Did I spend my time at Yale, yes, at fucking Yale, getting As in all my coursework, falling in love with dead languages, learning to become myself and the woman I had every right to be, did I spend this time mourning and regretting my decision? Of course not.

I labored for years to get into Yale. I was the president of the French Club and humiliated myself by wearing a beret that did not suit me at all. I lettered in volleyball, basketball, and softball even though I was short and not naturally athletic or even coordinated. I studied diligently for tests that were painfully, moronically stupid.

And they took me. They took me and I became who I became and the cost of it was a baby that never got to be born. That was the price and I paid it.

And yet when Lorrie Ann decided to keep the baby and marry Jim, everyone was deeply surprised. It was such a patently stupid thing to do. And Lorrie Ann was not a stupid girl.

As for why Lorrie Ann did ultimately marry Jim, her thinking pretty much ran like this:

The question was not, Would marrying Jim make her happy? But, Should one kill an unborn child? Or, more important, Should one kill an unborn child just because one has dreams of being a beatnik in San Francisco?

She decided early on that one probably ought not to do that. She felt instinctively that if she killed an unborn child in order to go have fun in San Francisco, horrible, horrible things might happen to her in retribution. After all, her father had been taken from her just because she had eaten pepperoni and laughed at poor Brittany Slane's downy hair. So then, if one couldn't kill the baby, should one give up the baby for adoption, or should one raise it oneself?

This was the main sticking point for Lorrie Ann. As she had been considering all this, she had looked up "children for adoption" online. There were hundreds of them, all black little boys. She showed them to me in the public library one afternoon. The descriptions of them were heartbreaking, and for weeks she was haunted by their nervous smiles. "Renaldo is eight years old and looking for his forever home. He has some anger management issues, but is seeking counseling and makes good grades in school. His mother is currently incarcerated, and his father . . ."

There were page after page of them. From this she knew two things. One: her baby would be snatched up because it was white. And two: there was an army of young black boys who were being raised in the worst imaginable way, unloved, unseen, angry, and poor. She wondered when they would rise up. She wondered if anyone else could see it coming. She wondered if she prayed for them whether it would actually do anything, whether they would feel it, on their worn-out mattresses, in their foster homes, with the fear running through their veins, under scratchy blankets and broken moons.

I hadn't known what to say to her, as we wandered, dazed by the bright sun, away from the public library. My instinct, stupidly, was not to go out and protect those boys, but to protect Lorrie Ann from knowing about them.

"How can this be going on? How can no one want these boys? Are they not human?" Lorrie Ann was literally pulling her hair. I guided her toward the window at the 76 station where I bought us 5th Avenue bars.

"The thing is," I said, "you can't do anything about it now, right? So better to work now, go to college, become someone who does have power, who can help. Right? I mean, isn't that the only way? Just—just—try not to think about them right now."

But where I was callous and intellectual, Lorrie Ann was all heart.

"I can't stand for her to ever feel unwanted like that," she said. (She felt instinctively that the baby inside her was a girl.)

"But you saw," I argued, my mouth stuffed with candy bar, "she would be adopted right away. It wouldn't be like with those boys."

"But don't all adopted children feel unwanted?"

"I don't think so," I said, dizzy, blinded by the white glare of the side-walk, by Lorrie Ann's perfect, smooth skin.

"Well, they should. They weren't wanted. They were given up. They're stupid if they don't feel unwanted." She began the laborious process of picking all of the chocolate off her 5th Avenue bar in flakes, which she ate separately. Only when the peanut butter center was completely nude would she begin to ingest it, and only then in tiny, butterfly nibbles.

No, she would not give the baby up. She just couldn't. She wouldn't. So then, if she was going to keep the baby, would it be better for it to have a father, or for it to not?

Having loved and lost Terry the way she had, how could she not want a father for her child?

Jim was a good guy, and so having him in the child's life would be a good thing. It would have been different if Jim had been less good, if he had been mean or sneaky, but he was decent. And she felt that it would be easier if she and Jim were married.

So she married him.

The day she finally decided, Jim was working at his restaurant, a small, fairly high-class Italian place where he had learned the word "amuse-bouche," which he loved to say, senselessly, over and over again into the skin of her neck to make her laugh. He was stupid and childish like that, and for some reason it delighted Lorrie Ann. He had called her because the kitchen had run out of baby powder. The restaurant was housed in an old converted private home, and the kitchen was not properly ventilated, and so with the fryer going and the stove going and the oven going, it was often more than 100 degrees in there, and the boys, from standing and running around, suffered horrible ball chafe and ass chap, which they attempted to combat by dumping loads of baby powder down one another's pants. Lorrie Ann was familiar with this practice (there was no hiding the white powdery stains on Jim's chef pants when he got off work), and so when he called her to say they had run out of baby powder, she had known that it was serious business and immediately stopped off at the Rite Aid to buy them a bottle.

She peeked her head in the back door of the kitchen.

"Your girl's here, Jim," the salad guy said when he saw her. She waved at him, showing the bottle of baby powder. "You're my savior!" he called to her.

Jim came around the side of the line and into the little hallway. "There's a beautiful woman in my kitchen!" he said, his cheeks red. Because of the stifling heat of the kitchen, Jim sweated constantly at work, which made his skin unnaturally clear and babylike. It also made him smell like mice, which Lorrie Ann had objected to at first, but which now gave her an erotic thrill. I disliked hearing about this, but it is also one of the facts about Jim I have been unable to discharge from my memory, even now, all these years later.

"I brought you baby powder," Lorrie Ann said. She was nervous about being in the kitchen, didn't know if she should step all the way inside, if she was allowed to be there. She didn't want to get Jim in trouble.

He took the bottle from her and set it on a rack, then turned to the salad guy: "I'm going to go outside and have a cigarette. I'll be back in five."

Outside, even the summer heat was a relief from the temperature of the kitchen, and Jim dusted off a cobwebby milk crate for Lorrie Ann to sit on while he smoked.

"You really are glowing, you know. They always say pregnant women glow, but some of them don't. Some of them get all pimply and nasty."

These compliments made Lorrie Ann shy, and she dipped her head as she laughed. Once, Jim had told her she had such pretty eyes and that they reminded him of Dentyne gum, "like if I chewed on them, they'd be minty." She found his lack of guile charming. "It makes the compliments mean more," she told me, "because he must really mean them."

"But," I had objected, "he's imagining eating your eyeballs."

"So?" she asked.

There was a silence between them then, both awkward and intimate. Lorrie Ann half wanted it to go on forever. She liked not having to talk. Sometimes her favorite thing was just to meet Jim after he got off work at eleven and lie on his futon with him, watching TV. Food Network, mostly, and sometimes Animal Planet. There they could just rest next to each other, two tiny worlds, separate but at peace.

"I don't mean to be trying to sweet-talk you," Jim said finally. "I really want you to go to Berkeley. I'll move, you know. If you want to just defer a year. Or you could apply to UCI. We'll make it work."

Lorrie Ann searched his face for any sign that he did not mean what he said. "My mom says that having kids is like getting a double helping of gravity," she said. "Twice as hard to move, twice as hard to get things done."

"I like your mom," Jim said. He did. Dana and he got along famously. It almost pained Lorrie Ann that Jim had done everything so right. Didn't he deserve to get what he wanted? Didn't he deserve to be happy? And he said his happiness would be in marrying her. This made the equation in her mind awfully unbalanced. On the one side of it was the life of an unborn child, Jim's happiness, and doing the right thing, and then on the other side of it was drinking coffee in San Francisco and driving up those scary streets so steep it seemed like your car was on a roller-coaster track. She had pictures of herself in the city: all the things she would do there, the person she would grow up to be. A life of bookstores and cut flowers and tiny glass bottles arranged on window frames and trolley cars and everything she wanted.

"I love you," Lorrie Ann lied. (Was it a lie? I never knew, exactly. I couldn't understand her love for Jim and so I made my peace with Lor's decisions by assuming her feelings for him were either feigned or a delusion, but perhaps they were not. Perhaps she loved him with the same animal part of herself that couldn't let that baby go.)

"I love you too," Jim said, "but you know that. Lorrie Ann, let's be honest. You could probably find a guy ten times better than me. But you won't ever find one who loves you as much as I love you."

And that was what clinched it. It was like a branch snapping inside of her, or so I must imagine. It must have been unavoidable, an almost physical fact, her decision. It must have been nonrational, or else I can never forgive her. How could it be that I wanted those scary narrow streets and books and coffee shops for her so much more than she wanted them for herself? But she stood up, and she grabbed him, squeezed him in his sweaty chef's coat in a tight hug. "Yes," she said into his apron.

"Yes? Like yes-yes?" Jim said.

"Yes," Lorrie Ann said. And then Jim reached his arms around her and squeezed her so that she was lifted off the ground, and he began jumping up and down with her pinioned to the front of him, screaming and whooping and hollering. He let her go and opened the kitchen door and yelled at the salad boy: "The most beautiful girl in the world has agreed to marry me!"

The salad boy came toward them, stuck his head out of the doorway. "You really did?" he asked Lorrie Ann.

She nodded, blushing.

"Well, shit," he said.

"Can you believe this?" Jim asked him, gripping the salad boy by the shoulders.

"You're one lucky fucker," the salad boy said.

"I am," Jim said, crushing the salad boy to his chest. "I'm the luckiest fucker in the world."

It was a bit rushed, since Lorrie Ann wanted to get married before she was really showing, but they managed to put together a pretty good party at the community center, where the surviving members of Sons of Eden played one last reunion show, and everyone brought potluck, and Lorrie Ann looked so beautiful that for a while there it seemed like maybe she had been right, and maybe there was something in Jim that no one else could see, and maybe everything was going to be wonderful. It was impossible to imagine bad things happening to Lorrie Ann. There was just something about her. I remember at the reception, egged on by Jim and the bassist of Sons of Eden, she sang an old Kitty Wells number, "If Teardrops Were Pennies." I shivered to hear her voice, a slender silver thread of sound in the heavy dusk of that California August, but as time kept unspooling and the years passed, I wondered if somehow Lorrie Ann had sung her own curse, had prophesied all that was to come.

In Istanbul with Franklin, when I was translating the Sumerian myth of Inanna, I would think of my old friend.

Inanna sings:

> *My father has given me the* me:
> *. . .*
> *He gave me the art of the hero.*
> *He gave me the art of power.*
> *He gave me the art of treachery.*
> *He gave me the art of straightforwardness.*
> *He gave me the plundering of cities.*
> *He gave me the setting up of lamentations.*
> *He gave me the rejoicing of the heart.*

Inanna sings on and on about the different *me*, a Sumerian concept that has no direct English correlative, but can best be described as a mode of being. While her father was drunk, she tricked him into giving her everything, all the *me:* the art of the woodworker, the art of the metalsmith. He gives her the art of travel and the art of the secure dwelling place. The art of kindness and of deceit. It was this that reminded me of Lorrie Ann. The girl had all the *me,* had been given herself as a gift, so that everything she did was absolutely hers and hers alone.

But I also wondered what happens to the songs we sing, even after we are done singing them.

Which is not to say that I approved of her marriage to Jim. I never did, and in all of her wedding pictures my eyes are like black, smoldering coals. I was so angry that at the reception I got horribly drunk and brutally fucked a boy named Garrett in his car, riding him in the backseat, my hand clamped over his nose and mouth, pushing his face to the side and smashing it into the upholstery so that he couldn't look at me.

The thing was: I was supposed to go to Berkeley too. That had been the plan, for both of us to get into Berkeley and move to San Francisco together. But I hadn't gotten in.

I had procrastinated. It is impossible as an adult to even reconstruct the kind of magical thinking that seventeen-year-olds are capable of, but somehow I left my essays for both Berkeley and Yale for the last night before the deadline. I had sent in nothing applications to UCI, Santa Cruz, and UCSD earlier in the week. Maybe their deadlines were earlier; I don't know. But I remember very specifically that I had one night to write the Yale and Berkeley essays, the two that were most important to me. (I had told no one I was applying to Yale, no one except the school guidance counselor, who told me I was wasting my time.)

I waited until everyone was asleep, and then I snuck out to the patio with my mother's pack of Camels and a glass of red wine, and I spent the next nine hours writing my Yale essay. I told them about the horrors of French Club, and the letters in sports, and the As, and the AP classes, and I told them that I had done all of this not because I wanted to make money or have a good career, but because I was sure that there must be, somewhere in the world, a place that I belonged, somewhere where I wouldn't feel like I was hiding behind the mask of my face, somewhere where my mind could stretch out instead of being shunted back inside me by the trick sliding doors of multiple-choice tests, somewhere where I could find peers, where our ideas could come out of us and form a kind of glowing golden mesh between us of shared mental energy, just like in Plato's dialogues, somewhere where what I was would not be a problem for anyone, where I wouldn't be a "smart-ass," or a "smart mouth," or a "smart aleck," but just fucking smart.

In the morning, I cobbled together something to send in to Berkeley, something that, evidently, wasn't good enough.

Maybe if I had been going to Berkeley with her, Lorrie Ann would have chosen differently: Berkeley would have seemed more real, had a stronger gravitational pull. Or maybe it was the shock of hearing I was going to Yale, the betrayal, that kept her from going. I still remember the afternoon I told her, breathless, having run all the way to her house and then straight up those wooden steps and into the circle of gnomes, the admissions letter clenched in my hand. I had profoundly misunderstood how hurt Lorrie Ann would be that I had kept a secret from her, and such an important one. The look on her face when I told her gave me the sudden jolt of stepping off a curb without meaning to. But applying to Yale had been as private for me as masturbating. In a weird way, it had never occurred to me to tell Lorrie Ann at all. But I was leaving her. Was it insane to think that my betrayal was at least part of what made her think it was such a good idea to partner up with Jim?

CHAPTER FOUR

A Miracle

At Yale, I began to drift away from her. Part of it was my inevitable involvement in the life of the college: I made friends; I started dating; I fell in love with translating Latin and Greek. (The elegantly playful way that Horace used the ablative case, the garish ugliness of Greek contrasted with the gorgeous things it said, as though butterflies were hidden in monstrous stone gargoyles!) Everything at Yale was so wonderful that I felt a perpetual impostor. It seemed sometimes that I was the only one who had routinely shoplifted from Victoria's Secret in youth and who knew all of the words to every song by Sublime.

But part of why we drifted apart was that talking to Lorrie Ann about her pregnancy and her life depressed me. Perhaps it was my own abortion that annexed any feelings of excitement that I might have had on her behalf. Perhaps it was that I felt, but could not say to her, that she had made a mistake, that she should have gone to San Francisco, just as I had gone to New Haven. Perhaps it was just that every phone call confirmed for me that Lorrie Ann was good and I was bad. I spent my days lazing in a boy's dorm room, eating microwave waffles and a can of frosting, trying to invent new sexual positions and discussing Catullus, while Lorrie Ann spent her days researching strollers and agonizing over which car seat to ask her mother to buy. I was growing tired of being bad and bored with her for being good. So this was what it was like to grow apart, I thought.

But when she called to tell me the baby had been born, I understood that we had not been growing apart but had only been becoming more equal and opposite, and through our symmetry had been becoming even more deeply connected. The baby, a boy they named Zachary, had been born blue. The birth had been bad. An emergency C-section. There would be a brain scan, but not until tomorrow or the next day, when the baby was more stable. She told me these things and then neither of us could speak and the phone was filled with the staticky hiss of Lorrie Ann's jagged breathing and my own high-pitched hyperventilation. Something in the universe was flawed and great masses were careening through space unchecked. I wanted so badly to keep this from happening to her, but it had already happened. It had already happened and nothing could undo it. "I'll be there tomorrow," I said, though I had no idea how, how I would afford a plane ticket, what I would say to my professors. I had not even come home for Christmas, that's how broke I was.

"Okay," she said.

"I'll be there tomorrow," I repeated.

"I believe you," she said. "You'll be here tomorrow."

As it turned out, I was able to buy a standby ticket on Delta with a combination of cash and a newly activated credit card, and I was indeed by Lorrie Ann's hospital bed the following afternoon. I had written all my professors a strange, overly intimate account of why I would be absent from their classes for the next two weeks and asked for mercy. What I had not done was do laundry, and so my suitcase was filled with dirty clothes, and somehow I could smell them even through the duffel bag in the antiseptic clean of her hospital room.

When I got there, she was asleep. There was no baby, no Jim, no Dana: just Lor, alone in her hospital bed. I had come with a pathetic bouquet of daisies I bought at the airport, forgetting entirely that I would be able to buy flowers at the hospital. Lor looked weirdly swollen. Her cheeks were chubby, her chin softly doubled, her lips so swollen the bottom one had a split in it. There were yellow circles under her eyes. Her hair was lank and greasy. Why hadn't anyone washed her hair? She was wearing a hospital gown that was, I was astounded to see, flecked with blood. Why had no one brought her a nightgown of her own? Or at least insisted on a clean hospital gown? I found a spare water pitcher in the nightstand by her bed, filled it with water, and did my best to fluff the ragged daisies. There were no other flowers in the room. When I saw Jim, I would deck him.

Except that when I saw Jim, he was in the nursery holding a tiny baby who looked exactly like Lorrie Ann, with tears of joy just streaming down his steamy, pink face. Not wanting to disturb Lorrie Ann, I had left the daisies by her bedside and gone in search of the baby. (Truthfully, it was only that once I had run out of things to fix or think about fixing, and I was left only to look at her, my Lolola, the pain of it was excruciating. I knew no answer to such pain besides action. That was what I had always done. Find your mother passed out in the bathroom? Pull her up and put her to bed, laughing to yourself because the tiles left a pink grid on her cheek, but for God's sake, don't think about it, don't dwell on it, don't allow yourself to fully know how terribly out of control your life is. It was best, in my opinion, to try to feel nothing at all.)

I was on the other side of the big glass window that separated the nursery from the hall, but Jim caught sight of me right away and raised the baby in his arms slightly, so I could see, so I could admire what looked like a perfectly normal little baby boy. Jim was smiling and crying at the same time in a way that made him look perfectly idiotic, but was also, of course, deeply touching. I had never dated a guy like Jim, a guy who was firmly "a nice guy." For the first time, I wondered what it would be like.

When he gave the baby back to the nurse and came out into the hall, he said, "Sorry, that was just the first time they let me feed him. They just took him off the IV. And the more he suckled at that little bottle, the more I thought: He's gonna live! He's gonna live! It's just been— oh, Mia."

He threw an arm over my shoulders as we headed down the hall back to Lor's room. "How's Lorrie Ann been?" I asked.

"A trouper. An absolute fucking trouper. She's doing so great."

I understood from this more that Jim approved of Lorrie Ann's stoicism than that she was actually "doing great." With his arm around me, I could smell the vague mice-smell Lorrie Ann had complained about. She was dead-on: he smelled like a hamster cage.

"He kept choking, but he got some of it down. They said if he didn't get better at it, they'd start feeding him with a tube, and we don't want that."

"He looks beautiful," I said. "He looks just like her."

Jim looked over at me. "That's funny. Everybody says he looks like me."

The baby looked nothing like him. He looked like a miniature version of Lorrie Ann. If he'd spent as much time perusing her baby pictures as I had, he would know that. "Well, of course he looks like you too," I said.

I began to understand that Jim's reality was highly dominant. Through his will, the baby was made to look exactly like him. And also through his will, what was obviously a tragedy, or at least a trauma, was transformed into a miracle. Their little boy had survived. Everything would be all right. That Lorrie Ann couldn't yet pee on her own, or even stand up, that there was a seven-inch incision in her abdominal wall, that she hadn't gotten to hold her baby for longer than twenty minutes, all of this was deemed inconsequential.

When we returned to Lorrie Ann's hospital room she was awake and there was a nurse at her side.

"Mia!" she said.

"Is this your friend? Do you want her to stay?" the nurse asked.

"Yes, let her stay," Lor said.

"You, out," the nurse said to Jim.

"Yes, ma'am," Jim said, and popped back out the doorway.

"She's gonna help me stand up," Lor explained. "I haven't stood up yet. I can't believe you got here so fast."

"All right," the nurse said. "I'm gonna put a pad down here on the floor because you're gonna gush, all right? And you, you take her hands."

"I know," I said. "I got the first flight out. I was lucky."

The nurse levered Lorrie Ann's bed all the way up, so that she was sitting, and then helped Lor turn and put her feet on the ground. I was given Lorrie Ann's hands to hold.

"Pull!" the nurse cried, then softer, but insistently, to Lorrie Ann: "You can do it, you can do it, you can do it."

Lorrie Ann's face was suddenly white and waxy, wet with sweat; she was biting her lip, but as she finally came all the way up to her feet she let out a yelp, a deformed little sound that seemed indicative of more pain than if she had been screaming. Her hands were squeezing mine so hard that our knuckles were white. She was shaking and trying to look down.

"Don't look," I said, and she turned her gaze up to the ceiling. Blood was running down her legs and pooling around her feet.

"Is this normal?" I asked.

"I'm just gonna wipe you down, okay?" the nurse said. "This is totally normal. Then we'll get you in the shower and your friend can help you get cleaned up."

"I think I'm going to pass out," Lor said softly.

"You're not gonna pass out," the nurse said, as she swabbed down Lorrie Ann's legs and folded up the pad soaked with blood. "So are you her friend? Did you say you flew in?"

"Yeah, I flew in," I said.

The nurse glared at me and made a motion with her hand to keep going. "It was an easy flight," I said, "but it was so weird to be in California again. It's snowing in New Haven. You know, everything feels so familiar that it's like I never left, and yet I've missed it all so much that it almost hurts to look at things. I was getting weepy just driving on the 405."

"You were?" Lor asked.

"Oh yeah. And I had the Beach Boys playing in the rental. I was a wreck. You should have seen me, you would have cracked up."

The nurse pushed the IV pole toward me after she hooked the catheter bag on. "Just make sure she doesn't get tangled," she said, and moved out of the way so that Lorrie Ann and I could scoot toward the bathroom.

Every step, I could tell, was its own agony, but she made it to the bathroom. The nurse had gotten the hot water running in the shower, which was really just part of the room, so Lor could walk right into the spray once she got her hospital gown off. As I was untying the little ties behind her back, Lorrie Ann said, "I've missed you."

I put my mouth against the back of her neck. "I've missed you so much it feels like it's crushing my internal organs." I could also smell the unique smell of her skin, which of course I had memorized deep in the cells of my childhood, but had not been conscious of until now: the smell was sweet, like baby powder, and faintly bitter, like Swiss chard.

"I'm so scared," she said. "I'm so scared that this is normal. That you can just have all your organs unpacked from your torso and a baby ripped out and then you are expected to stand up and take a shower. The surgeon wasn't nice. Did you know that? That they can just be rude to you right after they do that to you? It's insane. I'm on a lot of painkillers. I'm sorry, I don't know what I'm saying."

"It's okay," I whispered. "Let's wash your hair."

I helped her pull down the weird mesh disposable underwear and get rid of the monster pad that had done nothing to absorb all that blood but just sat there between her legs like a fucking sofa. I could tell she started feeling better when we got her in the water. She actually laughed when I first lathered up her hair. "This feels so good. I didn't think anything could feel good ever again."

I tried not to look at the staples that went up her belly like she was some Frankenstein office document. They weren't gory or anything. Really, it was their neatness that was upsetting, their inorganic regularity.

I got completely wet helping her shower, but I didn't mind. To feel the lather, thick and sweet in her long hair, to help her turn under the hot spray, to watch her splash her face again and again like a duck diving down underwater, to help her become clean so that no part of her was bloody or oozing, all of this was more intimate and more satisfying even than sex.

When we got her out of the shower, the nurse gave me a fresh hospital gown, and we dressed her, then got her into bed. She closed her eyes the minute her head hit the pillow. "I'm not sleeping," she said, "I just have to close my eyes."

"All right," I said, as I pulled her hair out behind her so that I could comb it out, "keep them closed."

"I'm not sleeping," she said again, just before she fell asleep.

"Of course not," I said, and kept combing.

The baby. Zach. What to say about the baby? He seemed just as much the hairless, pink neonate as any other recently born being. His legs were a little stiff, and his fists were always clenched, but most babies clench their fists. The stiffness would only get worse; Dana would jokingly call him the Christ child because his natural position was highly reminiscent of crucifixion. But when he was first born, he really did seem almost completely normal. The only noticeable, really noticeable, difference was that when he drank from a bottle he splashed and sputtered and choked and gasped and managed to get formula absolutely all over his face. But we all thought it was kind of cute. I don't think any of us really knew what was coming. Not really. Not even after the brain scan came back bad. The doctors kept making seesaw motions with their hands: it was impossible to know how completely Zach would recover. Some babies suffered massive traumas and grew up normal; others suffered seemingly minor brain injuries and wound up with debilitating cerebral palsy. In the face of such endless equivocation, Jim's reality became our reality: there had been a miracle. The boy had lived.

As to the details of what happened to Lorrie Ann, what had happened during Zach's birth, I didn't understand enough about labor and delivery then to ask intelligent questions and piece together what had gone wrong. I knew that she had been induced and that her labor had stalled and that then she had passed out and an emergency C-section had been performed. That was why her stitches went straight up her belly instead of side to side. The only hint I really had about how awful things had been was from Dana.

We were eating chili fries together in the hospital cafeteria. Jim was upstairs napping with Lorrie Ann. Zach was, of course, in the nursery. There was a lot less to actually do than I had imagined, and it was still only the first day. By day three, I would begin to feel completely useless. But at that moment, it felt profound to be eating chili fries with Lorrie Ann's mother in the hospital. Perhaps the word "profound" makes me seem immature or egocentric, but I was immature and egocentric. I was only eighteen. I felt like a grown-up in a way I never had before. It was quietly, tightly thrilling. I wanted so badly to be capable, capable of being Dana's confidante, capable of being Lorrie Ann's true friend.

"I swear," Dana said, "hospitals just weren't like this when I had Lorrie Ann and Bobby. Something's not right about it."

"What do you mean?"

"I just, I seem to remember my doctor being there for, not my whole labor, but definitely long stretches of it. Her doctor came only to perform the surgery. Otherwise, it was just this silly little nurse. Sweet thing, but couldn't have been older than twenty and not exactly bright."

I would find out later from Lorrie Ann that this nurse had been wearing shimmery purple eye shadow that reminded her of My Little Pony. The girl had been almost completely incapable of getting the fetal monitors that were strapped to Lor's belly to pick up anything. Every time Lor shifted in the bed, they would go offline and the girl would come and tighten, always tighten, the elastic bands. Lor had bruises and even small lacerations on her belly from these straps, that's how tight the girl had them, and still she couldn't pick up the baby's heart rate clearly. Several times an older nurse had to come in and do it for her.

Dana stared off into space for a bit, twisted free a chili fry. "It was like being in a nightmare," she said finally. "A nightmare where everyone is trying to be polite and doesn't know what to say."

For some reason this observation frightened me in a way that no amount of Lor's blood in the shower ever could.

"Poor Jim is ready to declare that asshole surgeon some kind of saint," Dana said drily. "Sweet boy, but—"

"A little eager to please," I supplied.

"Exactly," Dana murmured, then pushed the chili fries away from her. "Stop me before I finish these. Jesus, I love chili fries."

Perhaps the most disorienting thing about that trip was seeing my own family. I hadn't told my mother I'd be coming. In fact, I hadn't even really planned on seeing them. I hadn't thought about where I would be staying, having just assumed that I would be somehow needed at the hospital twenty-four hours a day. When Jim and Dana made it clear at the end of the first day that I should go "home," I began to wonder exactly where home should be. I knew vaguely that I could pay for one or two nights on what was left of the new credit card's available balance, but I couldn't afford at all the two weeks I planned to stay. The only sensible thing to do was go home-home, and yet I did not want to.

Though Lor and I had always joked that I had a stone for a heart, I knew really that what I was trying to describe was a profound fickleness, a weird detachment from reality and other people. I could love someone profoundly and still hurt that person mortally. I had to actively, consciously try not to hurt the people I loved. I was, in some sense, simply too free. It was easy to not tell Lorrie Ann I was applying to Yale. It was easy even, in a mechanical sense, to schedule that abortion and break my toe. It was easy to wash down Lorrie Ann's blood-crusted and bloated body, to gently soap her bruised hips.

But what had not been easy, even for me, was to leave my brothers. Every day I kept myself from imagining what might be happening to them. I trusted my mother to take care of them not at all. The moment my mind landed on Max or Alex, when I remembered something they said or did or a look they often gave, my inner self would leap back as if burned. I did not want to go home to my mother's because I was afraid that their clothes would be dirty, that she wouldn't be home or if she was that she would be passed out, that they would hug me too tightly and whisper-beg, as they had when I first left, for me to please please stay. If what was in my mother's house was too bad, I would not be able to return to Yale at all. I could leave once, but it would be beyond even me to do it twice. I knew all this as I pulled up in front of my old house in the little green rental car, which had an engine as high-pitched and feeble as an ailing mosquito.

But what I found was disturbing in a completely different way. I pressed the doorbell and my little brother Max, who was the oldest, answered. "It's Mia!" he screamed, and clamped his little arms around me, pressing his face into my stomach. Inside I could smell spaghetti sauce. There was a new lamp in the living room. My mother came out from the kitchen wearing an apron. An apron! When she kissed me, there was not even the smell of wine on her breath.

It turned out that without me, everything had been fine. They had been thriving. My belief that I had been the glue that was keeping our entire little family together turned out to be a complete delusion. In fact, they all seemed much happier and at peace than when I had lived there. Even the bathroom was squeaky clean, with a new and really lovely shower curtain, cream with pink and brown flowers, satiny and rich people–ish.

I could have cried.

The next few days were frankly a little boring. In the mornings, I would head to the hospital, where more and more I received the impression that I was actually in the way. I was rarely alone with Lorrie Ann, as Jim and Dana were ever present. Even Bobby swung by every day, bringing In-N-Out burgers or burritos for everyone. Eventually, Jim stopped me in the hall outside Lorrie Ann's room. "How long are you gonna stay?" he asked.

"I figured I'd get some lunch around one," I said.

"No, I mean in California."

"Oh, I'm here for two weeks."

"Two weeks?" he asked. "Wow."

There was an awkward pause. I could hear Dana laughing inside Lor's room, and Lor murmuring something that made her mother laugh even louder.

Jim blinked his round, wet little eyes. "The thing is, Mia, I'm not sure this is really the best time for a visit, you know? Lorrie Ann's trying to recover, we've got the baby to take care of, it just isn't the best time for, like, guests, you know?"

I stared at him. "I guess I don't think of myself as a guest, Jim."

"Ach! See now?" he said. "Don't get offended. Lorrie Ann knew you'd get offended. Listen, it's just that we think it would be easier once she's been discharged and we're home if it's just me, her, and the baby."

I had pictured myself doing things like grocery shopping for them, fixing dinner, taking out the trash, but I suddenly realized Jim was capable of doing all those things. He was, after all, a chef and could probably make much better dinners than I could. Each time I was faced with a bell pepper, I had to re-derive the best method of slicing it. What really hurt was that Lorrie Ann had been part of this decision, but had opted not to talk to me herself. "You do it," I imagined her saying to Jim.

"Okay," I said. "No problem."

In fact, it was better for me to go back earlier: less time to fall in love with my brothers and their micro-suede skin, less time to fight with my mother and her new domesticity, less work to make up at Yale, less money to spend on the rental car. But on the plane back to New Haven, I felt jilted. I knew it was irrational. They were a family. They should be together and celebrate their new son, who had miraculously lived.

It just hurt to finally understand that I was not part of that family, that it would now be Jim and not me that Lorrie Ann wanted when she was in trouble. I wondered whether the flight attendant would card me if I ordered a scotch. Beneath me, America was visible only as a series of gray and brown rectangles, innumerable and strange.

CHAPTER FIVE

Dead Like Dead-Dead

After Yale, I attended graduate school at UMich and got a dog by mistake. What I mean is, my first year I had a roommate who got a pit bull puppy that she named Space Cake and who then promptly disappeared off the face of the planet, leaving me with the puppy and her part of the rent to pay. Space was solid white, and her pink skin shone through her creamy fur, making her look like a piglet. Her eyes were pinky blue like a white rabbit's.

That dog ate everything nice I owned. Space devoured cell phones, designer sunglasses, shoes. She loved most to suss out and remove the metal fettuccine curve of an underwire bra. Her mouth was pink and wrinkly and wet like a vagina. It was like being the owner of a small, sensual monster. She would angle herself wearily, then suddenly flop, completely limp, into your lap. Her body smelled wonderfully of yeast, and in her eyes was a terrible knowing, as though with her bloody pink eyes she were saying that her fate was entirely in your hands and that she would surrender as willingly to violence as to pleasure.

After she had been mine almost the whole year, Space got hit by a car on Washtenaw Avenue near Carpenter. It was a busy street and one I usually avoided walking along, but on that night I was in a hurry to get back home and change so I could go out on a date. It was already dark. I should have been paying more attention. I was distracted. We were walking toward another woman and her dog, a mirror image of ourselves, really, and Space suddenly stopped as I kept walking and her collar pulled right off her neck. I felt the tug, turned to look, and reached out my hand just as she bolted into traffic. She was hit twice, but made it to the other side, limping badly. I could still see her even though it was dark because of her white fur. The headlights of passing cars were a strobe. "Space," I kept screaming. "Stay there! Space! Stay!"

But she didn't. She ran to me. She was hit three more times on the way, and the last time she was hit so hard that she skidded on her side maybe fifteen yards past me. The woman and her dog who were our mirror image were both frozen, watching all this, horrified. The woman had her hand over her mouth. She had very curly hair, the kind that is difficult to take care of without it getting frizzy, and it was undulating around her head in the wind. When I got to Space, she was not moving, but her eyes were darting wildly about. I dragged her by her ankles farther to the side of the road, and knelt beside her. I tried to lift her head onto my lap, but the bottom side of her face was missing. She began shaking in such a way that I guessed she was having a seizure.

"She's not dead!" I screamed at the woman who was watching us. "Oh God, she isn't dead!"

I would have given anything to be able to kill Space, but I didn't know how. How could I break her big thick neck? With what could I put her out of her misery? I had only an iPod and a house key. I had nothing. What was worse was how afraid I was to touch her, as though her body were dirty. I kept trying to make myself rest my palms on her body, to let her know I was there, that I loved her, but she was as foul to me as if she had been any anonymous roadkill, some infested carcass. She was still warm! And yet no matter how hard I tried, I could not keep my hands on her body, but kept pulling them back up and bunching them in fists under my face.

"My friend's dog just had puppies!" the woman with the curly hair said.

"I don't want puppies," I said. "What do I do? She's too big to carry!"

"I don't know. Can you call someone?" the woman asked.

But I had no one to call. Eventually, a kind woman in an SUV stopped and offered to give me and Space a ride somewhere. The woman had one of those windshield sun protectors that are shiny metallic paper-fabric and look like they should line the inside of a rotisserie oven. I tugged Space's body onto it and then loaded her into this woman's SUV. We were on our way to the vet when Space finally stopped shaking and her body became still. Instantly, the smell in the car changed. After a brief consultation, the woman reversed her direction and instead took me and the corpse of my dog to my apartment.

I had never before this understood the horror of death. I found poets and writers who wrote on themes of death to be slightly melodramatic. For myself, I looked forward to death. I was curious if there would be anything. If there would be a bright light or heaven or hell or nothingness. I thought it was going to be kind of cool to find out, and I had no worries that I would die whenever I was supposed to and that it would be fine. Before Space, I did not understand zombie movies either, or what makes vampires frightening. I didn't understand how very dead dead things were.

The night of Space's death, I called the only person I knew to call.

She picked up on the third ring.

"Hey, Mia, what's up?"

Quavering, I told her the story. "And now I can't stop seeing it happen in my mind, just over and over again. I'm not being melodramatic. I just keep almost seeing it. Do you know what I mean?" I could hear screaming in the background, child screaming.

"No," Lorrie Ann said, in a way that I could tell was not meant for me, but for Zach. "Listen," she said, "Jim gets home tomorrow in the morning and the house is a fucking wreck. It's insane. The sergeant on Rear D only called me like half an hour ago."

"Rear D" was the rear detachment, or the group of soldiers who were left behind on a deployment. Jim had joined the army during my last year at Yale, so by now I knew all the lingo. They were living on base at Fort Irwin in San Bernardino, one of the most remote and desolate of all army bases, surrounded on all sides by the Mojave Desert. Lorrie Ann spoke of this isolation often in tones that implied quiet persecution, by which I was completely baffled. Jim had not been drafted; he had enlisted. I didn't have a terrible amount of sympathy for the Jim-Army decision.

Purportedly, he had done it so that they could have insurance for Zach, whose CP, it turned out, was diagnosed as more severe almost every time he was taken to the doctor. By the time he was two, Lorrie Ann and Jim were several hundred thousand in debt. Jim earned too much for them to qualify for Medicaid, but no private insurance would take them. I'm not saying their premiums would have been inhumanly high, I mean the insurance companies were actually saying no. Jim's restaurant, being privately owned, didn't offer any insurance to their employees. So he and Lorrie Ann were up shit creek, until Jim got the brilliant idea of joining the army.

If you asked Lorrie Ann, he'd practically martyred himself on behalf of their miserable little family, but, truthfully, he could have just gotten a full-time job with a corporate restaurant that offered its employees insurance. Hell, he could have gotten a job at Starbucks! (Lorrie Ann became so violently upset with me when I suggested this that I could hear the spittle flying from her mouth even over the phone, as she went on and on about how good the army insurance was and how the army was taking care of them and how cheap food was on base and their free housing and how naive it was of me to compare it to working at Star-bucks. Yes, I wanted to say, but Starbucks doesn't ask you to kill people. But I didn't say that—how could I?)

In the end, I suspected, Jim joined the army because it seemed like it would be exciting, noble, violent, and also get him away from their claustrophobic little house, where Zach was refusing more and more to live up to Jim's hopes for him, and where Lorrie Ann was slowly trans-forming into some kind of dim-witted saint. She had begun blogging. I'm not kidding. Lorrie Ann had begun blogging a terrifying admixture of casserole recipes, updates on Zach's surgeries, and weird poems that alleged that Zach was an angel sent from the Lord to teach her and Jim about the beauty of sacrifice. Some days it was just a creepy one-liner: *Zach's life is more important for those around him than it is for himself.*

"I'm sorry," I said to Lorrie Ann. "I just really needed someone to talk to." Space's body was on my balcony. What to do with it? In the morning I supposed I would call the vet and see if they did cremations or if I needed to call Animal Control. I had never dealt with an animal's dead body in a legitimate way. When our pets died when I was a child, my mom would have us put the body in a cardboard box and drive around until we found a construction site with a Dumpster.

"I know," she said, "I know, it's hard when a pet dies."

"But if you don't have time . . ." I trailed off, shamelessly trying to guilt her into talking to me. She was my only friend! Actually, I had made many friends at Yale, even at UMich, but they were have-a-drink-at-the-pub friends, not my-dog-is-dead-on-the-balcony friends.

Lorrie Ann sighed. "Mia," she said. "I know you really don't want to hear this, but . . . it's just a dog. I know it feels like this big profound thing right now, the nature of mortality and all that, but it only feels big and profound because it just happened, like just now. It won't feel like such a big deal tomorrow, and in a couple of months it won't seem like a big deal at all. So, just, you know, like, have a drink and rent a movie or something."

I am sure that my eyes bugged cartoonishly out of my head. Lorrie Ann had never, not ever, said anything so cold to me before. Lorrie Ann was always nice—that was her role, to be caring and sweet and kind and call me Mia-Bear. What was even worse was that what she said reverberated with the chilling, metallic ring of truth. I would remember forever what Space's dead body felt like in my arms, but eventually the experience would shrink until it fit in line with the other events in my life.

"I've gotta go," she said. "Sorry for being such a bummer."

When Jim was killed during his second tour, I was in Rome on vacation. One of my Latin professors was married to a woman whose family was deeply connected to the Vatican and somehow he had gotten me reading privileges at the Vatican library, and had even arranged an adorable, if decaying, flat off the Piazza Barberini.

It was Dana who called to tell me.

"The funeral is next week," she said. "And, of course, you're welcome to stay with us or with Lorrie Ann. Your mama moved out to Fontana, didn't she?"

I hesitated. I had only two more weeks in Rome. I didn't particularly want to take a week and fly all the way back to California. More practically, such a last-minute international ticket would be insanely expensive, and I was a graduate student. I'd had to beg my father for the money to come to Rome in the first place.

"I don't know if I can make it," I said. "I'm in Rome."

"I know you're in Rome. How on earth do you think I called you?"

"Right," I said. Just then a strip of wallpaper came unglued and peeled down in my living room, making a thick, wet unsticking sound. I watched it sway, dangling from the wall across from me. "I just, it was a really big deal that my professor set this up, and I don't really know them well enough to explain, you know, and I don't want him to think I'm jerking him around, and on top of that, you know, I actually don't know if I'll have the money for a ticket."

"I'll pay for your ticket," Dana said.

That stumped me. It wasn't just that I didn't want to return to California for Jim's funeral—I somehow already knew I wasn't going to.

"Okay," I said. "But that feels like too much. That's too generous."

"Don't be silly," she said. "I'll have Bobby go online tonight."

In what was the middle of the night my time, Dana called back to say that she'd had no idea what a flight from Rome to LA would run, and that she was sorry—she just couldn't do it.

"Don't worry," I told her. "I kind of figured. Last-minute flights are crazy expensive."

"I know you never liked him," Dana said, "but he was a good boy."

It was three in the morning and I hadn't clicked on a light when I picked up the phone. I blinked in the darkness. "I know. He was a really good guy," I said.

"He loved her," Dana said, her voice trembling. "And he loved that little boy."

"I know he did."

"Well, good night," she said. "It'd be nice if you called Lor."

"Of course," I said. "I didn't know if she was . . . ready to talk, or—"

"She's ready," Dana said and hung up.

Once I was off the phone, my eyes adjusted slightly to the darkness and I felt less disoriented, able to make out the faint outline of my white curtains, the curling brass bed frame, the black ceramic lamp on the table. A wave of relief washed over me. I would not have to go. I would not have to eat tiny weenies swimming in barbecue sauce. I would not have to hug the other army wives who had been brainwashed to accept such happenings and who would whisper to me, "She's got strong shoulders." And most of all, I would not have to stand there like an idiot as Lor became more and more distant from me, sealed off behind the plate glass of grief. I knew that I should go, that I should find a way to go.

But instead, the following day I stayed in the apartment drinking two bottles of wine and then went out around dusk and ate so much gelato that I made myself sick.

I called Lor the next day, but I only got her voice mail. She didn't call me back. I figured that she was busy, bereft, any number of things. I called again once I was back in the States, and again she didn't return the call. I knew then that she was angry at me, cold, frozen angry with me, for not coming to the funeral. I wrote her a long, long e-mail, apologizing, trying to explain, and she wrote me back a clipped one. It was fine; she understood. But I knew it wasn't fine and she didn't understand. Who could understand? I had behaved terribly. Even I knew that.

So the following Christmas, I made it a point to visit her.

She was living in Costa Mesa. After Jim's death, almost all the "death gratuity" (such a creepy phrase!) had gone to collections, and though she would receive another $400,000 over the coming years, she had already signed this money over to the collections agencies in a settlement that would leave her broke but finally debt-free. She was allowed to continue living on base for only six months after Jim's death, and it was Zach's social worker, Mr. Kawabata, who had come to their rescue and found them a place to stay, a complex with specially prorated rent for people on disability.

At first I had been amazed, because the location was really good, convenient and in a nice area, but as I parked and walked to her door, I began to understand that this was a sad place. There were plants on the porches, but they were dying plants. There were tiny hibachi barbecues moldering and filled with pools of rainwater. There were sun-bleached and dirty American flags hanging limply from mini flagpoles flaking with chipped paint. Several dogs barked at me as I made my way to her door.

As I waited on the stoop, having rung the doorbell, in that tense moment before the flurry of kisses and hugs and meaningless compliments, I realized for the first time that Jim was dead. His being dead became real to me. I had known, obviously; I had even cried about it, thinking those two bottles of wine and bucket of gelato were somehow my tribute to him. But he had never seemed deader than in that moment before that door was about to open. Dead the way Space had been dead. Really and truly dead. My heart began to race. My friend had been living here, all this time, with Jim dead, with a disabled child, with no money. How alone Lorrie Ann had been through all of this stunned me. My own selfishness in failing to be there for her was overwhelming and made me close my eyes the way one does to get through a passing wave of nausea.

When Lorrie Ann opened the door, her smile huge and open and absolutely the way I remembered it, I suddenly smelled pot smoke. We hugged and she invited me in, gesturing to a couch that was already inhabited by a Middle Eastern–looking man crouched before a large bong. He was missing both his legs from the knee down and in their place were fascinating mechanical contraptions that looked as if they had been designed by NASA. I wouldn't have been surprised if he could leap over cars and ponies, so impressive did they look. He had waist-length black hair hanging loose that shone like a dark mirror, and a thick silver chain around his neck, from which a miniature silver skeleton dangled. Zach's wheelchair was in the corner, arranged as though it were an easy chair placed there to complement the sofa. I couldn't take my eyes off him—Zach was beautiful. He had Lorrie Ann's nose, upturned and elfin, her oceanic eyes, her skin, white and satiny as heavy whipping cream.

"This is Arman," Lorrie Ann said, gesturing to the man on the couch. "He lives next door."

"Hi," I said, feeling suddenly more awkward than I had in years. Was Lorrie Ann sleeping with this man? She couldn't be. Jim had been dead only six months. Was it all right to smoke pot in front of the child? Was I going to be offered some of the pot, and if I was offered some, did I want to get stoned here? I had not been this unable to read social cues or this unsure of my own desires since undergrad.

Uneasy about joining Arman on the couch, I slipped to my knees in front of the coffee table, clutching my purse. I kept looking and then trying not to look at Zach in his wheelchair in the corner. He was wearing a Christmas sweater with pompoms on it. He seemed so much smaller than six, and he was thin, skeletally thin. His lips were a little spitty and glistened, red and curly—a woman's lips on a boy's face.

"Can I get you something to drink?" Lorrie Ann asked. "Beer? Milk? I don't think I have anything besides beer and milk."

"Beer, please."

And Lorrie Ann disappeared into the kitchen, leaving me alone with Zach, who was silent but kept opening and closing his mouth, and Arman, who said nothing and did not acknowledge me in any way. I looked around. There was a small bookshelf positively weighted down with what I could already tell from across the room was an eccentric collection of books. I saw several popular science books, Stephen Hawking and that kind of thing, but I also saw *1001 Arabian Nights,* a few mystery novels, a copy of *Light in August* and a volume of poetry by Rumi, as well as several books on kabbalah. I noticed that the carpet was actually three different patterns of carpet, all thin and industrial, like the kind installed in elementary schools. They were joined at the seams by neat-looking lines of duct tape. I could also smell, distinctly, that somewhere in this house there was a cat. On the wall, a large cheaply framed Magritte print hung: the one of a man in a bowler with his face, if indeed he really has a face, obscured by a levitating apple.

Lorrie Ann returned with three cans of Bud Light.

She knelt easily beside me as she handed out the cans of beer, and then we both sat on the floor, facing Arman. "It's so good to see you!" she said, in a kind of singsong, smiling at me, chipper as a little fucking Girl Scout. Was she still angry at me? Had she ever been angry at me?

"It's good to see you too," I said, "but it's also really weird."

"It's weird?" Lorrie Ann asked.

I nodded. "Yeah, it's weird. I don't think I really understood how dead Jim was until I was ringing the doorbell, and then I was like, 'Shit, he is dead-dead, like all the way dead.'" I was rapidly spiraling into some kind of perverse truth-telling mode as a highly ineffectual defense mechanism. "That came out awful, but what I mean is that when you are a half a world away, it seems more like something happening in a novel, you know, and we've lived apart for so many years now that you are kind of like that for me, except when I see you, then you are suddenly terribly real, and that made Jim's death real and now I feel like I can't catch my breath because everything is too real for words."

Lorrie Ann looked at me critically for a moment, as though I were a gem she were assessing through one of those tiny eyepieces. Then she said, "I know exactly what you mean. For most of the year you are just a character in a book I'm reading. And then when you do show up,

I think: Oh, God, it's *her*! It's *her*! The girl I knew when I was a kid. My friend." She nodded then, smiling, her eyes damp, and I thought: She forgives me. She understands me. Perhaps that was what I loved most in Lor, nothing in her, but the very fact that she seemed to always understand me.

"And I'm sorry," I said, "but this housing complex is depressing. I don't like you living here. I know I should lie and say it's cute, but it just makes me sad. If you have to live without Jim, I wish it was in a house with a white picket fence somewhere."

Lorrie Ann laughed. "It is depressing here. It is. And I'm really fucking poor," she said. "I thought I was poor growing up, but this! Jesus. But, no debt! I can't even tell you what a relief it is to not be getting calls three times a day from twelve different hospitals. I will take poor any day over that."

Arman raised his can of Bud Light, and he and Lorrie Ann clinked. "Who, being loved, is poor?" he asked, and dimly I registered that he was quoting Oscar Wilde. Who was this guy?

"You know, Mia," Lorrie Ann said, "I actually really like my job waiting tables. If that makes you feel any better."

"Shut up, you fucking liar, waiting tables is awful and you know it. It's a horrible, killing job that makes you want to hit people in the face. I've waited tables before. You can't fool me."

Lorrie Ann guffawed. "You really weren't suited to it, were you?"

"No," I said.

"Well, I like it. I'm like a plow horse or something. What I do is so physical. All I do is move things through space, but just for really short distances. It's odd. People think it's so important too. I can make them happy or sad just by the precise way I move an object, like a plate or a cup, through time and space."

Personally I thought she was deluding herself, trying to find metaphysical grandeur in work that was truly unspeakably boring and difficult.

Arman grunted, packing a new bowl on the bong.

"Mostly," she said, "I like it because it's so impersonal. Nobody knows what I'm thinking. I don't have to tell anybody. And so the inside of my head has become this sort of wonderful, private garden almost."

Her eyes filled with something then. It was so obvious that she was thinking something, and whatever it was that she was thinking about seemed to be immense and magical and important. It just made you wish you could climb inside her head. As though the inside of Lorrie Ann must be the most interesting place in the world, a veritable Shangri-la. How did she do that? And did she know she was doing it?

"I don't really fucking buy it," I said finally.

"Good call," Arman said, and raised his beer to clink with me.

"Thanks, man. Yeah, I call bullshit, Lorrie Ann. All that just sounds to me like shit you made up to feel better about how awful your job is."

Lorrie Ann laughed, wild and loud. "Maybe you're right."

Just then Zach began to make horrible sounds, choking, asphyxiating sounds, and Lorrie Ann scooted over to him on her butt, reached up, and stuck her fingers in his mouth to feel around for anything in there as she kept talking to us. "Still, I don't have any regrets. I don't. It's not worth it to regret any of it."

"Eh," I said, "maybe."

"I regret everything," Arman said. "Almost every single thing I've ever done, I regret."

"That's really shitty," I said.

Arman nodded. "Well," he said, "I make really shitty decisions. So they're worth regretting."

"I'm too selfish to make poor decisions," I offered.

"So it's not actually a virtue?" Lorrie Ann asked, having apparently reassured herself that Zach was not choking on anything and now wiping his mouth with a burp cloth. "Your good decision-making power is actually a function of your little, black heart?"

"Yep, pretty much."

"I don't know, your life sounds so exciting," Lorrie Ann went on in a gush "I picture you walking around campus, your mind alive with all these ideas and texts and, I mean—I know I don't really know what you do, I can't even imagine it, so you must think I'm so stupid even saying this—but I picture you in, like, this big library, like some library from a Borges story or something, an infinite library of all of human knowledge. It makes me happy thinking that."

I was slack-jawed at her generosity of spirit.

"More beer?" she said, just at the moment that Arman held out the bong to me.

CHAPTER SIX

Accidents Happen

I got drunker that night than I had in years, and I had more fun than I'd had in even longer. We drank beers, shot the shit, told Arman all about Brittany Slane and her downy hair and constant, preposterous, but probably true, genealogical claims. I noted that Lorrie Ann no longer had any problem laughing at Brittany Slane. She didn't seem to feel nearly as guilty as she used to. As the night progressed, she and Arman slowly began to act more and more like a couple, laughing at inside jokes, letting their hands rest easily on the other's thigh or shoulder. There was something about the impropriety of Lorrie Ann's relationship with Arman that reassured me: she would make sure that she got what she needed. Gone were the days of casserole blog posts and self-imposed sainthood.

Lorrie Ann seemed happier than she had since before she married Jim. She was silly in a way I didn't remember: making crazy voices, not just for Zach, but in general. She had even adopted weirdly exaggerated arm movements highly reminiscent of Chris Farley. She and Arman, who was also a musician, had been obsessively rehearsing adaptations of Boyz II Men songs with insanely complex harmonies, which they sang for me ad nauseum. "The nineties were dope!" Arman kept saying.

Arman, as it turned out, was Armenian. I asked about how his family escaped, his story of coming to America. It seemed to surprise Lorrie Ann that there had been a massive genocide perpetrated against the Armenians. "What?" she cried. "I didn't know! You all act like I've been to college or some shit."

"Don't worry, baby," Arman said, "we moved here when I was four. I'm about as Armenian as you are."

It was a silly night. We all took turns dancing in front of Zach, who laughed wildly. The stupider we looked, the more he laughed, and his laughter was so wonderful that we lost all inhibition. Elvis Costello was blaring from surprisingly good speakers, Arman was moonwalking (an eerie sight on his mechanical legs) and doing the grocery cart, I was doing the chicken dance, Lorrie Ann was doing some weird combination of the Macarena and the sprinkler, and Zach was laughing so hard sometimes we had to stop to make sure he could breathe okay.

Zach was soon to have another operation on his calf muscles to lengthen them, and yet it did not seem that anyone expected this operation would make him able to walk. It was being done for its own sake or for some other reason I did not understand.

Lorrie Ann, despite the three beers and small amount of pot she smoked that night, seemed to be a good mother, and genuinely cared for Zach. I witnessed their rather revolting bedtime ritual. He had a feeding tube now because he hadn't been able to get enough nutrition from eating solids, and I had to look away from the place where it entered his abdomen. I was both touched and alarmed by how easily and naturally she tickled him, cajoled him, kissed him on the forehead, and in other ways covered his poor twisted body in small affections. He was, after all, her kid, and even more moving than seeing how much she loved him was seeing how much he loved her. Every time he looked at her, he got moon eyes and seemed to tremble with the excitement of looking at her beautiful face.

I thought: Me too, kid. Me too.

Late, late in the night, long after Zach had been put to bed, I noticed that Lorrie Ann had been gone from the room for an unusually long time. "Where is she?" I asked Arman.

"Bathroom," he said, reloading the bong.

I crawled there on my hands and knees. How many beers had I had?

"Lolola?" I called, tapping at the door with my fingernails.

"What?" came her muffled voice. I could already tell, just by the timbre, that she'd been crying.

"Please open up," I said. "You can cry, but you aren't allowed to cry alone."

The door cracked open and I could see her sitting on the toilet, blowing her nose into a wad of toilet paper in the bright yellow light of the bathroom.

"It's hard," she said, suddenly hiccuping.

"It must be so hard."

"He's never going to grow up," she hissed into the wad of toilet paper. There was nothing to say to that, there was nothing at all, and so I just pushed the bathroom door a little farther open and crawled in and crouched at her feet, hugging her ankles. I don't think I understood until that moment that Zach wasn't going to grow up, that he was going to stay like this, unable to walk or talk, wearing increasingly large Christmas sweaters, having his diaper changed. How long could it go on? How long was he expected to live? I was too afraid to ask.

"And I miss Jim," she said. "I miss him so much, and I'm also so mad at him that I can't even stand to think about him. Fucking playing war games. Getting himself fucking blown up. What an idiot. What a fucking idiot! How could he? How could he leave us like that?"

"I know," I said, hugging her feet. "I know."

Arman found us like that: Lorrie Ann's blue eyes glittering, myself prostrate at the feet of a goddess. He used two forearm crutches to help aid his balance on his mechanical legs. "There's Goldschläger in my apartment," he said, "and I'm willing to share."

I found out that night that Lorrie Ann had had her uterus removed when Zach was born. This was long after the Goldschläger. We were all sloppy drunk.

"Oh yeah," she said, "and it just killed Jim. He wanted to have another one. To try again."

"Why did they have to remove it?" I asked.

"They don't explain shit like that to you," she said. "They just said that my uterus had been damaged too much to repair and so they removed it. I was unconscious when they did it."

Arman and I sat, thinking about that. I remembered Dana and the chili fries. A nightmare in which everyone is trying to be polite and doesn't know what to say. That was what she had said.

"I feel like," Arman said, in a dreamy contemplative voice, "technology is causing new moral dilemmas."

Lorrie Ann nodded. "I know what you mean," she said, but I had no idea anymore what they were even talking about. I was lying down with my cheek pressed into the industrial carpet, looking up at the Magritte poster, wondering if there was a face behind that apple, wondering where Lorrie Ann's uterus had gone, where it physically had gone. Did they throw out things like that? Did they incinerate them? Did they make such items of the body vanish entirely from this world?

"I love you," I said suddenly. "I love you so much, Lorrie Ann!"

"I love you too," she said.

"Promise?" I asked, because it seemed impossible that Lorrie Ann could really love me. She was so perfect, so beautiful.

"Promise," she said.

I found that I did not worry as much about Lorrie Ann after that. It seemed to me that the bad luck vultures had come and gone. They had finished with her. Jim's death had been the final blow, and she had survived, had perhaps even become better for it. We talked on the phone perhaps once a month, sometimes letting it go longer, but whenever we did talk there was an easy intimacy that it felt like we'd earned. This, this was what friendship was.

———

I had just moved to Istanbul after getting my PhD when I got the call.

"Mia," she said, her voice quiet but vibrating with tension.

"Hey Lolola," I said, yawning and pouring myself a cup of coffee from the French press. The window was open; Franklin liked to keep the windows open, especially when we slept, and I remember that the breeze that came in was too cold, but tangy with salt from the Bosporus.

"I don't know what to do. I'm going to explain to you, and then you have to tell me what to do."

"Okay," I said, easing myself into a chair at the kitchen. I knew then, as one always knows in such moments, that the news would be bad.

"My mother is in the hospital and Zach is afraid of hospitals. He screams, bad, whenever we have to go in one, and there's no one to watch him. I can't get ahold of anybody. What do I do?"

"What about Arman?"

"He's not there. I don't know where he is."

"What happened to your mom? Is she okay?"

"I don't know. I don't know, that's why I've got to get down there. It was the sheriff's office that called me. Our apartment got broken into."

"The Larkspur place?"

"Yeah."

The thought of someone breaking into the Larkspur place sent a ripple of outrage through me. I could feel the hairs on my arms stand on end.

"Someone broke into your apartment and hurt your mother?"

"I don't know. I guess so. I don't know," Lorrie Ann said. "Just tell me what to do with Zach. I can't leave him here, right? I can't leave him in the car. If I take him to the hospital, he'll start screaming. He screams and screams. It's just awful when he does. For the last surgery they had to sedate him right away."

Franklin came up behind me then, began to rub my left shoulder with one of his huge, warm hands.

"Can you call the hospital and just . . . I don't know, explain? Get your mom's nurse on the phone and at least ask what's happened to her?"

"Yeah, yeah, I can do that. I haven't called. I just called you. I just needed you to tell me what to do."

"I know. I know. Okay, well, call the hospital. Where is she, Hoag? You know, maybe they have some sort of day care center there or some kind of—"

"Right, okay, then I'll call you back," Lorrie Ann said, and hung up.

As the story evolved over the next few hours and the next few weeks, it turned out that Bobby, Lorrie Ann's older brother, had, without anyone quite being aware of it, gotten into a bit of trouble. Probably this should have been evident from the fact that he was thirty-two and still living in the gnome-filled apartment with Dana, but this state of affairs had been going on for so long that no one really questioned it anymore.

Why hadn't Bobby married?

Was he gay?

No, he didn't seem to be gay. And he did always have a girlfriend, who was usually sweet enough, always in her mid-twenties, still struggling through undergraduate in an effort to one day become a teacher/ nurse/counselor. These girls of his were often ponytailed with athletic legs tanned from being out and about. They were the sort of girls still young and pretty enough to get by looking all right in discount clothes from Marshalls and T.J.Maxx. In five years' time, they would begin to look dumpy and uncared for, but Bobby managed to somehow get rid of them before this ever happened, and he seemed to have an almost unending supply of new ones to choose from.

Bobby himself worked for a smaller, rival company to Junk to the Dump, and had risen in the ranks just enough to have control of his own truck and crew. It was a job he didn't hate that paid decently and allowed him to bring home miraculous things that other people had thrown away: a chair shaped like a giant baseball glove, a statue of the Buddha, extremely cool bead curtains made of those Chinese coins with squares punched through the middle. He still fiddled with his Fender Stratocaster, but his days of playing in bands and trying to get gigs were long over. (Besides, everyone knew that Lorrie Ann, of the two of them, had been the inheritor of their father's talent.)

Evidently, though, this life had not been entirely satisfactory to Bobby, or else he had just begun dealing crystal meth and marijuana for no reason. According to Bobby, it was the latter: he had never meant to become a drug dealer—it just sort of happened. The normal party scene of his twenties had gradually morphed into something darker, but no less ordinary. The good ducks among his friends had married, had children, stopped drinking. The friends who remained unmarried, without careers, and ready to party every weekend with Bobby were naturally of a more sinister bent. There was something a little bit wrong with them. And that thing that was a little bit wrong with them caused them to sometimes want to do blow on the weekends with nineteen-year-old girls, and caused them to need to take several bong hits before work, and caused them to pursue these pleasures with a regularity no longer spontaneous, but routine. Bobby had gone from being someone who sometimes knew the right people to an outright hookup to a small-time drug dealer.

And so one day, a dumb seventeen-year-old named Carlos had driven with his friend from Santa Ana to Corona del Mar and shot up a lot of speed while waiting for Bobby to leave for work. Once Bobby had finally left, driving off in his Jeep, Carlos had run up the stairs to the Swifts' apartment, only to delightedly discover that the lock didn't even need picking! The door was open!

He had no idea that Bobby lived with his mother. He had no idea that Dana would be home. His intent was, thrillingly, to rob Bobby of either money or drugs. Already, one can imagine, Carlos was on edge, and the gnomes must have been a frightening surprise in their own right, so when Dana startled him by emerging from the kitchen in her bathrobe, he had grabbed the biggest gnome at his disposal and whacked her over the head with it. What was not explained was why he kept on whacking her, even after that gnome (ceramic) had broken, with another, lighter weight, but equally large wooden gnome. Kept on whacking her even when she was motionless on the floor.

"I don't know," Bobby later told Lorrie Ann, "the kid must have been crazy high."

And while Carlos was successful in downing Dana, he did not carry out his mission, having become too spooked to do anything but run back downstairs, jump in his friend's car, and shout, "Drive! Drive!"

What I didn't understand when Lorrie Ann first called me about the Zach-hospital problem was that, if it was nine o'clock in the morning in Istanbul, which it was, then it was eleven at night in California, which is precisely why Lorrie Ann did not know of any day care that would be open to take Zach while she made her way to the hospital. It was also why it upset her so much that she couldn't find Arman. Where was he?

Lorrie Ann had been notified so late in the evening only because Dana had not been found until Bobby came home that night around eight o'clock, her head swollen to almost twice its size and the color of an eggplant, but her breathing still coming, shallow but regular, her lips smeared against the pink shag carpet of the living room, shards of broken gnome all around her. Bobby, as anyone would, called 911. As he waited for the ambulance, however, he became concerned: cops would be coming and there was a half pound of crystal meth in his "bedroom"—really the same annexed corner of the living room that Lorrie Ann had used as a girl. He did not just want to flush it—really, there was too much of it to flush—so he ran down and put it in his car, thinking the cops would not, at least not right away, have any reason to ask to inspect his car. Then the paramedics arrived. There was a flurry of activity. Everyone agreed that Bobby should follow the ambulance in his own car to Hoag, where they were taking his mother.

Once in the car, however, Bobby just did not feel good about driving all the drugs to such an official place as a hospital. He couldn't put the drugs back upstairs; the house was still crawling with cops who were fingerprinting things and collecting evidence. It was a nightmare. He decided that the best thing to do was take a "slight" detour to his buddy Seth's house in Mission Viejo and leave the drugs there. Seth, as it turned out, was only too delighted to play host to the drugs, and suggested that what Bobby really needed in order to brace himself for the hospital and recover from such a traumatic thing as finding his mother on the floor with a head the color of eggplant was to get a little high. Not a lot, just a little. Just a bump.

And so it came to be that Bobby never returned to the hospital that night, but instead had his buddy Seth pretend to be the sheriff's office and call Lorrie Ann, cryptically telling her to go to the hospital, where her mother was in critical condition.

It took days to sort this full story out, especially as Bobby, out of shame, kept lying about his end of things. What ultimately happened that night was that Lorrie Ann was able to find out the basics of her mother's condition over the phone: traumatic brain injury, induced coma, a surgery called a ventriculostomy already performed, where a small tube had been inserted via a hole in the cranium into one of the ventricles to allow fluid to drain. It would take Lorrie Ann several hours to understand that they were talking about a hole they had made in her cranium, not just a hole that was naturally there, and it would take her longer still to realize that by "into one of the ventricles" they meant: into a part of the brain itself, a part they just hoped wasn't very important. Lorrie Ann explained to the nurse that she had a child with severe CP and a phobia of hospitals. No, there was no special day care open at that time where Zach could stay while Lorrie Ann visited Dana. But, the nurse reassured her, her mother was not conscious and was stable for now, and so Lorrie Ann could come absolutely whenever she could make it there. "Even if it's really late?" Lorrie Ann asked. The kindness of this nurse was making her break down crying.

"Even if it's the very middle of the night," the sweet nurse said.

———

And it was the very middle of the night, past the middle of the night, really, by the time Lorrie Ann made it there.

Around three, she heard Arman come home. By that time, she had already begun drinking whiskey. Zach was in bed. He was sleeping. She wanted, badly, to leave him sleeping there while she went to the hospital, but she knew she absolutely could not. And so she poured herself a bowl of Lucky Charms and, while she was at it, she also poured, into a Winnie-the-Pooh mug, a couple of fingers of whiskey.

Even though she did not know precisely where Arman was, she knew where he was. And every hour that he stayed out made her angrier and angrier, so that her blood was circulating through her body at what felt like twice its normal speed. When she heard him come home at three, she even debated whether or not she should go over there and knock. She might explode at him. She could, after all, be mature and wait until morning.

But she was too angry for that, and so after just a few minutes, she was pounding at his door.

"Come in!"

She pushed the door open.

"What do you want?" he asked her. His eyes were bloodshot. She knew that if she got close to him, where he was sitting on the couch, she would smell pot on him and possibly other things, fruity perfume or the rawer, salty smell of sex. They were, as he constantly reminded her, "not in a relationship," and so these trysts of his were perfectly within the rules.

"Can you just watch Zach while I go to the hospital? My mom's in the ICU."

Arman's sneer melted completely. "Of course," he said, scrambling to get to his feet, and quickly following her to her apartment, with his swinging gait, caused by the forearm crutches, but which Lorrie Ann now found charming, now loved.

"He's asleep," Lorrie Ann said. "You don't have to stay up or anything, but if you could just sleep in my room so you can hear him if he wakes up?"

"What happened?" Arman asked.

Lorrie Ann told him about Dana's head injury, about the tube inserted into her brain, about the induced coma. If she had had access to details, such as Bobby's vivid and descriptive "eggplant," she no doubt would have used them on Arman to make him feel bad, but she did not, and so her explanation was technical and unemotional.

"Why would someone break into your mom's place and try to beat her to death with a gnome?" Arman asked.

"I don't know," Lorrie Ann said.

"I'm sorry, girl. I don't know what to say. Just: embrace the suck." Lorrie Ann understood that this was soldier slang and that it meant something along the lines of "The world is shitty, but we've got to deal with it." She was too tired to accept Arman's platitudes.

"Is that what you were out doing?" she asked. "Embracing the suck?"

"Every day I embrace the suck," Arman said.

"Oh, bullshit," Lorrie Ann said. "Fucking teenage girls that wander into your fucking stupid smoke shop does not count as embracing the suck."

"First of all, they aren't teenagers. They are fully in their twenties. And second of all, may I point out just one more time: I have no fucking legs."

"Wah, wah, wah," Lorrie Ann said. "Poor Arman got his legs blown off."

"That's right, bitch," Arman said. "It sucks to have no legs."

"Cry me a fucking river," Lorrie Ann said, grabbing up her keys and stalking out of the apartment. She did not slam the front door, but she definitely closed it aggressively, before making her way to her car, saying a small prayer that she would not be pulled over for a DUI, and turning the key in the ignition.

It was dark in her mother's room, and Lor approached the bed suddenly out of breath. She became aware of how much her mouth tasted of whiskey. I'm drunk, she thought. She stood at the side of the bed. Was it her mother? Was she in the right room? In the bed was a small figure with a head swathed in bandages, tucked under a thin sheet, with many tubes going in and out. Lor simply could not recognize her mother's face, not in the dark, not with all the bandages. She sat in the chair. Certainly the bandages around the head seemed to indicate that it was her mother, but what if there was another woman about the size of her mother who had also had a head trauma? Lor told herself to stop being silly and just admit to herself that this was her mother, but the more she sat there, the more she worried that she was sitting at the bedside of a total stranger.

Finally, she stood up and slowly peeled back the blanket, more of a sheet, really, from her mother's feet. She saw the neon orange toenail polish, the thin white tan line on her mother's second toe from the silver toe ring with a shamrock she habitually wore. What had they done with the toe ring? Cut it off? Something about the feet looked so forlorn. Her eyes had adjusted somewhat to the dark, but her vision was still drained of color, like one of those black-and-white photographs where only certain parts were colored in: there were her mother's gray feet, the shadows rich and lustrous over her high arches, the toenails a sudden neon orange, breaking the gray scale.

She touched them, gently pushing her thumbs into the arches, wrapping her warm hands around them. She sat one hip on the edge of her mother's bed and rubbed her feet, long and slow and mournfully. She thought of Zach's feet, twisted and pointed as though he were mid-leap in a ballet. She thought of Jim's feet, dead and cold in dress shoes under the ground. And then, of course, Arman had no feet at all.

She thought of her own feet, which for once were not aching, and the way they vibrated in her shoes slightly, as though they longed to have real contact with the ground, not the hospital floor, but real dirt, real earth. She thought about monkey feet and human hands and human feet. With a jerk, as though remembering an appointment, she remembered that human beings were animals. Nothing more than animals. It was because of this fact that Dana might die.

As Lor rubbed Dana's feet, she whispered to her mother, "You are going to need these feet, Mom. You are going to wake up and you are going to walk and even run around again. You will need these beautiful feet."

It was true; Dana's feet were beautiful, far more beautiful than Lor's. Dana was a perfect size six, with high arches and magnificently even toes, like a doll's. Lor's feet were wider and flatter and bigger than her mother's. She pulled on Dana's toes individually, rubbing the bulb of each between her fingers. Suddenly she remembered the night she refused to break my toe, and the image of my foot flashed before her, the horrible split bulb, the cracked asphalt, the sudden explosion of blood and screaming, but she pushed it away.

CHAPTER SEVEN

Let Them Eat Cake

If anything, it was Istanbul that created distance between me and Lorrie Ann. The international calls were outrageously expensive, and Lorrie Ann's dial-up connection in the sad, subsidized apartment was so slow it rendered Skype some kind of slow-motion, avant-garde collage. Lorrie Ann could hardly ever afford to call me, and I could afford to call her for only twenty minutes once a month or so. Franklin and I were living off a grant, and Turkey wasn't as cheap as we'd been hoping. So I didn't hear all that much about Lor's life after Dana's attack. I knew only that Dana recovered but was classified as disabled, and that she had moved in with Lorrie Ann and Zach, which actually solved some of Lorrie Ann's babysitter problems. In fact, Lorrie Ann seemed preternaturally relaxed about all of this the few times I talked to her.

And so my life became my own again. The narrative concerned only myself, Franklin, and the wonders of ancient Sumer, and I did not have to worry about my opposite twin, who was unlucky, or who else was being punished for sins I did not understand. Left to my own devices, I was richly, deeply, quietly happy.

I was attending the excruciatingly boring reception at which I met Franklin only to steal food. This was back at UMich, during my second-to-last year there. I intended merely to gather a few cheese cubes and chocolate-covered strawberries on my miniature paper plate and snag a glass of wine before hightailing it back to my office, where I could put some Queen on my fabulous new computer speakers and get back to work on my article. But the chair, a man I adored, whose name was Dr. Wooly, and who was perfectly rubicund and always smiling, much like a 1950s illustration of Santa Claus, insisted that I go shake hands with Franklin.

"It would be good for you to date someone like him," Dr. Wooly said as he steered me by the elbow, his great mane of white Santa hair cascading down his tweed-clad shoulders. Normally, I rather enjoyed the avuncular way in which Dr. Wooly affected to advise me regarding my love life, but nothing Dr. Wooly could have said would have set me against Franklin so completely. I did not like doing things that were "good for me." Not even yoga.

And Franklin himself turned out to be a complete snooze. He was nice. He shook my hand. He was, of course, very red haired, a true ginger, with hair the color of Cheetos and skin absolutely covered in freckles of a more muted orange. He was of slightly above average height and with an unusually athletic build. I noted that he was good looking, despite his freckles, but good looking was not everything for me, was not even a must. The most interesting thing about Franklin looks-wise were his eyes, which were an almost iridescent brown that was dangerously close to being orange, like a Halloween cat's. I have never, before or since, met someone with eyes that color.

It would have ended there, except that, for whatever peculiar reason, Franklin liked me. Later he would say, "I fell in love with you from the moment I saw you." At first, I thought it was only his romanticism talking, a confusion between lust and love. But later, I came to believe him.

(I am sentimental about only two things in this world: Franklin and Lorrie Ann.)

He began to hang around outside my office, to pop his head in and ask me questions, to stay late working, knowing I stayed late working. This kind of puppyish interest, if anything, made him less attractive to me. Indeed, I had to be wary because most men who were interested in me were masochists who wanted me to flagellate them in ways both physical and spiritual, which was, perhaps surprisingly, not in my line at all. If anything, I sought the reverse: men who would overpower me, who could make me feel small and frail and helpless, and for whose love I had to clamor and beg, whine and snivel. They were usually dangerously self-involved, the men I made lovers, one a Russian novelist with a recurrent alcohol problem and delusions of grandeur but with a remarkable and encyclopedic knowledge of Husserl, another a tortured African American painter (quite talented) who found his very interest and indeed love for me, a white girl, to be yet another form of his debasement and mental colonization by the white man. In short, Franklin was just not my type.

And then one day, Franklin asked me out.

"Remember the day I asked you out?" he often asks me, even now, years later.

"Yes," I say.

"I was so nervous."

"You didn't show it," I say.

And he didn't. He came into my office, casually leaning against the door frame. It was about eight at night, and he had been monitoring me, I suppose, and must have known that I had taken no dinner break.

"You are going to have dinner with me," he announced.

"I am?"

"I really hope so," he said, his brow lifted, his smile wide.

And so he, feigning nonchalance, as though none of this were planned, escorted me out of the building and around the corner to a not-inexpensive Italian place that had candles on the tables and where I ordered the farfalle and asparagus with gorgonzola cream sauce, and where he ordered a steak, and where we drank a bottle of wine.

Our rapport was not immediate. In fact, there were several points during dinner when I zoned out completely and returned to the conversation with no idea of what he was saying. He was speaking, of course, about cuneiform, which should have been interesting to me, but Franklin was so good, so orderly, and so polite that it was difficult to tell at first that he was brilliant. But he was.

After dinner, we returned to campus. "I've got to stop by my office," Franklin said, and, unthinkingly, I waited with him while he unlocked his door. Inside, all was lit by candles. There was a bundle of lilies on the desk.

"For you," he said, handing them to me without any kind of fanfare.

"For me?"

He nodded eagerly. On the floor there was a blanket spread out, another bottle of wine, a plate set with cheeses and crackers, a box of chocolates. Some kind of chamber music was playing softly, what I later identified as a concerto by Fauré. I was so surprised by all this that I didn't know what to do but laugh, not derisively, but nervously, girlishly, hiding my face in the lilies. I had never had anyone make such a gesture before. Not in my whole life. Not even when I went to prom.

"Will you . . . stay and chat?" he asked.

And so I began to take Franklin seriously as a suitor. And as time went on, I would take him more and more seriously, as a suitor, as a scholar, as a man.

When we began working together on the Inanna project, I worried we would wreck things by spending too much time together, but we seemed unable to disappoint each other. How often had I sat across a table from some man or other and realized, in the elision of the moment, that they were about to disappoint me terribly?

I remember once finding several Polaroids of a naked woman in my mother's nightstand. I had no idea who the woman was; she was a stranger, someone I had never seen before, yet she was clearly posed on my mother's bed—I recognized the tiny rosebuds of the bedspread. The first two were of the woman alone, and then there was another one of she and my mother, both naked, and artfully kissing each other, in the

watched, passionless way familiar to firmly heterosexual women participating in polite threesomes. The photographer, I guessed, had been my
stepfather, Paddy. I must have been around eleven when I found these
photos, and I remember, not feelings of shock or scandal, but a sickening
recognition of something I had known all along, this awareness of my
parents' base dirtiness. I slid the photos quietly back in the drawer, imagining my mother and Paddy pathetically showing these three washed-out
Polaroids to one another after the "kids" were put to bed: my two wild
little brothers and me, sleeping in a heap on our air mattress. This feeling of resigned disappointment, a kind of contained disgust, was present
throughout the rest of my life in almost all of my human relationships.
Always, people were turning out to be a bit less than they could have
been, a bit more what you had uncharitably suspected. Even I was less
than I had hoped I would be, and it was Lorrie Ann, in large part, who
made me aware of this, not through her own perfection, but because she
was the only witness to the thing I regret most in my life.

When I was twelve, Lorrie Ann and I were pretending to be best friends
with this other girl, Meghan Farmer. With a callousness that is common
in twelve-year-old girls, but would be shocking in adult women, we ver-
bally agreed that our friendship with her was "just pretend." Truthfully,
the idea had been mine and Lorrie Ann had fought me, stubborn as a
donkey, every step of the way, but together we lured Meghan into the
friendship, pooling our money to buy a Best Friends Forever necklace
with three interlocking charms from Claire's at the mall in order that
she be part of a dance routine we were doing for a talent show. The
three of us choreographed a horribly sexual bump-and-grind routine to
TLC's "Waterfalls," which miraculously won first place.

Also, we admired Meghan's breasts, which were already huge. Unfor-
tunately, the more we got to know Meghan, the more we didn't like her.
She wasn't very good about brushing her teeth. I had also noticed that
she seemed to wear the same pair of underwear for multiple days in a

row. She loved to make the "Whoot-whoot!" sound for no reason. At first this had seemed festive and exciting, a kind of wonderful conversational punctuation mark, but after a while, it was just loud.

In any event, Lorrie Ann and I had agreed to meet Meghan at Auntie Anne's Pretzels at the mall, and so, since Lorrie Ann and I lived just a few blocks apart from each other, she was supposed to come by my house around two so that we could walk the mile and a half to the mall together.

It was fall, which, frankly, is almost meaningless in Southern California. But I remember that it was fall because I remember that my little brother Alex, the youngest one, had just had his second birthday the weekend before. I also remember that it was a Sunday because the reason that we couldn't all meet in the morning was because Lorrie Ann was at church.

Normally my mother didn't work Sundays, and so I had counted on her being home to watch the boys. We had a sort of informal understanding: my mother absolutely took advantage of me as free help with the boys, abandoning them to my care six days out of seven, and in exchange I was entitled to be as rude and demanding as I wanted. It was also understood that she would keep me in makeup and nice clothes, or the nicest we could afford. Since my mother was slender, we often shared clothes anyway, and it was from her that I developed a taste for fine fabrics. In any event, when my mother had unexpectedly announced that morning that she and Paddy were taking the day to go to the beach and "rekindle their romance," I was infuriated.

"Why are you going to the beach?" I asked. "It's fucking cold! It's almost winter!"

"We're going to the Fun Zone. We're going to ride the Ferris wheel and play skee ball. We hardly even see each other anymore, Mia."

"I don't care!" I said. "I don't care if you two never fuck again!"

My mother was calmly putting on makeup in the bathroom, and I watched her in the mirror from the doorway. She finished with her eyebrows, then turned and sat on the pot to pee.

"You can go with your friends to the mall another day."

I felt Paddy move behind me in the hall, walking swiftly, just the current of air as he passed. He and I hardly ever spoke. I watched my mother pee, thinking that every year she began to look more and more porcine, her fake-blond curls more and more reminiscent of Miss Piggy.

"You know who you really never see? Your sons. Why did you even have them? You obviously don't care about them."

I heard Paddy crack a beer in the kitchen. Alex and Max were watching *Barney* in the living room. They watched a lot of TV in those days, and the glowing screen kept them in an almost perpetual coma.

"You think you're all grown up," my mother said, wiping herself. "But you're not. You're just not, Mia. You don't understand the adult world."

I laughed, a big fake laugh then, a stage laugh. "God," I said, "you really think you're an adult, don't you?"

"I do," my mother said, yanking up her jeans. "Because I am."

I leaned farther into the bathroom, getting my head close to hers, so that she jerked back. I breathed in her face. "Poor thing," I said. "You have no idea what you're doing. You're just like a teenager playing pretend at being a grown-up."

Her mouth opened, but she said nothing.

"Have you figured out yet that Paddy doesn't really love you?"

"That's enough, Mia," my mother said.

"Oh, how cute," I said, pulling back so I was no longer quite so close to her face, but instead leaning in the doorway. "You still think he does."

"I'm leaving," she announced, pursing her lips so that faint frown lines appeared in her artificially preserved skin.

"Of course you are," I said, swinging away from the doorway and stalking along the wooden floor of the hallway, smacking the floorboards with my bare feet, before collapsing on the black leather couch with my brothers.

As my mother passed me on her way to the front door, she called out for Paddy. "Are you ready?"

I was grateful when they'd gone.

Except, a few hours later, when the boys got hungry for lunch, I realized that there wasn't really any food in the house. The only money I had was the ten dollars of my allowance. The supermarket really wasn't far, perhaps a mile at the most. But we didn't have a double stroller, and taking Max and Alex anywhere was a huge ordeal. In particular, Alex, excited but also confused by his birthday the previous weekend, had decided he wanted nothing but cake.

"Cake!" he screamed.

"We can't have cake," I said.

"CAKE!!!!"

"We can't have cake because your mother is a vicious, selfish alcoholic," I told him. "What about a pickle?"

"No," Alex wailed. "No!"

I looked in the fridge some more. "What about a slice of bread with yummy ketchup on it?"

"NO!!!!! CAKE!!!!!!!"

"No more screaming," I said. "What about . . ." I trailed off. I remember I was looking in the freezer and seeing that we had frozen peaches. I was wondering if maybe I could make something out of the frozen peaches and Bisquick and water that might be cake-ish, or at least cake-ish enough to fool a two-year-old. But just then Alex bit me, hard, on the thigh just below the hem of my jean shorts, breaking the skin. I screamed and started hitting him on the top of the head to try to make him let go. When he finally drew back, his mouth was smeared with my blood.

"Cake!" he screamed.

"NO!" I yelled, grabbing him by the arm and dragging him into our room. Looking back, I'm surprised I didn't dislocate his shoulder. I didn't know what I was doing; I had no plan. I remember he was wearing nothing but a diaper, and I wanted to spank him, but everything was happening too fast for me to take off the diaper. I threw Alex facedown on our air mattress, and I grabbed a wire hanger from the floor, and I began beating him with it, whipping him across the back as he screamed. Max watched from the doorway, sucking his thumb.

It was this scene that Lorrie Ann walked in on, when she thought she was coming to meet me to walk to the mall. When I saw her I froze, the hanger still upraised in the air.

And so Lorrie Ann knew exactly how much less I was than what I could have been, how far I had fallen from the mark. Lorrie Ann knew and, somehow, went on loving me.

We never spoke of what had happened. Mutely, she helped me apply Neosporin to Alex's back and to my thigh, and without discussion we pooled our money and took Max and Alex both out for pizza at Gina's over on Iris. They loved pizza. They still do. We didn't notify Meghan Farmer of the change in plans, and that day when we stood her up at the mall was the marker of the beginning of the end of our threesome, which was later punctuated by Meghan hurling her portion of the friendship necklace at me on the playground as I shouted, "At least I wash *my* vagina!"

And yet, no matter how many times I steeled myself, pitted my gut, prepared for Franklin to suddenly reveal himself as selfish, as small hearted, as foolish or puerile, he always failed to say what I expected him to say, or do what I expected him to do. I never stopped being surprised by his goodness, just as I could not stop myself from being surprised by Lorrie Ann's goodness. I held both of them in a fierce and irrational esteem that owed more to the veneration of the collector than the easy gratitude of a friend. They were my trophies, my prizes, my miniature gods. I did not pursue my relationship with either for personal reasons, but because I sincerely believed they were the two best specimens of humanity I had yet to run across on the planet.

I knew too that I was not worthy of them, but then, I had not been worthy of Yale either, worthy of any of my accomplishments. I knew full well that I had stolen them, stolen all the beauty of my life, stolen scholarship itself, and I had resolved simply to be very careful that no one find out. Even in my most genuine moments there was a whiff of artificiality, a tremor that belied the force with which I was pretending to be myself.

Once, when we were about ten, Lorrie Ann had been given too much change at the Chevron snack shop: she had paid with a ten, but the man must have thought she gave him a twenty. Lorrie Ann didn't even notice until we were five blocks away, and then insisted we walk all the way back so that she could give him that unearned ten-dollar bill, which as I recall was soft and wrinkled like wilted lettuce. I am sure Lorrie Ann would never remember that day, such an insignificant anecdote, but in my mind it became a central organizing allegory about the differences between us. Everything I had in life was half stolen, a secret, wilt-y ten-dollar bill that Lorrie Ann would have been too good to keep, but which I could not force myself to give away.

Incidentally, Franklin had been with me the very last time I ever saw my biological father. Paddy I still saw intermittently, whenever I would go to visit my half brothers, but my real father was doing God knows what in San Francisco. I no longer bothered to monitor his activities.

He was a yacht salesman. He had started in cars, and gone through a brief RV period when I was in my teens, but now he did yachts and nothing but yachts. He was short, and he had worn a mustache since before I was born. It helped to balance his huge proboscis, which was the same red sunburn color as his face, but ovular and soft looking, as though it were made of foam like Bert's nose from *Sesame Street*. I am grateful that I did not inherit his nose, but I always worried I would inherit his temperament.

Basically, he was crazy. That's the short version. Throughout my childhood I would see him once, maybe twice a year. I would be flown up to San Francisco and he would meet me at the airport, usually alone, sometimes accompanied by whatever bimbo he was dating. They were all blond and all about twenty-five. It was unclear to me how my father, who was not even very good looking, and not even very wealthy, managed to pull such young pussy. When I was a teenager and rebellious enough to give voice to such questions, he would scratch his ear, stare out at the wharf, and say, "I don't know, pudding. It doesn't hurt that I'm well endowed."

"Gross, Dad."

"Well, it doesn't," he would say.

But really I think women dated my father because he was exciting. Whatever he did, he did 200 percent. That meant when he was interested in you or what you were saying, you felt like the only person in the room. And when he was no longer interested in you? You might as well have been exiled to northern Siberia. He was filled with whims and caprices, sudden passions and equally sudden aversions. He went on a kick where he decided he loved chocolate soy milk and he drank nothing else for six weeks. He would keep four or five cartons in the fridge at a time, so quickly did he go through them. He decided, one weekend when I was fifteen and visiting, just after Christmas, that he needed a new look. He made me help him dump all of his dresser drawers into garbage bags that we left at Goodwill. He refused to keep so much as an athletic sock. Then we went to Macy's and bought him an entirely new wardrobe. (This was an unfortunate period, what I refer to as the Ed Hardy Years. There were a lot of sugar skulls and tattoo panthers and rhinestones on my father's clothes for a while there.)

And so I think these young women, most of whom were making up for their lack of any real direction or education with their hair color and grooming and slutty clothes, found it exciting that my father could decide at eleven p.m. on a Tuesday that he wasn't going to go to work for the rest of the week, and moreover that the two of them were going to Atlantic City! Or he might decide that you should let him cut off all your hair. (He did this to me when I was thirteen.) Or he might decide, as he did on the trip where he met Franklin, and which was the last time I ever saw him, that you harbored secret animosity toward him.

That Sunday, he took Franklin and me out to brunch, where he behaved sullenly, refusing to speak or to answer our questions. He kept leaving to go outside and smoke one of his Swisher Sweets. I couldn't tell what it was about, if it was just some sort of elaborate way of saying he didn't approve of Franklin. I hadn't brought a serious boyfriend around in years, but when I had dated in high school and college, my dad hadn't been the least bit protective. Finally, I lost patience. "Dad, what's your deal? Why are you being such a grouch?"

"A grouch, Mia?" He gave a derisive bark of a laugh and rubbed his toast into his egg yolk aggressively, as though he were scouring the plate with it.

"Yeah, and frankly, you're being rude," I said.

"Well, pardon me. All of this is just a little hard to swallow."

"What is hard to swallow?"

"I'm betrayed by my own flesh and blood and then I'm made to sit in it, like a dog, sitting, in, in, its own—*shit*." He punctuated this outburst by putting on his sunglasses, even though we were indoors.

"I have no idea what you're talking about," I said.

"You act all sweet and harmless," he said, "but I know what you really are. I know what you think of me."

"I'm your daughter," I said. "That's what I really am."

"I never entirely trusted your mother on that one," he said.

"What is your problem?" I was beginning to be rattled. Sometimes my dad would get into an irrational funk that required extreme cajoling, but this was over the top even for him.

"You're a little traitor," he said. "You should have been an actress." Then to Franklin: "Don't trust her. Don't trust her for a second. Get out while you can."

Franklin just raised his eyebrows and smiled. Though I was mortified and upset, Franklin still seemed utterly good-natured. "I'll take that under advisement," he said.

"You smug bastard," my father said.

"Daddy," I said, wringing the napkin in my lap, "I really don't understand what this is about."

"Why don't you run and go tell your mother that I'm behaving 'irrationally'?" he sneered, making elaborate finger quotes in the air.

As it turned out, my father had seen a note I wrote on my mother's Facebook page for Mother's Day. I had written: "Thank you for being my mother. I could always depend on you, even if I couldn't agree with you. Thank you for being there day in and day out. Thank you for loving me."

My father, of course, took this to mean that if my mother was dependable, he was not, and if she was there for me day in and day out, this was a jab at him for not being there. And if I needed to thank my mother for loving me, it was only because I must think that my father hadn't loved me enough.

"Daddy," I said, "none of that's true! I had to thank her for being there because that's all I could thank her for! You know me and Mom never got along. I was just desperate for something nice to say!"

"I think you know," Franklin said suddenly, butting his head in where perhaps it didn't belong, "that Mia loves you and that loving her mother doesn't make her love you any less. I'm positive you understand that." I watched as he stared my father down, Franklin's orange cat eyes almost flickering with rage.

I tensed myself, sure that my father was going to throw a gigantic fit. I wanted to correct Franklin: you couldn't strong-arm my father into doing the right thing, you had to slowly manipulate him by catering to his ego, flattering him bit by bit until you had gotten him to shift his position. I had spent a lifetime manipulating my father's moods. I knew what I was doing.

"Of course I know that," my father said, and I thought I must have misheard him.

"Because you and Mia have such an incredible bond. I know you couldn't ever doubt that."

"Of course not!" my father said.

I sat between them, just staring in slack-jawed wonder.

"I hate Facebook," Franklin said, seemingly apropos of nothing.

"So do I!" my father said.

And just like that, Franklin vanquished the dragon that was my father.

When I got him home that afternoon, I leaped on him like a hungry creature: I couldn't even speak or verbalize my gratitude, I just covered him in ravenous kisses. And ever after that, I just didn't care quite as much what my father thought of me or what my father felt. We exchanged a few more phone calls and e-mails, but none of them moved me particularly. I was like a marionette clipped free from the wooden cross of its control.

On the day that Lor called me, I had just bought a pregnancy test. If I was indeed pregnant, then it would be the first time since my unfortunate tryst with Ryan Almquist in tenth grade. At this point I was twenty-eight, and you can imagine it took a certain level of scrupulousness on my part to remain so infertile over the years, especially since I was rarely without a sexual partner, in fact, rarely without several. Until Franklin. Franklin, I loved. Franklin, I simply could not lose. I did not know what would happen if I were pregnant, what we would do, and so I was contemplating the test box with my heart in my throat, when the phone rang.

"Hey Mia, it's Lor," she said when I answered. "Are you still in Istanbul?"

"Yeah," I said. "Why?"

"I'm in town! I wanted to see you!"

My mind was like a frozen computer. I hadn't seen Lorrie Ann in two years, but I suddenly realized we hadn't even spoken in perhaps six months. I felt like I had lost the plot of a novel I was reading. How could Lorrie Ann be in Istanbul when Zach could not fly and, moreover, they had no money. How the fuck had she gotten here?

"That's great!" I said, trying to cover my confusion.

"How far are you from the Grand Bazaar?" she asked. "I don't know my way around super well, so I'm worried I'll get lost if I try to go to your place. I'm calling from a pay phone."

Stranger and stranger. Who even used pay phones anymore?

"Not far," I said. "I'll come get you. I'll meet you in the booksellers' stalls."

And just like that, Lorrie Ann walked back into my life.

CHAPTER EIGHT

Loving a Loser

The crowds in the main market, at any time of day, were simply crushing, but the booksellers' stalls were sleepier: ancient old men sitting high up on stools, overseeing their hodgepodge of knowledge, religious tracts and decaying erotic manuals smashed together with out-of-date math textbooks and cheap romances. I imagined these men as the guardians of all human knowledge, and each piece of knowledge had value, was worth something, if only a single Turkish lira. When I found Lorrie Anne, she was browsing through an edition of *In Search of Lost Time*. She was wearing a yellow sundress that came to mid-calf and a long blue cardigan that hung from her shoulders. She'd lost weight. Her hair was pulled back in a sloppy braid that looked like it had been slept on.

When she saw me, she said, "Oh my God!" and waved both her arms at me, as though I were very far away, across a crowded airport, instead of just a few feet from her. Suddenly, I noticed that she was barefoot and her feet were bleeding.

"Isn't this crazy?" she said.

"Yes," I said. "Why aren't you wearing shoes?"

"I had to leave them behind," she said, as though that sentence made any sense.

"Do you want to come back to our flat? Have some tea, or, how long will you be in Istanbul?"

"I don't know," she said and laughed. She gestured at the sky, which was a bright, almost Technicolor blue, with the book she was holding. "It's great here! You have Proust and everything!"

My God, I thought, this must be what Inanna looked like when she came back from the underworld: beautiful but mad.

After deciding to visit my apartment for tea, I steered her back inside the Grand Bazaar, where I ducked into a side alley and purchased her a pair of pink cloth slippers because they were cheap and because I, bizarrely, thought she might like them as a souvenir. They had the traditional pom-pom on the toe. On impulse, I also bought a child's tea set that was for sale in the same shop. It was time Bensu had a real one, I thought, and I also thought this particular tea set was beautiful and cunning: a bright yellow ceramic with gold geometric tracings. It was so pretty I wanted a full-size one for myself.

Once Lor was shod, I led her through the streets of Beyazit to our apartment. Where was Zach? I felt the need to ask this urgently, and yet I sensed it would be cruel to, that in order for Lorrie Ann to appear alone in Istanbul, terrible things must have happened.

"What are you doing in Istanbul?" I asked instead.

"I don't really know," she said.

"You don't know?"

"No, I'm sorry, that seems dramatic when I say it like that. I just mean, there isn't really a good reason for me to be here. I was traveling."

"For business or pleasure?" I asked, though I couldn't imagine what business Lorrie Ann might have here, or anywhere for that matter.

"For my friend's business," she said.

"Arman?"

"No," she said. "I don't think he'd ever visit Turkey. Maybe I'm just here to piss him off." She gave a little laugh. I had forgotten somehow that of course he was Armenian and would never want to come to Turkey.

"Do you have a hotel?"

"Yes," she said, "but I can't go back there."

"Are you on drugs?" I asked her, in a soft voice, so that we wouldn't be heard on the street. We were just passing a street vendor grilling corn and kabobs. The scent of burned corn was intoxicating. "Are you hungry?" I asked, before she'd had time to answer, gesturing at the corn. Perhaps I did not want to hear her answer. I did not want to put Lor in the same category as my mother and her drinking. I did not want to think of her that way, the way I thought of animals: beings that were charming but were not in control of themselves, incapable of being responsible for their actions.

"I'm starving," she admitted, and I bought us both an ear of corn and steered us toward a bench, where I could set down the tea set. I sat down, but Lorrie Ann stayed standing upright, the corn cob held in both hands.

For a moment we just ate, greedy for the smoky, burned, sweet corn.

"This is so good I could cry," she said.

"It's my favorite," I said. "So is that what this is—drugs?"

"Of course not," Lorrie Ann said, so easily that I believed her completely. "It would probably be easier if it was about drugs. I was traveling with this girl. Woman. Whatever. And we just hit this point where—you know how complicated it can get? Traveling with somebody, and their world becomes your world?"

I nodded, still neatly shearing the rows of corn with my teeth like a typewriter going across a page. I wanted so badly for her to have an answer that made sense.

"It sounds so ordinary," Lor said, "but somehow it was absolutely too much, and I started to realize that she was crazy, like the big things that she believed in were terribly warped, and then we had a fight and she went crazy and threw all my shoes off the balcony into the river and kicked me out of our hotel."

This was insane, but I kept nodding. Where was Zach? If he was dead, wouldn't she have called me? Had she called me? Had I simply not gotten the crucial voice mail? She paused and chewed on her corn for a bit. The mid-morning sun was pure and drenching as honey.

"I'm sorry," she said suddenly. "I don't know why I lied to you. Of course I'm on drugs. I shouldn't have lied. I'm sorry. It's just a reflex, but then I felt so bad for lying that I could hardly concentrate on what I was saying."

"What drugs?" I asked.

"Opiates," she said.

"What opiates?"

"Whatever opiates are available." She shrugged her narrow shoulders. Her breasts seemed much smaller. She was thin, really thin. "I know it sounds bad, Mia," she said, "but it's not all *Basketball Diaries* and *Trainspotting*."

"So what is it then," I asked, "if it's not that?"

"It's like the ordinary way Americans eat themselves to death. It's like anything."

I listened, squinting. I knew in part what she meant: the war on drugs had fooled all of us. The first time I tried cocaine at a party at Yale, I had thought: That's it? That's all? That's what we've all been afraid of? But I still thought of opiates as something altogether different. You didn't casually do heroin. You didn't do heroin on the weekends.

"I won't be sick on your couch or have hallucinations or anything," she said.

"All right." I was looking at her pink slippers and thinking of her bleeding feet underneath.

"I won't steal your TV."

"We don't have a TV."

"We?" she asked.

I was brought up short. I was thinking so many things that I wasn't saying that I was having difficulty keeping track of the conversation. "We?" she had asked. What on earth did she mean? What did the sound "we" signify? Then, just as quickly, I understood. "Franklin," I said, upset. Lorrie Ann knew about Franklin. I had told her all about him.

"God, that's right," she said. "I didn't realize you two were living together."

"For a year," I said tightly.

"For a year," she echoed. Her half-finished corncob dangled from her hand like something dirty or ruined, as though she no longer wanted to be touching it.

"Where can I put this?" she asked, holding it out to me like a child. My stomach clenched. The bad luck vultures were not done. They had come to stay.

As it turned out, it was the helpful Arman who had first initiated Lorrie Ann in the ways of opiates. Together they abused the medication he was given for his legs, or for the absence of his legs, which was oxycodone, generic for OxyContin. Through the crippled-vet grapevine he was also able to procure fentanyl suckers and patches, which they occasionally abused while watching comedies from Redbox as all the while Zach spasmed in his chair nearby.

"We weren't wild or anything," Lorrie Ann said. There is no way she could imagine how much more revolting I found her quiet addiction than any Dionysian revelry she could have indulged in. It made me angry to think of Lorrie Ann high, in sweatpants, watching National Lampoon movies, her head in Arman's lap, her eyes glazed. It made me angry because it made me so sad. I imagined his dark hand, stroking the fine gold filaments of her hair.

"What a fucking loser" was all I could say to her.

"He wasn't a loser," she said. By this time we were at my kitchen table. I had hidden the pregnancy test in a drawer with the place mats.

"He was a fucking loser," I said, blowing on my tea.

"You women, man," Arman said, the first night he had come over to Lorrie Ann's. "You're like Luthers with vaginas."

"Luthers with vaginas? Like New-Testament-Luther Luthers?" Lorrie Ann asked. She could not imagine what Arman meant, but she was interested because it seemed to her like an unexpected thing to say. She was prepared to like Arman simply because he was legless and her next-door neighbor. If he was interesting, that would be a bonus. So few people she met were ever interesting.

"Yeah, like, I don't know, it just seems to me that women have been part of the slave class for most of history, right? But now they have all this freedom they don't know what to do with, and it's kind of like the period of reformation in a religion. You know, women have access to this reset button."

"Reset button?" Lor asked.

Arman sat back on the couch, lolled his head to the side, smiling, that long black hair of his shimmering like water. "You know, like, women used to be born into their destiny. That determined them, usually. But now, they're educated and shit, and they have an opportunity to reassess the world, and once they have reassessed the world, they can reassess the way they belong to the world, and from there they can reinvent themselves so that they fit into the world in the way they want to, so that they can control how they will belong to it. Reset button. Not a linear journey either. More like Leibniz. There's monadic stuff happening with women."

"What is 'monadic'?" Lorrie Ann demanded. She was excited. It had been so long since she was intellectually excited that she didn't even understand exactly that this was what she was feeling. She heard the timer ding in the kitchen, but she didn't get up to get it. She was making cinnamon rolls, the kind with orange-flavored frosting. It was one in the morning on a Tuesday.

"Oh, a monad?" he said. "Monads are weird. Okay, basically, there was this guy named Leibniz. And he invented this idea of metaphysical atoms. So monads are to the metaphysical world what atoms are to the physical world. Only, that's just a way into thinking it, because it's not quite that. Leibniz didn't actually believe that there was a divide between the physical and the metaphysical. Most philosophers, from Plato on, believe there is this distinction between the world of ideas and the world of things. Leibniz thought they were the same thing and the monad was how it was architecturally organized."

"But what is a monad?" Lorrie Ann asked. "Like, would the concept of 'red' or 'blue' be a monad? Give me an example."

"Do you mind if I . . . ?" he asked, pulling a pipe of marijuana from his pocket. Lorrie Ann waved at him to go ahead, and waited impatiently as he took a few puffs. "Okay, example of a monad," Arman said, leaning back again into the couch. The cinnamon rolls were burning. "Well, it's not a concept. So it's not red or blue or pretty or ugly. It's more like each human being is a monad, and the existence of God is a monad, and the thing about the monads is that each one is a tiny mirror of the universe, and it fits in harmoniously with all the other monads, so that they all reflect and affect one another, no matter how far removed from one another they are in space and time."

"Is a tree a monad?" she asked, almost breathless with the beauty of this concept.

"I think so. Yeah, I think everything that exists would be a monad, kind of. I don't know. I haven't read Leibniz in years."

Lorrie Ann just stared at him. She wanted to pick him up and shake him up and down until all of the amazing things inside of him came out, so that she could paw through all the ideas like a kid going through the fallen candy from a piñata.

"So with women, it seems like this monadic thing, like the universe is actually going to change in response to the way they are changing themselves, and they are actually changing themselves by changing the way they look at the universe. They are so much more in tune with their intuition than men, and their sense of destiny is more holistic and that demands this kind of integration, not only within society, but within themselves. They are looking to be right sized. So that they work right with all the other monads and they are all in harmony like they should be. So I guess when I said they were Luthers with vaginas, what I really meant is that they are going to take the holy book and translate it, so it isn't in Latin anymore, but in their own tongue, and that's going to change the nature of the book itself. Shazam!"

It was with these sorts of stoner sophistries, these eccentric flashes of insight, that Arman managed to win my Lorrie Ann.

She just stared at him. "I vote that you never stop talking," she said.

Arman laughed. "Usually girls want me to stop talking."

"No," Lorrie Ann said, "I would actually pay you to keep talking."

"Well," he said, "you don't have to pay me."

"That's lucky, I don't have any money."

She was a goner from then on. An absolute fucking goner.

Together they ate the burned cinnamon rolls, and Lorrie Ann wondered all night why he didn't try to kiss her.

But it wasn't Arman's style to kiss Lorrie Ann. Instead, he waited for her to kiss him. If I had to guess, I would say that even Arman's trysts with young stoner chicks who wandered into his Costa Mesa smoke shop were motivated by a profound insecurity. He had, after all, lost his legs. It was no longer comfortable for him to have sex in any position but with the woman on top, and he felt emasculated by this.

"He can't just take off the thingies and rest on his stumps like they were knees?" I asked Lor in one of our phone calls.

"It hurts too much," she said, "and besides there's something wrong with, like, the ballast. Without the shins there to stabilize, he has to keep himself entirely up with his arms, and his arms are really buff from the crutches, but it's so physically exhausting that he can't come like that, and honestly, it just isn't very fun."

"Hmm . . . ," I said.

"So I always have to be on top," she said.

"Do you mind?"

"Not at all. But I think he does."

"Why should he mind?"

"I'm not sure," Lorrie Ann said, and I wished I could read her face. "Does he just get bored of it?"

"Not exactly," she said. "He just has a really hard time coming."

"That's kind of odd," I said.

"So I usually have to finish him with my mouth."

"That's really odd," I said.

"I don't know," she said. "I guess I only really slept with Jim before."

"Yeah, well, I've slept with like thirty guys and I'm telling you: it's weird."

"Shut up."

"Prude."

"Whore."

"I love you," I said, laughing.

"I love you more," she told me.

From what I could piece together through many such conversations, Arman was the sort of man able to achieve orgasm only when the woman was in a subservient position. Submission and dominance were his game, and Lorrie Ann riding away on top, bringing herself to climax like the brave cowgirl she was, was just not hot to him. I wished that I could show Lorrie Ann the legions and legions of wonderful men who, upon hearing of this, would have cried out in horror, "What a shame! What a waste!" For who wouldn't want to be ridden by the beautiful, buxom Lorrie Ann? Only a fool, and Arman was most definitely that. Though he was a very, very smart fool.

Arman was the rare, true autodidact. I have always been secretly envious of such people, since my own education, while extensive, also has the orderly nature of an English garden. I was educated in an entirely purposive way. Arman, though, Arman had filled his mind with a vagabond mixture of trash and treasure. He had read all the major philosophers from the pre-Socratics on, but he had also read those more minor figures, like de Tocqueville, who were no longer in fashion. He read H. P. Lovecraft voraciously and had gone through an intense Hermann Hesse period, which centered, predictably, on *Steppenwolf.* He venerated obscure fiction writers like Harry Crews and had absolutely arcane taste in poetry. He worshipped *Les Chants de Maldoror* by Comte de Lautréamont, but he adored Milton above all others. In fact, when he wrote lyrics to songs, for he played the bass and Lorrie Ann the guitar, and much of their relationship took the form of smoking pot and fiddling with their instruments together, composing songs that never were more than half finished, his cadences and word choice were disturbingly Miltonic while remaining as emotionally immature as any Matchbox Twenty song.

Predictably, perhaps, he took himself painfully seriously.

"I am a man of many sorrows," he wrote Lorrie Ann once, in a letter explaining why he could not be faithful to her even though he loved her. "I am torn between the notion of love as some grand a priori concept and love as a living, cultivated reality. You are real, Lorrie Ann. Real as a hand, real as a pillow. Which is precisely what I cannot stand in you, and why I cannot abide as your kept man. I must be free to explore the infinite potentiality of the universe. You simply cannot be my muse. You don't inspire me. And yet, I love you. Honestly, what am I to do? I am being torn asunder like Dionysus."

I am being unfair in presenting him this way, so coldly showing only the worst parts of Arman. For Lorrie Ann did fall in love with him, and she had her reasons, though I suspect a large part of her love was really pity in the cloak of love.

For instance, here is how Arman lost his legs:

He and his "battle buddies" (how bizarre and troubling I found this term, as though his comrades were action figures or some other child's "my buddy" toy) were clearing a building. He walked into a room and saw his "brother" (one of his platoon) in a face-off with an eight-year-old holding an Uzi. The child and his comrade were both stock-still as in the building all around them there were screams and bursts of fire. What could Arman do? He shot the boy and saved his friend.

"He was just a child," he sobbed to Lorrie Ann one night. "He was just a little boy."

After that, Arman stayed perpetually drunk. He went on all his missions drunk. He spent all his pay on alcohol, which was difficult and costly to procure. A bottle of Crown Royal could cost upward of two hundred dollars. He was often so drunk in combat that he would fail to keep coherent grasp of the mission and would wind up stopping somewhere and just vomiting into a corner. When they fought in cities, he mostly hid behind buildings, hoping not to have to kill anyone, hoping also that a muj would stumble across him and end his farcical existence. Once, he lay down in an alley for the duration of a firefight. "I was just napping," he explained, "but everyone thought I was dead. Even my guys were surprised when later I got up." But Arman was not reprimanded or punished for this behavior, extreme as it was. "The leadership had unraveled" was his enigmatic explanation.

It was during one of these drunken missions that Arman was accidentally left behind in a building destined to be blown up. In the explosion, one of the support beams fell on him, severing his legs at the shins. "I was so happy to finally be dying," he told Lorrie Ann, "that when one of my buddies came and tried to get me, I actually threatened to shoot him. 'I'll have no legs,' I begged him. 'Please don't save me. If you have any mercy, just shoot me in the face, please. Shoot me in the face, brother.'" But his battle buddy did not, could not, in the end, bring himself to do it. Once they were back stateside, the young man had come to him in the hospital, crying and apologizing. He knew that Arman had meant it, and that it was because of him that Arman would now have to live out the rest of his days as a crippled child-killer.

"I could have been a happy dead person," Arman summed up. "But instead, I'm this."

"He wasn't a loser," Lorrie Ann said, that day at my kitchen table. Her eyes seemed glassy. Was she high? Or was she just tired? I didn't know. I didn't know a lot about drugs, really. "He was just lost."

"I'm sure," I said. "I'm not saying he was consciously malevolent or something."

"No, but, I just kept thinking, what if Jim had come back and I wasn't there? What if he'd been alone with all of that, with everything he'd done? Wouldn't I want some girl to try to love him, even though he was so broken? Wouldn't I barter my soul itself for a girl to do that for him?" She brought her thumb to her mouth and began to nibble on the nail. She still chewed them, after all these years.

I didn't know how to answer her. I wanted to say that Jim was different, that Arman had never been half the man Jim was, but I couldn't, because the truth was, I didn't think Jim had been much of a man anyway. Granted, in comparison to Arman he was like Prince Charming, but still. What I really wanted to say was that no man was worth Lorrie Ann's soul. That she shouldn't give herself up for anyone ever.

"In the thing I'm translating," I said finally, "there's this part where this goddess, Inanna, goes to the underworld. She just develops this craving for death, to know death. And as she goes, deeper and deeper, she has to give up everything. All the gifts she's been given, all the wisdom of her father, all her armor, everything. And each time, she asks why, she says, 'What is this?' And she's told, 'Quiet, Inanna, the ways of the underworld are perfect. They may not be questioned.' And finally she's naked, and she stands before the goddess of the underworld. And the judges of the underworld surround her and pass judgment over her. They kill her. It says, 'Inanna was turned into a corpse, a piece of rotting meat, and was hung from a hook on the wall.'"

"Does she really die there? That can't be the end of the story. Stories just don't end like that," Lorrie Ann said.

"She escapes," I admitted, impressed by Lor's canniness. "Her servant begs the gods for help, to go and get her, but each god says no. Her father says no because he says she chose this. He says, 'My daughter craved the Great Above, Inanna craved the Great Below . . . She who goes to the Dark City stays there.' Finally her uncle decides to help."

"So does he go and get her?" Lorrie Ann had made her thumb bleed and was now sucking on the wound.

"Weirdly, he doesn't go himself. He fashions little genderless creatures out of dirt and then gives them instructions on how to save her. They act all friendly to the queen of the underworld, sympathizing with her pain. And when she decides she likes them, she offers them a gift, and they ask for Inanna's corpse. Then they bring her back to life. They resurrect her. After that it gets complicated—the demons follow her out. The *galla*, they follow her back out into the world."

"How weird."

"I know."

We were silent then. The tea had turned bitter in the pot, and I flinched when I took a sip.

"Mia, do you think I'm a corpse hanging on the wall?" Lorrie Ann asked. "Is that it?"

"A little bit," I said. "Maybe."

I looked into my cup of tea. There was a pattern of sediment on the bottom, and I thought about the practice of divining things from tea leaves. Were women so desperate to know what would happen to them that they would tell themselves such lies, such fairy tales? Certainly, for most of history, women had not had control over what would happen to them at all, and so perhaps it was as effective as anything else to try to read the future in tea leaves. The next time I looked up, Lorrie Ann was crying.

"Where's Zach?" I asked.

"I'll tell you," she said, "but can I please, please, please go shoot up in your bathroom?"

CHAPTER NINE

Men Who Die Again and Again

Of course I said yes. There was a deep instinct in me, left over from the years with my mother and Paddy, I guess, to avoid conflict with any person who was not sober. A drunk could insist that the moon was green, and I would do nothing but nod affably. Certainly, I knew enough not to try to take away the bottle from someone trying to see the bottom of it. So there was no way I would tell Lorrie Ann she could not shoot up in my bathroom, even though I am sure that would have been the sane thing to do.

The thing that most disturbed me, and what I hadn't wanted to get into with Lorrie Ann, about the underworld section of Inanna was that when the demons follow her out of the underworld, they want to take someone in her place. A life for a life. The most ancient form of mathematics.

At first they want to take her best friend, but Inanna says no. "She is my constant support," she says. "She is my *sukkal* who gives me wise advice. She is my warrior who fights by my side." They ask for her two sons, but again, Inanna says no. She faces those terrifying *galla*, who I could not help but imagine as wooden gnomes like those Lor's mother collected, and staring deep into their wooden, inhuman eyes, she refuses to give them her sons.

But who will Inanna give up? She has to give up someone. Who will it be?

It is her lover, her husband, her mortal man, Dumuzi.

"Inanna fastened on Dumuzi the eye of death. She spoke against him the word of wrath. She uttered against him the cry of guilt: Take him! Take Dumuzi away!" And the demons fell on Dumuzi. The Sumerian descriptions of violence disturbed me—they were obscene in some way that was new to me precisely because it felt so old. The passages described the demons seizing him by the thighs, pouring out his milk, gashing him with axes.

Was that the choice—your friend, your son, or your husband? I think I had become fascinated with Inanna because I saw so much of Lor in her, or so much of her in Lor, but now, as I opened the drawer where I had secreted away the pregnancy test, a blue box with curly pink script reading "Yes or No," I feared the Inanna in myself. I feared my ability to betray—to betray Lor, to betray Franklin, to betray the bean of life that might be inside me.

How to excuse the way that Lor had betrayed Zach? If, indeed, that was what she had done. That night four years ago, when I had visited Lorrie Ann and Zach and the loser Arman in the sad, subsidized Costa Mesa apartment, there had been a moment when she was putting Zach to bed that stuck with me.

She had been lifting Zach out of his wheelchair and up onto the bed with its spread-out blanket, where she prepared to feed him through his feeding tube, holding the little bag of formula aloft so that it would flow down the tube, led by gravity, into her son, where it would give him sustenance. "At some point, I'm not going to be able to lift him anymore, and I have no idea what I'll do. Literally, I can't imagine what I'll do."

Was that what had happened? In some literal or metaphysical way, had Lorrie Ann been unable to shoulder the load?

I could hear her running water in the bathroom. Lorrie Ann was here, was in my magical sublet apartment where nothing matched and where all the knives were dull, and what should have been happy was terrible. She was shooting up in my bathroom and I was so paralyzed I didn't know what to do but pretend everything was normal.

Even with that test in my hand, I was having trouble holding the thought of a baby still enough to look at. Did I want a baby? The one time Franklin and I had talked about it he had been vehement: he had no desire for children, he didn't see himself as a papa type. It had been part of a discussion about his ex-girlfriend, Elizabeth. Her desire for children had been what made them break up. And I knew that, and so even considering keeping the child felt like a betrayal.

My own feelings were more like a swarm than a coherent position. On the one hand, there was the feeling of the miraculous, the tender and tangled, the impossible and yet ordinary division of cells that must be protected, safeguarded. On the other hand, there was Zach's infant body, gray-blue and still, all that could be taken from you when you risked wanting something. There was my crushed toe to contend with and the microsuede of my brothers' skin, my mother's puffy eyes, the possibility that I would be like her, or worse, the hanger, the horrible hanger that I had used. It was complicated, it was unspeakably complicated.

But I was afraid that no matter what happened, I would wind up betraying somebody: Franklin, or the bean of life, or myself.

I picture them in her kitchen, sometime after the Goldschläger night, Arman at the table and Lor doing dishes.

"There were complications."

"Yeah, but what complications?" he would have asked. "I mean, something specific must have happened. It's not like some percentage of children are randomly born with brain damage."

"There were problems with my uterus."

"What was the problem with your uterus?" Arman insisted, even as Lorrie Ann's shoulders became rigid.

"You're really not going to stop asking, are you?" she said, slamming the dish she was washing back into the sink.

"I told you how I lost my legs," he said, still sitting easily at her kitchen table, playing with a fork, rubbing the tines with his thumb.

"And I'm telling you: there was a problem with my uterus." She shook suds off her hands and into the sink, dried her hands on a dish towel. For a moment they just stared at each other in the small kitchen.

"Please," he said. "Please trust me."

"I don't know. I don't know what was wrong with my uterus. There just was. There was just something wrong, okay?" Lorrie Ann clutched the dish towel so that the veins and tendons in the backs of her hands danced just under the skin.

"Do you want me to do the dishes?" Arman asked. Lorrie Ann knew it was a peace offering, but it also took Arman hours to do dishes because he had to do them one handed so he could use his other hand to keep himself upright on a crutch.

"No." She sighed, turning back to the sink.

But then later in bed:

"Please just tell me the story."

"Why do you want to hear the story?"

They were in the dark, though the door was open to the lighted hall so they could hear Zach if he started to cry. He needed the hall light left on or he would get night terrors.

"Fine, don't tell me."

"Arman."

"No, if you want to stay closed up inside yourself forever, that's your choice. Not my business."

"Arman."

But he didn't speak to her. He didn't turn away; he let her keep lying there, nestled in his armpit, her head upon his chest, his long hair spread out under her like a blanket, but through some sort of voodoo he made his body unnaturally still, until it seemed he might be made of clay like a golem.

"I needed to be induced," Lorrie Ann said. Her voice sounded so tiny, so high in the darkness, even to herself, like a child's or a puppet's.

Immediately, she could feel Arman's body come back to life. She could almost hear the blood gush through his tissues. He squeezed her arm.

"I was late. I was three or four days past my due date and they kept saying Zach was going to be a big baby, that we needed to get him out of there. They said he would be nine pounds at least. He turned out to be only seven, but I guess the ultrasounds really only give you a rough estimate." She stopped for a moment, reining herself in. It was so difficult to talk about pregnancy and birth and babies because the details mattered only to people who had done it themselves. Arman wouldn't care about birth weights; he wouldn't know about how they told you the baby would be wrinkly and weird if it stayed in there too long.

"I was excited to be induced," she said. "I was huge. I was like a house. It was the middle of winter, but I was sweating all the time. I was just like: Get this baby out of me."

"Sure," he said, squeezing her arm again.

"So we go in, and they start the induction drugs, and I go into labor pretty quickly. A couple of hours, really. And right away I ask for the epidural because it hurts. I had thought I could handle it because I normally have a really high pain threshold, but—no."

"Right."

"Jim was there, and he was cute, he was like, 'Get the drugs! This is why we live in America, baby!' "

"I've always been curious—is the epidural just a nerve block or is there anything awesome in there?"

"Oh, there was definitely something awesome in there. Either that or they were giving it to me intravenously. I'm guessing fentanyl. Something like that."

"So you got the good shit!"

"Yep," Lorrie Ann said into the darkness. "I had the good shit."

For a moment she just lay there, Arman's arms around her. She wondered if Jim were looking down on her from heaven and if he would mind this man touching her, holding her in the dark of night as she told this story. Her instincts told her that Jim would hate it, that Jim would come back from the dead and charge into the room to stop it. But Jim wasn't watching. Jim was gone.

"For about the first two hours, I was like: This is great. And then I started feeling really weird. I felt panicky, like my heart was racing, just this overwhelming feeling of wrongness. And then, even through the epidural, pain started coming—pain like a knife. It felt like someone was sitting on my chest. I kept telling Jim: It hurts, it hurts. The next parts I don't remember very well, but they turned up my epidural because I wouldn't stop screaming. I remember the nurse rolling her eyes because she thought I was just being a baby. I kept saying: Something's wrong, it hurts. Everyone kept saying: Yeah, it hurts—you're having a baby. My labor had completely stalled and they were frustrated with me, I remember. I couldn't breathe because that heavy feeling on my chest was getting worse and worse, like an elephant sitting down on me. And then . . . I passed out."

"What happened?"

"Emergency C-section."

"But why did you pass out?"

"My uterus just tore. And all the amniotic fluid started to leak out into my stomach cavity, and I guess I had a seizure."

"But why did your uterus tear?"

"We don't know."

"Uteruses can just tear?"

"I guess so."

There was silence, and then suddenly Lorrie Ann heard Arman sniffle. When she turned to look at him, she could see by the light on in the hall that he was crying. She was surprised. "I'm sorry," she said.

"No," he said, wiping the few tears away with the back of his hand. "It just kills me: that nurse rolling her eyes at you while your uterus was splitting open."

"She didn't know," Lorrie Ann said.

"She should have."

"How could she have known?"

"They should have listened to you. They ignored you."

"Everyone ignores a woman in labor," she said.

There was silence again. Lorrie Ann was surprised at how defensive she felt. She couldn't afford, emotionally, for Arman to take her side in this way. She couldn't afford it because Jim hadn't done it. It had never occurred to Jim that everyone had ignored Lorrie Ann. That she had tried to tell them something was wrong, that an elephant was sitting on her chest, that her heart was racing. Jim had only been kind and never tried to make her feel bad for having a defective uterus that tore. But he had never, not even for a moment, suggested to her that she had been worth listening to, that she had been mistreated.

"What did the doctor say?" Arman asked.

"He said I was lucky," Lorrie Ann said, hoping like hell Arman wouldn't hear the quaver in her voice.

Then again, if he really wanted to cry, Arman could have just started doing a little bit of Internet research. The drug they gave Lorrie Ann to induce her labor was called Misoprostol. If Arman had Googled it, he would have seen that it was an oral medication for stomach ulcers that doctors had discovered also had a weird side effect of inducing labor if you stuck it up a woman's vagina. Misoprostol was only eight dollars a dose; the next cheapest induction drug was almost two hundred dollars a dose. It wasn't illegal to use Misoprostol; the FDA had approved it. For stomach ulcers. Taken orally. No one had studied exactly what it would do if you put it up a woman's vagina, but it seemed to work great.

Arman wouldn't have really found much online back when all this happened to Lorrie Ann. Doctors had just started experimenting with Misoprostol, and, anecdotally, it was a miracle drug. The best thing about Misoprostol was that it would bring on labor so hard and so fast that a woman could be induced at eight in the morning and the doctor could be home by three in the afternoon. "Let's just get this over with," doctors would say to women, and the women agreed: they wanted to get it over with too. They were scared. All they knew of labor was women screaming and almost dying in movies and on TV. All they wanted was to be safe, and safety was doing what the doctor said.

If he had looked into it later, when Zach was six, and when he first started banging Lorrie Ann, Arman would have found troubling indications that Misoprostol had been linked to uterine rupture, especially in cases where the mother had had a previous cesarean. The uterus would contract so violently from the drug that it would literally be ripped apart inside the woman's body. The babies often drowned to death inside their mother's abdominal cavities.

But Lorrie Ann hadn't had a previous C-section. What had happened?

It was the kind of puzzle that would have bothered Arman. He would have wanted to figure it out. God knows, I did.

Was it that Lorrie Ann's doctor had given her four doses of 100 milligrams, when the standard dose was 25 milligrams? Or did she perhaps have a placental abruption or weakness that some careless ultrasound tech had missed? How big had the tears in her uterus even been? Had the complete hysterectomy the doctor performed during her C-section truly been necessary? Would things have turned out differently if anyone had actually listened to Lorrie Ann when she told them something was wrong, that there was a new pain? If the nurse with the My Little Pony eye shadow had been a bit better with those fetal monitors? If they had rushed her to surgery the moment she alerted them, would Zach have been born blue?

Lorrie Ann would say that no one could know the answer to that question and that it wasn't worth asking anyway. But I say that it was fifty-seven minutes between the time she first told them something was wrong and the time the C-section was performed, that was what the log in her records said: fifty-seven minutes. And those fifty-seven minutes were what cost Zach his brain. Fifty-seven minutes of drowning in Lorrie Ann's stomach. Fifty-seven minutes, during thirty-five of which Lorrie Ann was conscious and begging. Thirty-five minutes of rolling their eyes at her. Of telling her to calm down. Of counting off Lamaze breathing techniques for her. Of telling her to focus. Just focus. Calm down. Stop screaming. Stop screaming. Thirty-five minutes.

I would have suggested that Lorrie Ann sue, and would have offered to pay for the lawyers, if my preliminary research hadn't already shown me how fruitless Misoprostol lawsuits were. I did all this research in the years after I saw Lorrie Ann and Arman in the subsidized Costa Mesa apartment and she told me she'd had a complete hysterectomy. I hadn't known before that her uterus had torn. Was it standard to remove a woman's uterus in an emergency C-section? I started to look into it. I asked Lorrie Ann for her hospital records. I told her I was looking into getting some kind of compensation for Zach to help pay for his physical therapy. And in a way, I was.

But you couldn't prove it was the Misoprostol that had caused the uterus to rupture. There wasn't any science to establish a connection; no studies had been done; it was an ulcer medication. The doctors couldn't be blamed for using an FDA-approved medication, even if its FDA approval was for the drug as used orally to treat stomach ulcers. There wasn't any protocol in place since the drug was being used off-label, so you couldn't even get doctors for using an inappropriate dosage.

And it's true: everyone ignores a woman in labor.

This was just the way babies got born.

This was just the way women were hung, like meat, from hooks upon the wall.

When Lorrie Ann came back into the room, I slammed shut the drawer that hid the pregnancy test. I didn't want to tell her I might be pregnant. I didn't want to take the test in front of her, to find out yes or no, and then to have her ask, to have to tell her, what I was thinking, whether I thought: yes or no.

"So did I tell you about the Indians?" Lorrie Ann said.

"Indians?"

She swept past me to the table and resumed her place before her tea-cup. She looked phenomenally better. She had redone her braid and splashed water on her face. Her eyes were bright and sparkling.

"That's the first part of the story," Lorrie Ann said, "of how I lost Zach. By the way, I love the plants in your bathroom."

"Thank you," I said, coming to sit at the table with her, as the understanding of what she had said settled inside me like a heavy stone. So this was the Story of How I Lost Zach. I found that my lungs would not inflate fully.

"So when my mother came out of her coma, she claimed she had had a vision."

"A vision?"

"A vision about the genocide of the Native Americans."

"Like a dream? Is there a difference between a vision and a dream?"

Lorrie Ann sighed. "I don't know," she said, "but my mother got all fired up about the injustice of what we did to the Native Americans. She told me parts of it, the dream. She had some kind of guide, an Indian that, like, I don't know, showed her all of history? She claims to have been adopted by the Blackfoot tribe in her dream. It's—none of this matters, it's just something that happens with traumatic brain injury. The pressure from the swelling—it made her brain fire in all sorts of weird ways."

"But after she came out of the coma? Was she okay?"

"Well. Yes and no. I mean, she wasn't seeing things that weren't there or anything, but she became convinced that the reason Zach was born blue was because our ancestors had participated in the genocide. Cause and effect. Karma. Whatever you want to call it, like history is some big Rube Goldberg machine. So now we had to go around doing good works in order to lift the curse off our family."

"This is just so weird," I said.

"Actually, apparently lots and lots of people have visions about the Native American genocide. They have a Web forum. She goes on there all the time. She's obsessed."

"Holy fuck," I said, setting down my empty teacup.

"I know," Lorrie Ann said, letting a trill of laughter escape. The drugs were making her feel good, I could tell. She was enjoying talking, leaning toward me. Her pupils were tiny. "She can't work anymore. Her old work wouldn't hire her back after the accident."

"Just because of the Indians?" Lor's happiness was eerie, as though she were actually enjoying her mother's misfortune.

"They say she can't be trusted around children," Lorrie Ann said, waving her hand dismissively. "That part's bunk. I think she'd be fine around kids. The worst she would do is tell them about Indians being slaughtered. But because of stuff at the hospital, she had to see a shrink and then Social Security and on and on, and now she's in the system as being mentally disabled. She bit a nurse."

"She bit a nurse?!"

"Yeah, when she first woke up. She claims not to remember biting the nurse."

"It's totally impossible for me to imagine your mother biting a nurse," I said. Underneath my almost overdone exclamations of surprise was a strange, furtive seed of doubt: What if Lorrie Ann were making all of this up?

"Honestly, I suspect the nurse provoked her in some way."

"And there are Web forums for these people—for people who have visions about Native Americans?"

"Oh yeah," Lor said. "Can I have some water? Or juice? Do you have juice? There's a ton of them."

"I have seltzer." I got up to pour her some from the fridge. All the hairs on the backs of my arms were standing up.

"Not a ton of Native Americans, obviously. But a ton of people who become obsessed with them, or haunted by them. I mean, not any kind of large-scale movement or anything. But more than you'd think. At least hundreds of them."

"And so do you know why she bit the nurse?"

"It's unclear," Lorrie Ann said, using both hands to accept the glass of seltzer, like a child. "My mom was in a lot of distress, and she was shouting things about there being blood on the nurse's hands, and the nurse was trying to hold her down, so she could be strapped to the bed because she was thrashing, and I guess my mom bit her."

This didn't seem terribly unreasonable to me. No disoriented person likes to be held down so they can be strapped to a bed. "Still," I said, "you'd think they would have experience with things like that. I hope the nurse didn't take it personally."

"Actually, the nurse was black, and for some reason she got really upset with the whole thing. She yelled at me about it, and what she was most upset about was being accused of killing the Native Americans. My mom was raving, and I guess she kept calling the nurse a white devil, which really freaked the nurse the fuck out. 'My people didn't have anything to do with that,' she kept saying. And she felt it was unfair that my mother's anger was centered on the genocide instead of on slavery or any of the other awful things white people did."

"So then Dana came to live with you."

"Exactly."

"And how was that?"

Lor paused, and her eyebrows flared as she considered her teacup. "It was bizarre," she said finally. "The whole last year has been fucking bizarre."

CHAPTER TEN

A Bad Mother

Over the breakfast table:

"I'm just saying," Dana insisted, spreading apricot jam on her English muffin, "four hundred treaties—not a single one of them kept. On not one did we keep our word."

"Doesn't surprise me," Arman said.

"Well, it should."

"Anyone want coffee?" Lor asked, holding out the pot.

"After Cain and Abel, who can really afford to be surprised by anything? Genocide?" Arman scoffed. "My people were victims of one of the most successful genocides in modern history and no one even knows about it."

"But America parades around as the good guy!"

"So does Turkey," Arman countered. "And Hitler would have too if he hadn't lost the spear of destiny."

"Oh please," Lor said. "Let's not talk about the spear of destiny. It isn't even eight in the morning yet!"

"What is the spear of destiny?" Dana asked, chewing her English muffin with gusto. For some reason, ever since the attack, Dana's jaw clicked every time her mouth closed, not just a tiny click, but a low, deep click that seemed to imply a bone structure much larger than Dana's and made her sound like a cow or a horse masticating. It drove Lor slightly mad.

And so Arman explained the spear of destiny, the holy lance that pierced Christ's side and that, it was said, gave dominion over the whole world to whoever possessed it. Today there were six alleged spears, though which, if any, was the real historical relic remained unknown. Hitler had started World War II in order to capture the spear, with which he was obsessed, or so said Trevor Ravenscroft's 1973 book, *The Spear of Destiny*. At the end of the war, Hitler lost the spear and it fell into the hands of U.S. general George Patton. Part of the lore of the spear was that losing it would result in death, which is perhaps why Hitler committed suicide.

"What did the United States do with it once they got it from Hitler?" Dana asked.

"Do you see what you've done?" Lorrie Ann asked Arman. "This isn't good for her."

"No one knows," Arman said. "But most people believe they've still got it. After all, look around. Crazy world run by fat-fuck Americans. Don't make no kinda sense."

Meanwhile, before Dana even got out of the hospital, Lorrie Ann, in the scramble of trips to visit Dana, doctor's appointments, and attempts to get Zach to day care, had shown up to work late three days in a row, and then, on the fourth day, had had to call in. Roberta, the bartender, had answered the call.

"No, sweetie, I can tell him. He's pissed right now because he can't find the box of silverware he thinks he ordered, but I'll tell him. It's crazy you've even been coming in with things as nuts as they have been. It's a Tuesday. We'll be fine."

The shameful truth is that Lor had had to call in not because she needed to bring Dana home from the hospital and spend the night getting her settled in as she claimed—Dana wasn't coming home until Friday at the earliest—but because she didn't think she could emotionally handle waiting on people for one minute more. She couldn't smile and say, "My name's Lorrie Ann. I'll be your server tonight. Let me just tell you a little bit about our specials." She couldn't pretend to laugh at the new head chef's jokes. Instead, she stayed home in sweatpants with Arman and Zach, getting high and watching *Watership Down*, which terrified Zach and sent him into hysterics.

Roberta didn't call Lorrie Ann that night to say that Zipper had fired her. (Zipper was the owner of The Cellar. I had met him once or twice. He was a greasy, middle-aged cokehead who had been the proud owner of John Travolta good looks in his youth, of which all that remained was the braggadocio.) Roberta hoped that Zipper would change his mind in the morning when he was sober. After all, Lorrie Ann had worked there ever since Jim died and she moved back to Costa Mesa, almost four years ago. It would be insane to fire her for calling in sick when her mother was in the hospital, as everyone well knew.

But that was precisely the kind of insane Zipper was, apparently. When Lor showed up for work the next day, even more tired from her all-night vigil with Zach, the chorus of which had been, "Bunnies aren't really like that, baby, I promise. They don't hurt each other like that. I'm so so sorry, baby. Mommy didn't know," Zipper asked her what she was doing there.

"I'm the five-to-ten shift."

"You don't work here anymore," Zipper said, coldly stapling a stack of receipts together behind the bar. "Or were you too busy to read the memo?"

"There was a memo? Wait, what are you talking about, Zipper?"

"We had one server on, Lor. One!"

"My mother is in the hospital," Lor began. "She—"

"I don't really give a fuck," Zipper said. "I need reliable servers. You are no longer reliable. End of story. We'll find someone else who can be reliable."

And so that was that.

When Lor got back to her apartment, still in her blacks, Arman was surprised to see her. "You get cut early?" he asked. He was making an egg-salad sandwich in her kitchen.

"I got fired," she said.

"No," Arman said.

"That's what Zipper said."

"He's just mad," Arman said. "Give him a couple days and he'll change his mind."

But he didn't. And so, by the time Dana moved in, Lor was unemployed, and she, Dana, and Zach lived mostly on Lor's unemployment and relied heavily upon Arman's kindness.

The state of Arman's finances was always slightly mysterious to Lor. He owned the smoke shop, but not really. In order to keep receiving his disability, he had to seem unable to work, and so his family, more precisely his uncle, "owned" the smoke shop and filed all the taxes. All of Arman's family owned 7-Elevens, and they had offered him one of these, but Arman had wanted the smoke shop. "It's more 'me,'" he had explained to Lorrie Ann. "Can you even picture me running a 7-Eleven?"

In any event, Arman turned over the majority of his income to the family and kept some small amount for himself. Always there was drama regarding this amount. Sometimes, Arman would begin to cook the books and cheat his uncle; other times, he would claim that his uncle took everything and that he made next to nothing on top of his disability checks, which were by no means extravagant. "It doesn't pay very well to get your legs blown off for your country," Arman said. "You'd think they'd at least keep me in booze."

"They keep you in opiates," Lor pointed out.

"True," Arman admitted.

Whatever the true state of Arman's poverty, during this period of crisis, he did genuinely help Lorrie Ann. He filled her fridge with groceries. He sent in the payment on her car insurance. Eventually, he pointed out, Dana would probably get some sort of settlement for having been beaten nearly to death. Perhaps he was generous with Lorrie Ann because he assumed he would get a slice of the pie.

Wasn't that how it worked? When you got nearly beaten to death, didn't someone give you a ton of money? Lorrie Ann had just assumed it was so, and Arman assured her that eventually it would work out this way, but in fact, it never did. For one thing, though Bobby found out it was Carlos through the grapevine, he never gave the boy up. The case remained unsolved. For another thing, even if Carlos had been tried, what damages could they have squeezed in a civil suit from a boy who had less than nothing and was not even a legal U.S. citizen? In the end, Dana was simply put on disability, just like Arman and Zach. She spent all day on Jim's old Dell laptop. It ran so slowly that only Dana's fanatical zeal gave her the patience to wait through the boot-up, writing to various people on her American Indian forums and doing research on what she called "the biggest cover-up ever perpetrated by the American government. Lor, this makes Watergate look like child's play."

During this time Lor sank into a profound depression. In his boundless wisdom and generosity, Arman gave Lorrie Ann free reign with all of his prescriptions. Doubtless he thought he was easing her through her tough time. Dana never even noticed when Lor started taking her Vicodin to augment her high because she herself had stopped taking them, didn't like them: "They cloud my mind. You know, it just figures that the white man would invent this kind of poison and hand it out like it was medicine." Lor would spend days at a time in the same pajamas. Her relationship with Arman had become almost entirely platonic. (The opiates compromised his ability to get an erection.) If he noticed that she had stopped washing her hair, he said nothing. Neither he nor she attempted to wash the dishes piling up in the sink. Dana sometimes did them. One day the cat got out and was never seen again.

"He'll come back," Arman kept telling her. But Lor knew the cat was gone for good. She felt terrible that she couldn't seem to cry for the cat. Had she even loved the cat? She thought she had, but now she didn't know. It was unclear. When she tried to remember specific moments of intimacy with the cat, she couldn't. All she remembered was the way the cat kept its paws so white, and the way its ears seemed too large for its body. Was that enough? Was that love?

Lor spent a lot of time thinking about killing herself. Because of the availability of large amounts of narcotics, she didn't have to visualize hanging herself from the ceiling fan in the bedroom or slitting her wrists in the tub. She could just wait until the first of the month, when Arman filled all his prescriptions, and then she could take them all. (Actually, she planned to leave Arman the share she had determined he legitimately needed for his legs. She was thoughtful and prim even in wanton despair.) But the truth was, no matter how much Lorrie Ann longed for death, and no matter how peaceful and happy these fantasies made her, she knew she could never do anything so selfish. She had a child to take care of.

But it was also during this time that Lorrie Ann began to have trouble moving Zach. Dana had firm instructions not to lift anything heavy and Arman had no legs; there was no one she could ask for help. She could barely maneuver Zach between the chair and his bed, and several nights she let him sleep sitting up because she was just too tired. The child seemed to sleep just as badly in his chair as he did in his bed. What did it even matter? He hardly slept anyway. He was in constant pain. The muscles of his spine and legs were so tight that his hips were always on the verge of dislocating. Because his breathing was also compromised, the doctors worried about giving him pain medication that would further suppress his lung function, and so he was allowed nothing but Tylenol. (Even after his many surgeries, the boy was never given anything stronger than Tylenol, which may go some distance toward explaining his phobia of hospitals.)

In other words, moving Zach also hurt him, and every time Lorrie Ann did it, she worried she might dislocate his legs, forcing a trip to the ER. Every time she had to change his diaper, she worried similarly. And so she changed his diaper less. He got a rash; she tried to treat the rash, but still, the rash persisted. Eventually, the rash turned into sores, perhaps also from sitting all day without being able to shift position. The worse the boy got, the guiltier Lorrie Ann felt, and the more, the very more she considered simply ending it, either by killing herself or else by killing Zach.

For the record, she considered killing Zach to be the more ethical of the two options. As far as she could tell, the only profit on Zach's continued life was his continued agony. She seemed to be the only one who questioned why and for what they were keeping him alive. Even Dana shushed her, saying, "Don't even talk that way. He's a beautiful boy."

But with every day he grew older, his body grew heavier, and the pressure on his joints increased. Every day he lived upped the amount of pain he was in. These days, he moaned almost constantly. She gave him the Tylenol, the highest doses she was allowed to give him, but she suspected he had long ago become resistant to the drug. She made his life a continual cycle of things that he loved: SpongeBob, playing cars (Lor moved the cars for him, driving them up and down his body and making the noises), walks around the housing complex, chocolate pudding (one of the few foods he loved enough to even try to eat). She tried to avoid or limit all things he did not like: baths, doctors, her being out of sight. But he was not happy. Sometimes he could not even bring himself to laugh when she made the elephant puppet sneeze, which was his favorite, his very favorite thing. He just smiled at her tiredly, as though to say: "I know you're trying." Yet, if she killed Zach, she had no doubt that she would be tried and convicted and sentenced to life in prison.

If, on the other hand, she killed herself, she would merely be passing the buck, and Zach would go to people who would continue to foster him in his agony, his body itself like a torture chamber for the soul within it, only those people would not even know enough to weep, would not love him, would not suffer with him. He would then be utterly alone. Lorrie Ann could not imagine anything more horrible.

If she were a good person, Lorrie Ann believed, she would kill Zach in the kindest way she knew of, which, she decided, would be to grind up OxyContin and feed it to him through his feeding tube, mixed into the formula, and then suffer the consequences. Wouldn't life in prison be easier than this? Wouldn't she feel better at least knowing that Zach was in heaven? Or, if there was no heaven, as she more and more suspected, knowing that Zach was at least not in any active pain?

But she was scared. She was scared to do it, scared something would go wrong. What if she only half killed Zach and they had to go to the hospital and they found out and took Zach away? Then all would have been in vain. She couldn't let that happen. But what if Zach needed more help dying? Could she really bring herself to put a pillow over his face? Could she press down? Even if he were moaning, were screaming, were making those noises that sometimes sounded so achingly close to "Mommy" that it sent shivers down her spine?

She worried also that her mother or Arman would walk in on her in the act. Could she possibly make them understand? She suspected that by crossing a line like that, she might cause reality to buck and sway. No one would be able to see her and forgive her. She would be beyond the pale, living in a world entirely on her own.

At my kitchen table, Lor went on, talking calmly, a steady stream of words, as tears simply ran and ran down her face. I had never seen any-one cry like that before: just the tears, without the sobbing. She didn't even reach up to brush them away, and so they flowed down her chin, her neck, and wetted the neckline of her sundress.

I felt sure then that no matter what happened, no matter what she told me, I would be able to take her side, to understand, to agree. I even felt at peace with the way she had fallen into taking Arman's painkillers. Of course, I thought, of course. I understood completely.

Dana, Lor went on to explain, was from another time, and she wasn't afraid of cops. She didn't have any native distrust of authority. In fact, she assumed that such people took positions of authority out of an innate goodness and desire to serve the community. In Dana's world, people became prison guards out of Christian charity toward the inmates. Do you see? And so, upon being assigned a social worker, Dana set about trying to befriend the woman. She held nothing back, but was frank and scrupulously honest. It was this behavior, actually, that convinced the social worker that Dana was, indeed, quite mentally ill. No one except for crazy people reached out and squeezed a social worker's hand after having served them tea and mint Milano cookies. No one volunteered so much highly personal information. And, of course, no one went on so about the genocide of the American Indian.

Lor herself had a social worker because of Zach, but Mr. Kawabata seldom visited. Dana's social worker was not a bad woman, Lor made sure to point out to me. She was a lesbian.

"How do you know?" I asked.

"She looked like a lesbian," Lor said. "I don't know. Maybe she wasn't. Maybe she just looked like one."

Kerry McDonough, which was the social worker's name, was not tall for a woman, but stocky, with short salt-and-pepper hair and a potbelly. Her skin was pink, as though she scrubbed it with steel wool, and her nose was so shiny you could see your reflection in it. She wore little oval glasses with black metal frames. Of course, since Dana really was a wonderful woman, even if she was crazy, McDonough got to like her, and Dana, being Dana, liked McDonough. The two of them established a rapport. Dana even began to call McDonough Dunny, which McDonough secretly liked.

"Oh, Dunny! Come in, come in!" Dana would cry, clasping McDonough's beefy hands in her own and leading McDonough back into the kitchen, where she would offer her muffins made of Bisquick or a cup of chili or whatever she happened to have on hand. McDonough, to her credit, managed to listen attentively to quite a bit of Dana's rambling about the Native Americans. What a shame, though, that McDonough assumed Dana was making it all up. In fact, almost everything that Dana said was true.

"No, Dunny, that first study everyone quotes was done by the government. In the only study ever done by independent researchers, they give a high and a low number. The low number is ten million. The high number is one hundred fourteen million."

"That's quite a variance," McDonough said.

"I know. Well, no one was keeping very good count, were they? They didn't think it was important. Can you imagine? But you see, it's a much larger number than the Jewish Holocaust."

"Wow," McDonough said. Not only did McDonough not believe 114 million Indians had been killed, she had a hard time believing there had ever even been that many Indians total. In point of fact, McDonough did not have any clear idea of exactly how many Jews had been killed in the Holocaust, so Dana's argument was moot.

And so it came to pass that one day when McDonough was over, Dana asked her for a favor. Lorrie Ann was out looking for work. In fact, she was interviewing at a gastropub that was set to open in the newly revitalized downtown of Santa Ana. She had expected the interview to take only an hour, including drive time, but when she arrived, there had been a line around the block: all young women, dressed in black, clutching résumés to their chests and chewing gum. She got in the line and she waited in it for two hours before she was allowed to interview. The most painful thing about it was not the boredom of the wait, but how alienated she felt from the other girls, who were all about ten years younger than she was. Instinctively, they ignored her as they made giggling small talk with one another. Lor felt frantic. She worried she wouldn't be hired because she was too old, that she would be put out to pasture like a horse. She was only twenty-nine! But in waitress years, that was like being one hundred.

Back at home, Dana was asking McDonough if she could possibly help Dana change Zach's diaper. Uneasily, McDonough agreed. Changing the diapers of ten-year-old boys with cerebral palsy was not normally something she considered within her purview. But for Dana, she would have done just about anything. I'm not saying she had a crush on Lorrie Ann's mother; we don't even know if Dunny was truly a lesbian. But a lot of McDonough's cases were depressing, and visiting Dana was not depressing. In fact, Dana's love of the American Indian and of ceramic gnomes and of blue eyeliner struck McDonough as downright charming.

And so it came to be that McDonough entered Zach's room for the first time and saw the heaps of undone laundry, the dirty bedsheets that were flecked with spilled feeding-tube formula, and the drawn mini-blinds, which made the otherwise ordinary room seem sordid and dim. She helped lift Zach from his chair and get his sweatpants off, but when she and Dana undid his diaper, and wiped away the shit, McDonough saw the sores. She saw that they were festering. She saw that his whole bottom was bruised from sitting all day. She saw that he was emaciated and his rib cage was showing. She saw that the area around his feeding tube was pink and inflamed. She saw what looked like a lesion on his testicles. It was enough to make her nauseated, and she had to let Dana do most of the work while she sat on the edge of the bed with her head between her knees.

She got up only when Dana announced that Zach was ready to go back into his chair. McDonough didn't think he should go back into the chair, but she didn't know how to say this. She needed to call Child Protective Services. She would call as soon as she got out to her car and have them come over right away. For now, she would help Dana and do as she was asked.

But as she was lifting him, she dislocated one of his legs. It popped right out of the hip socket, and suddenly the room was filled with the pure siren of Zach's agony, screams like McDonough had never heard in all her life.

So McDonough called 911.

So McDonough and Dana and Zach went to the ER.

So Child Protective Services became involved, and Zach never came home again.

CHAPTER ELEVEN

The Intervention

"It was probably only because McDonough liked my mom so much that they didn't press charges," Lor said. All of her earlier giddiness was drained away. Her eyes were glassy and distant.

"For what?" I asked, outraged.

"For negligence. Neglect."

"That's insane. What were you supposed to do? So then what happened?"

"Nothing happened," Lor said. "He's in foster care. A group home. Basically a nursing home."

I sat at the table with her then, just watching. She was leaning with her forearms on the tabletop, her shoulders hunched up around her ears as she squeezed at one of her cuticles. She had bitten it until it bled and now was trying to assess the damage. She blinked several times, as though her eyeballs were drying out. I got the sense that she was barely present.

"Did you appeal?"

Lor shook her head, still looking only at her bleeding cuticle.

"Well, that's the first thing we can do," I said. "Listen, I was going to head back to the States anyway. I could come stay in California and help you get this all worked out." Of course this trip to the States was being fabricated by me as I spoke the words. It did seem reasonable, in a way, to go back to the States for the abortion. It might be nice to have Lorrie Ann as an excuse. Just in case I decided not to tell Franklin. Just in case I needed, for some reason, to keep it to myself.

"I don't want to appeal," Lorrie Ann said, very softly.

"What do you mean?"

"I can't. I can't do it anymore. I can't go back to living that way."

"Of course. We'll get you proper help. Maybe an in-home nurse or something."

"Mia," Lorrie Ann said.

"We can do this," I insisted.

"No."

She looked up at me with eyes so empty and blue, I almost dropped my teacup. I felt immediate shame. I was like a child playing with a doll, trying to prop Lorrie Ann up at the tea party that was her ruined life, just so that I could avoid the pain of having to admit that it was ruined— and that Lorrie Ann was nothing more than a limp doll, a corpse upon the wall.

As it turned out, what happened was that Lorrie Ann had come home to the note from Dana telling Lor they were at the Hoag ER. The note did not say exactly why they had gone to the ER, but Lor knew that Dana had had her license suspended due to her brain injury and that, if they had gone to the ER, they had gone in an ambulance. (Bobby had taken over Dana's old Accord.) Because of this, and the fact that Lor knew Dana couldn't lift Zach, Lor honestly assumed much worse than a dislocated hip.

When Lor finally found them at Hoag, Dunny and Dana were drinking cocoa out of paper cups that had clearly come from a machine. When they told her about Zach's leg popping out of his hip socket, Lorrie Ann let out a trill of nervous and relieved laughter that made Dunny flinch. Lorrie Ann wanted to explain, but it was too complicated, and so she just made a waving motion of her hand. "I thought," she said, "I thought much worse. Okay. I'm sorry. Okay." She talked to the doctor, but she didn't remember what the doctor said. All she knew was that they were keeping Zach overnight and she should come back in the morning, so Dunny drove her and Dana home.

———

"Wait a second," I said, "I don't get it. How did you not know what they were going to do to Zach? How do you not know what the doctors said?"

None of this meshed at all with my notion of Lorrie Ann. Lorrie Ann had practically given herself a medical degree by reading articles about CP on the Internet. Lorrie Ann was deeply invested in Zach. She loved him. It didn't make any sense for her to just leave him at the hospital.

"I was really high," Lorrie Ann said.

"You went to the job interview high?"

"No, I went to the interview sober. I came home, found the note, got high, went to the ER." She said this easily, without guilt or shame, as though she were just clarifying a simple series of events.

"Why did you get high before going to the hospital?" I asked.

Lorrie Ann looked into her empty glass. She had drunk all the seltzer. "I thought he might be dead."

"Why would you want to be high at a moment like that?"

"So that I wouldn't have to feel it."

"Wouldn't you want to feel it?" I asked. "I mean, he's your son. If you really thought he was dead, wouldn't you race out the door and speed all the way there? I just can't imagine you actually reading that note and *not* jumping in the car."

Lorrie Ann didn't say anything. It was almost as though I hadn't asked her the questions. She didn't look at me either, but not as though she were avoiding my eyes—but like I wasn't there at all. She just rolled the bottom of her glass around on the table, letting the afternoon pass, letting the sun fall through the open window onto her shoulders, lighting up her blond braid in spangles.

"Lorrie Ann," I said, trying to shame her into talking to me.

"Lolola," I said, like someone reprimanding a dog.

"After you killed your little baby, you ate a hamburger," Lorrie Ann said simply, dispassionately. "So don't fucking talk to me that way, all right?"

And it was true. I had killed a little baby. And now I was considering killing another one. I was some kind of modern Medea. Who was I to judge Lorrie Ann? Who are any of us to judge? It went beyond throwing stones from glass houses. It wasn't just that no one was unimpeachable. It was that there was no such thing as judgment.

I thought about Inanna tossing her lover, Dumuzi, to the *galla* and how I judged her, could find no way around judging her. She had loved him so much. The passages of her courtship with Dumuzi were some of my favorite in all of literature. They had rung through my mind when I was first falling in love with Franklin, had become part of our own love story. The fact that she went on to betray him felt like an almost personal affront.

I remember first reading Franklin's rough translation of it in the bathtub of my apartment back in Ann Arbor. And even completely alone, in the dead of night, I blushed red as a beet.

The sexiness of it shocked me. I had never seen sexuality represented in such arboricultural terms. Inanna sings: "He has sprouted; he has burgeoned; he is lettuce planted by the water. He is the one my womb loves best."

As I read on, I became more and more scandalized. I couldn't believe these things had been written down, in some ancient language, lost for thousands of years, and then Franklin had copied them into a Rhodes composition book in his scratchy, childlike penmanship for me to read in an old scarred bathtub in a rental in Michigan.

Our system involved me looking at the cuneiform, which I could just barely read, as well as a copy of Franklin's translation, most of which was done by hand and then photocopied for me. My reading level in cuneiform was about like a third grader's: third graders can read Shakespeare in a technical sense, but in another sense they can't read him at all. So I needed Franklin's words in order to make sense of what I was reading, but I wasn't only reading Franklin's words: I was looking for the reflection I got between the two when I read them side by side. And then I tried to write down that thing—that magic thing that hovered between the two of them. "Make your milk sweet and thick, my bridegroom," Inanna sings. "My shepherd, I will drink your fresh milk . . . Let the milk of the goat flow in my sheepfold."

I had never, not once in my entire life, figured my vagina as a sheepfold. I was both horrified and powerfully aroused by the idea.

I often told Franklin he was my lettuce planted by the water.

(Had I killed a little baby? Had I really done that? Was there really a little baby growing inside me now?)

I wondered if Lorrie Ann had loved Jim the way I loved Franklin. Had he been her lettuce planted by the water? Had they watched in wonder together as her belly grew swollen and ripe, sure that they were owed the springtime of their lives, the bloody harvest of live-born young? Did he say something suddenly, offhand, as he was getting ready for work, or as he was rinsing a dish, that cut through the corridors of her loneliness? (I picture the inside of Lorrie Ann as one large colonnade, entirely of polished Carrara marble, every surface glittering like frosted glass or like the teeth of unicorns. In my mind there are no footsteps, no one wandering in this temple, for Lorrie Ann is the temple itself and not its priestess.) I remember them enjoying each other, surely, laughing. Jim could make anyone laugh. But had he known her? Had he really seen her, that frightening, wonderful, terrifying thing that was Lorrie Ann?

"So you got high and went to the hospital," I prompted. "And then Dunny drove you and your mom home again."

"And we ordered from Papa John's."

"Dunny stayed for dinner?"

"Yes," Lorrie Ann said. "She did."

"Was Arman there?"

"Yes," Lorrie Ann said. "He was."

"This is the weirdest night I can even imagine," I said.

"It was the weirdest night of my entire life. But at the same time completely normal. We were all just exhausted. I went to bed early, after we finished eating. Arman came in and just stroked my hair. He was really good at touching my hair, not like most men. He understood long hair because he had long hair, and he knew what felt good. He braided my hair and didn't talk to me at all. It was so kind. It was the nicest anyone has ever been to me."

I felt sure that I had been that nice to her, but I said nothing. I couldn't bring to mind a specific time I had been nice to her. But I had, hadn't I?

"But I guess Dunny and my mom stayed up talking," Lor said, wetting her lips with her tongue. I could hear how dry her mouth was, how thick her spit. "I guess they stayed up to chat."

Dana had confessed to Dunny that her Vicodin had gone missing and that it seemed to her like perhaps Lorrie Ann had been taking it. At first, she told Dunny, she had suspected Arman. After all, he seemed the drug addict type. But after some time observing her daughter, who rarely changed out of her pajamas, and who seemed content to spend all day every day watching *SpongeBob SquarePants* with her disabled son, Dana had realized that Lorrie Ann might have a problem. Did Dunny have any advice?

And so Dunny and Dana hatched a plan. Dunny confessed that she had already alerted Child Protective Services at the hospital and had recommended that Zach be taken from the home. She had worried about making this recommendation because she didn't know how Dana would feel about it, but Dana reassured her that she thought this was for the best. Taking care of Zach was more than Lorrie Ann was capable of these days. "It would have been different if my son-in-law had lived," Dana said. "He could have helped her."

"I'm so sorry to hear that," Dunny said. "I didn't know he'd passed."

"The war," Dana said. "War does not determine who is right—only who is left. Bertrand Russell said that."

Dunny, of course, had no idea who Bertrand Russell was. She only nodded, her brow knit, hoping to keep Dana from digressing into a rant. "I in no way blame her. I think she's trying the best that she can. That's what these systems are there for—a safety net. For when you just can't do it on your own."

"Exactly," Dana said. "I couldn't agree more. But what do you think we should do about the drugs?"

Dunny was more inclined to take the idea of Lorrie Ann as a drug addict seriously because of the way she had laughed at the hospital, had seemed so distracted, had been glassy eyed and distant all night. "You could ask her to take a drug test. You could confront her about the Vicodin. Have an intervention."

And so Dunny explained to Dana what an intervention was, and Dana was enchanted. It seemed like exactly what was called for. The very next morning she asked Arman to help her with the intervention. And so it was that Arman gave Lorrie Ann the heads-up about what was coming.

Lorrie Ann was shocked. "Who all is going to be at this intervention?"

"Dude," Arman said, "I don't know! Dunny and your mom, I guess. I told them I hadn't noticed anything but that you'd seemed a little depressed. What were you doing taking her pills, Lorrie baby?"

"I didn't take her pills!" Lorrie Ann lied. "She's just senile and she doesn't remember when she takes them!"

Arman shrugged. "What do you wanna do?"

"I want to curl up into a ball and go to sleep for a thousand years."

Arman was grinding up a 30 milligram oxycodone for her on a saucer. He laid the pill under a twenty-dollar bill to keep it from getting everywhere, then ground it to fine powder with the edge of his lighter. "Well, aside from sleeping for a thousand years."

"Can't I just say I don't have a drug problem? How would they know?"

"Your mom is clueless," Arman said. "But Dunny probably knows what high looks like." He scraped the powder into two lines using his

Blockbuster card, rolled the twenty into a tube, and handed it over to Lorrie Ann.

"Why did that fucking bitch have to get involved?" Lorrie Ann asked, snorting one line up her right nostril, then the other up her left.

Arman just shrugged, tapped his lighter against his fake leg, looked out the window.

"This is the last thing I want to be dealing with," Lorrie Ann said.

"You don't have a problem," Arman said. "I've seen people with problems. You just like to party."

"Exactly. And it's not like I'm fucking up or anything. Zipper firing me was some kind of act of God or something."

"Of course," Arman said.

"So maybe I just go in and I say, 'Mom, I didn't take your pills. I have no drug problem. This is all in your head.' I mean, she is technically diagnosed as having psychosis, right?"

"What if they want you to take a drug test?" Arman asked. He had, in fact, been told by Dana that she and Dunny planned to challenge Lor to take a drug test if she tried to deny taking the pills.

"A drug test for what?" Lor asked. "Where would they even get one?"

"Maybe Dunny has them. They could test you for opiates with just a pee test."

"They have that?"

Arman nodded, not looking at her, still slowly rubbing his lighter up and down the titanium pylon of his fake leg. It made a hollow scraping sound like sharpening a knife. "You could always, you know, just not show up," he said.

"Where would I go?"

"To your brother's?" Bobby was now living by himself in the Larkspur apartment.

"This is insane. They can't make me take a drug test."

"But what if they take Zach?" Arman said.

Because, of course, neither of them yet knew that Zach was already gone. In fact, as they spoke, Dunny was writing up her recommendation that Zach be removed from the home and faxing it over to Child

Protective Services. Earlier, she had been on the phone with the woman assigned to Zach, trying to arrange what nursing home facility he could be released to when he needed to leave the hospital.

"So what did you do?"

"I did what any woman would do," Lor said. "I told the truth. I begged for their forgiveness. I said I would do better. That I would do anything to get to keep Zach."

"And what happened?"

"They offered to send me to rehab. But when I found out that Zach was already gone, I just—what would the point be? Why would I even do that?"

"So then what?"

"It's—I was so honest. I was so sure that if I just came clean everything would work out okay. And then when I found out that my mother had actually agreed to this plan of taking Zach away. That she had actually given a report about the conditions of the house to the new social worker. Oh, God, I thought I was going to throw up. Arman was just furious. I couldn't even speak, but he was screaming, yelling, 'Is this what family is to you, you *Brady Bunch* bitches? Where's your loyalty?' It was a mess. I wound up dragging him out of there and spending the night at his place."

I imagined the two of them in the sudden silence of Arman's apartment. I imagined him making her food—frozen fish sticks. I imagined her drinking Gatorade, the blue kind, and eating the fish sticks, and crying and crying over her lost son. "We came up with this idea," she said, "that we would sell my car and sell Arman's car and go to India."

"India," I said. "Why India?"

"I don't know. I always loved *The Secret Garden* and *A Little Princess*. India seemed like a magical place. It seemed like a place you could lose yourself in." She stretched, raising her arms above her head, and I could see there was a hole in the armpit of her sweater.

"Tigers and monkeys and turbaned men with soulful eyes?"

Lor stared at me blankly, said nothing.

"What?" I asked.

"I'm just trying to understand," Lorrie Ann said slowly, as though she were in a dream, "why you would mock me right now. Are you angry at me? For what?"

"I'm not mocking you," I said. But I was angry at her.

"You loved *The Secret Garden* too. We both did." She reached out and put her hand on mine. I wondered if she had track marks. I wondered what track marks looked like.

"Yes, we did." I heard a sound then in the hall and for a moment I thought it was Franklin coming home and panic swept through me in a wave. But whoever was in the hall walked past our door and unlocked another.

"Do you hate me?" Lorrie Ann asked.

"No, I don't hate you," I said. "But I don't understand why you left. So Zach is in a home. Maybe that's even a relief, not having to take care of him every single moment. You could at least visit him. You could at least do that much."

Lorrie Ann's face assumed a strange blankness. "I visited him once," she said.

I waited for her to continue.

"Mia, the care he was getting there was worse than anything at my house. Worse. They changed him only every four hours, if that. He looked so thin. It was two weeks before they let me see him. And when he saw me, God, when he saw me, he just started crying and crying and crying. Mia, it was the most awful thing. It was like being eviscerated. It was the most awful day of my entire life."

"Which is why I can't understand how you left! How could you leave him?"

"I hate this fucking sentiment that you're expressing. It's a common one. The sacred child who must be cared for no matter what, no matter what the cost. You know, if this were a hundred years ago, Zach would have been left out in the woods. Because they knew—they knew no baby deserved to suffer like that, and no mother deserved to suffer that way either. But we've lost that. We've completely lost our fucking minds, so now the 'right thing to do' is to make him suffer pain we wouldn't wish on our worst enemy. That's the civilized thing to do. To torture him to death inside his own body by refusing to let him die. He can't even eat, Mia. He can't eat! What animal is kept alive past the point where it can eat? It's disgusting. It's foul. I couldn't watch it anymore. I couldn't be part of it."

"Okay," I said, stunned by her anger, her fury.

"I should have ended it," she said. "That would have been the right thing to do. To end it the right way. Where he would have been loved, and I could have—" she broke off, and I understood that she was having trouble speaking, couldn't get the words out. "Held him," she said finally.

There was a long slow stillness then. I thought about her feet, bleeding under the table.

"Tell me about India," I said.

CHAPTER TWELVE

Lorrie Ann's Love and Travels

After selling her own car and Arman's, after spending three hundred dollars in a sporting goods store on backpacks, after several blow-out fights with her mother and one long handwritten good-bye letter, after carefully hiding more than 400 milligrams of oxycodone inside a pack of ballpoint pens (the 30-milligram pills fit perfectly into the plastic barrels of the pens once the ink was removed, and through some obscure genius with an iron Arman was able to reseal the entire package of Bic pens so that it looked perfectly pristine), after a fifteen-hour flight to Dubai and a three-hour flight to Mumbai, after a multitude of tiny bottles of gin, after being sprayed with deet by distracted flight attendants, Lorrie Ann and Arman wandered into what seemed to them a half-demolished and largely abandoned airport.

Indeed, some kind of perpetual construction was at work in Chhatrapati Shivaji International Airport that was carried out by what seemed to Lor to be fifteen barefooted men. At first she did not understand what they were doing because they had no uniforms and so few and clearly improvised tools, but gradually it became clear to her that they were repairing the building whether they were wearing shoes or not. If she and Arman were supposed to go through customs, they somehow failed to go through the right corridor because they never did see anyone official before arriving in baggage claim, where they had no suitcases to wait for. They pushed out the doors and into the bright, muggy Mumbai day, where forty cabdrivers promptly began to fight for their business.

Those first few days, Lor worried she had made a horrible mistake. India was overwhelming. She had not been prepared for any of it: for the crowding, for the poverty, for the sheer difficulty of meeting basic needs. That first night she and Arman checked into their hotel, then decided to go for a walk, just around the block, to try to put off going to bed for at least another couple of hours in the hope that this would help them get over their jet lag faster, but even walking around the block with no destination in mind proved to be exhausting.

"I don't know if I can handle this many people staring at me," she said softly as they waited at an intersection for the light to change. The air was heavy with exhaust and something both ammoniac and salty, like cat piss or burned anise seeds.

"Ha," Arman said. "Everyone stared at me in the States. But here—do you see the way they look at my legs?"

"How are they looking?"

"They look like . . . like they think I must be important to have such nice fake legs."

"And to be walking with such a pretty blonde," Lorrie Ann said, as she watched a man with absolutely no legs at all push himself bravely into the intersection on a little mover's dolly, just a square of plywood with wheels that he propelled by pushing off on the pavement with his hands.

"Oh, they probably think you're a prostitute," he said.

"Why?!" Lor said. She noticed a kid goat tied up outside a jewelry store, chewing at the decorative shrubbery. A two-year-old was standing next to it, petting its back roughly. There was no adult in evidence.

"You've got your shoulders bare."

"It's a tank top! It's over a hundred degrees out!" she cried.

"Do you see a single other woman out here in a tank top?" he asked. Lor looked around. The streets were filled with women, most of them in salwar kameez in bright parrot colors, a few in saris, none of them with bared shoulders.

"But don't they just know I'm American?"

"Maybe," Arman said. "I don't know. Who knows, maybe they go back to the slums each night and watch dubbed episodes of *Friends*."

Just then a woman came up to them begging, holding out her hands, which had no fingers and so looked more like paws. Lor stared at the woman's hands for what felt like the longest time, trying to sort out what she was seeing, before she understood that all ten fingers had been meticulously removed. Lorrie Ann said, "I'm sorry, no," but Arman got out a few rupees and dropped the coins into the woman's palms.

"What do you think she did?" Lor asked, when the woman was gone.

"What do you mean?"

"What did she do to have all her fingers chopped off?"

"Does it matter?" Arman asked.

"I'm not saying you shouldn't have given her money. I would have given it to her. I just couldn't stop staring."

"Maybe she stole."

"Maybe," Lorrie Ann said, flaring her nostrils and breathing the twilight and exhaust fumes deep into her lungs. Did she even remember giving back that ten-dollar bill? Did she feel, like I did, that every moment of her new life, this wild romp through India, was something she had stolen? It occurred to me then that maybe Lorrie Ann had never been good, maybe I had been misunderstanding her. Maybe she had just been too scared to break the rules.

It was quite by accident that they stumbled upon the red-light district one night. It was not the first night they were in Mumbai (truthfully, no one called it Mumbai, preferring the older Bombay), but it was in that first clutch of nights when India was still new and overwhelming, when it seemed like a triumph to buy a soda or a pack of cigarettes. (Lor had taken up smoking.)

The red-light district was surprisingly devoid of red lights, but it was not difficult to figure out what it was because the women were displayed in cages, little prison cells that lined the street, and wherein the women stalked like bored tigers in their lingerie. Lorrie Ann felt they should leave and immediately, but Arman was fascinated.

"There're other white people," he pointed out. "It's safe."

In fact, the only place they had seen more tourists was Leopold Café, the famous expatriate bar. Ahead of them were a giggling German couple, and farther downstream in the sea of people Lorrie Ann could see a gaggle of Japanese, their cameras at the ready. And so they continued to drift, slowly, down the street, eyeing the hubbub and circus around them. The street was indeed crowded, mostly with young Indian men who were grinning foolishly and laughing at one another, gesturing to the girls on the balconies and in the cages, daring one another to approach. The prostitutes were decidedly less energetic. Some of them were quite old and fat, while others appeared to be no more than nine or ten and seemed malnourished. The vast majority, of course, were between fifteen and twenty-five, with skin that ranged from the darkest black to the palest snow. There were also boys for sale, as well as transvestites of both the obvious and the not-so-obvious varieties. The street was permeated by a deranged carnival feel that reminded her of Pleasure Island in *Pinocchio*, where all the boys slowly turn into donkeys.

"So is this legal?" Lor asked. "Is that why it's so . . . open?"

"It must be," Arman said, just as they passed a cop laughing with his arm around what could only be a pimp. "Do you want to get one?"

"What?" Lor asked, though of course she had heard him perfectly well. She was just surprised he had the poor taste to ask. She moved out of the way so that a water buffalo could pass.

"You've never made love to a woman," he pointed out. "It would be an adventure."

Her anger was so fierce and so intense that she didn't know what to say. These women were in cages with dirty mattresses wearing soiled clothes. Not to mention the burgeoning AIDS epidemic that was ravaging India. An adventure? Honestly? She watched the pavement under her feet as she walked and avoided stepping on a dead bird.

"Never mind," he said, clearly put out by her silence. "I forget how puritanical you are."

"I'm not puritanical," she said.

"Whatever you want to call it," Arman said, then chucked her on the shoulder. "I love you anyway, all right?"

The next day they visited Elephanta Island to look at the cave sculptures. They did not know who the gods depicted in the sculptures were, but they wandered through them, in awe, as around them massive figures, twice as tall as Arman, writhed in the stone, frozen mid-coitus or splitting into snakes. There were no plaques that explained any of it, at least not in English.

"This is incredible," Lor said. "But what does . . . I wish I knew what it meant."

"I think that's Shiva," Arman said, trying to be helpful.

"Right," Lor said.

Later, when they were buying a soda, they watched a monkey swing down from a tree and wrestle a bag of chips away from an eight-year-old. The startled child fell to the ground, but did not cry out, and then watched in wonder as the monkey ran away with her chips. Lor and Arman watched the monkey eat the chips up in the tree as they drank their Fanta.

"So Shiva is . . . ?" Lor finally asked.

"The god of destruction," Arman said.

"How appropriate."

Arman fished in his travel pouch and handed her a Starburst. This was their preferred daytime drug administration method: they carefully inserted a quarter or half of a pill of oxycodone into each Starburst, then wrapped it back up again. During the day you could simply unwrap the candy and chew it thoroughly, crushing up the pill fragment with your teeth, but keeping yourself from gagging by means of the sour Starburst flavor. At this point they were still not shooting up. That would come later.

When they began their descent down the thousand steps that led from the sacred caves to the docks, a man behind them began to take pictures of Lorrie Ann's hair. She became nervous and tripped, and unable to catch her balance, wound up falling down thirty or forty steps quite brutally as all the while the little man chased after her with his camera, taking shot after shot. He kept shooting even as she finally stopped herself from falling farther, panting on her hands and knees on a step, looking up at him, her nose bleeding. It took Arman a long time on his legs to catch up to them, and so for almost a full minute Lor simply looked at the man as he took pictures of her bloody nose.

She did not think he spoke English or maybe she would have yelled at him, at least said something indignant. At no point did he offer her a hand up. When Arman made it down to them, he shouldered past the man saying, "Show's over, buddy," and offered Lorrie Ann one of his crutches.

There were things about India that Lorrie Ann simply could not understand. Prostitution was legal, but not in some enlightened, liberal, secular wet dream, not in a Nevada Bunny Ranch or Amsterdam sex club kind of way. The women seemed to be in an obvious state of enslavement. Yet it was not hidden. Indeed, you could see vibrators and dildos on display, laid out in neat rows on blankets, at the electronics market near Victoria Terminus Station. India was the birthplace of *The Kama Sutra*, after all. Porn DVDs were sold on almost every corner. And yet most marriages were arranged; most women were virgins when they married; to bare your shoulders was to announce yourself as a prostitute. Bombay was undoubtedly dangerous, yet women walked around unafraid, even at night, even by themselves. Lor simply could not figure it out.

She also noticed how the women dressed. She loved their flowing salwar kameezes, their bright scarves, their proud lipstick. They seemed decorated not for the eyes of men, but for themselves. Even ugly or fat women took care with their appearance in this way. Part of it was the colors, which were wildly bright: blue silk pants with bright marigold tops and shimmering citrine scarves. Lorrie Ann couldn't get enough of it, and eventually she asked Arman if he would think she was foolish if she bought one.

"Buy one," he said. "They look comfortable."

And so, in a session of awkward, virginal haggling, Lorrie Ann bought a beautiful olive green and mango salwar kameez from a vendor on the street, down past Leopold Café in Colaba, where there were many white people and where she was sure she would be ripped off, but at least able to negotiate in English. She tried it on that night in the hotel room and was stunned by how light and breathable it was. The relief from the heat was almost instantaneous—the breeze moved right through the fabric.

"I'm never wearing anything else," Lorrie Ann announced and threw her wadded-up jeans in the tiny wastebasket in their hotel room.

"Good," Arman said. "You look beautiful."

She waggled her head back and forth like an Indian girl for him. "You think so?" she asked, in a fairly good imitation of a Hindi accent.

"Like a Bollywood star," he said.

"Yaar," Lorrie Ann said, "you lie like a rug."

Perhaps they would have stayed in Bombay longer, or perhaps not, but they decided to leave after visiting the Haji Ali Dargah.

The mosque was, quite simply, the most beautiful thing Lorrie Ann had ever seen. The mosque was built out at sea and was connected to the shore by a low seawall, so that at high tide it became an island, unreachable except by boat. At low tide, anyone could walk along the seawall and visit it. Her guidebook highly recommended it and told the story of the incredible Haji Ali for whom the mosque had been built, a saint who, it was said, met a woman in distress in the street who was holding an empty vessel and asked her what was wrong. She told him that she had tripped and spilled the oil her husband had sent her to get and now she was afraid to go home because she knew her husband would beat her. Saint Haji Ali asked her to take him to the spot where she had spilled the oil, and he stuck his thumb into the ground there and oil began to spout from the earth. The woman filled up her vessel, thanked him profusely, and went home. At first Haji Ali was well pleased with his act, but gradually he became worried he had harmed the earth in some way by so brutally jabbing it with his thumb. Full of remorse and suffering from constant nightmares, he soon fell ill and died. His coffin was sent out to sea, but through a miracle or else some trick of the tides, floated back to shore and so, where his coffin had been found, the mosque had been erected in his honor.

The whitewashed dargah stood like a mirage upon the shimmering sea, and to Lor its minarets and spires looked like something from her dreams. The afternoon sun was blinding, and it was difficult to feel she wasn't really in a dream as she and Arman slowly made their way along the seawall. Legless beggars were laid out on blankets, chanting, begging for alms. They made low buzzing sounds in their throats and waggled their amputated limbs in slow, rhythmic circles. Lorrie Ann asked Arman for money and he handed her a fistful of change. She gave a rupee or two to every beggar they passed. She did not know if they were lepers or if they had been disfigured another way. Some had faces that looked like heads of cauliflower. She stooped silently to place the coins on their towels, watching her own shadow move quickly over their prostrate bodies.

"Cover your hair," Arman said to her, very quietly and out of the corner of his mouth. Lor reached up and touched her hair, which was loose over her shoulders. She was wearing her salwar kameez, but she hadn't even thought about a head scarf. She took the long narrow scarf that had come with her outfit and tried to wrap it around her head.

"That's good," Arman said, though he still seemed nervous. They kept walking along the seawall. The dargah was more than five hundred meters from shore and it seemed they might never get there.

"I don't think we should keep going," Arman said finally.

"What do you mean?"

They kept walking forward but they slowed their steps.

"People are looking," Arman said. "I just don't think we should be here."

"The guidebook said we could—"

"I know, but—" he began to say, and right at that moment Lorrie Ann felt something hit the back of her head.

"Let's go," Arman took her by the arm and spun her around, walking her in the opposite direction.

"What was that?" Lorrie Ann asked, reaching to feel the back of her head.

"Don't touch it. Don't," Arman said, but it was already too late. Her hand had found the huge wad of rapidly cooling mucus stuck to her hair. Lorrie Ann snatched her hand away, looked at her fingers.

"They spit on me?"

"Yes, don't touch it," Arman said. "You don't want to get TB."

"They spit on me?" she asked again, unable to understand. She shook her hand, not wanting to rub it clean on her pretty outfit, but desperate to get the slime off her fingers. She began to hyperventilate, but she wasn't sure why. Another part of her was perfectly calm: So you were spit on, so what?

"Why would they do that?" she asked Arman, her voice quavery like a child's.

"Because you're an infidel," Arman said gruffly. "Let's go to McDonald's."

And so they went to McDonald's, where they bought Maharaja Macs and where Lorrie Ann was able to wash the phlegm out of her hair in the women's restroom. After frantically scrubbing her hands with the pale pink soap that seemed to be a staple of all bathrooms throughout the world, no matter what country you were in, she returned to the table and pretended to think it was funny and part of a great adventure that she had been spit on.

Arman laughed too. They giggled, eating their curried French fries, sipping their Diet Cokes. Neither of them commented on how odd it was that Arman, with his shorts, his Metallica T-shirt, his pierced ears, and his long flowing hair, had not been spit on. Nor did Lorrie Ann broach the wild panic floating just beneath the surface of her mind that somehow the person had known what she had done, had spit on her not because of her blond hair and her inadequate scarf, but because of Zach, because of Dana, because of the drugs, because of the way she let Arman touch her body at night, even the way she let him hold her throat while they were kissing in a gentle parody of strangulation, as though it were essential for his eroticism that he toy with the idea of killing her. She believed, on some level, that the man who had spit on her had seen all of this and had known, known as Arman had said, that she was an infidel.

She did not belong in God's house. That much she knew for sure, even as she ate the Maharaja Mac, even as she reached out a hand and snagged one of Arman's huge brown fingers and squeezed, smiling in his eyes.

And so they decided, later that night, to head down to Goa and they bought bus tickets the very next morning. Goa: land of untariffed beer and white sandy beaches, nesting place of American hippies, wanton sprawl of spice farms traversed by elephants wearing garlands of flowers, the spring break destination of every young Indian student. Goa, surely, would be kind to them and would restore order to what had increasingly become a jumble of events they were unable to interpret. Things had stopped leading from one to another. A monkey could just swoop down from a tree and steal your bag of chips. A man could spit on you or take pictures of you when you were bleeding and nothing at all would happen except that later you might go to Leopold's and drink what you thought was perhaps the best Long Island Iced Tea you'd ever had in your life. Imagine finding it in India! Of all places!

In other words, the proper scale of things was dangerously askew and reality was fraying. Goa was supposed to fix all of that, or at least Lorrie

Ann hoped it would. Between the malaria medication and the state of her life, she was having nightmares every night. She wasn't the kind to wake up screaming, but the kind to wake up silent and paralyzed, and so she rarely woke Arman and instead spent many two a.m.'s watching Bombay flicker outside their hotel window, smoking a cigarette, piecing together dreams that seemed to be about her mother, about the Native Americans, about Iraq and Jim and gunfire amid the floating minarets of impossibly beautiful mosques, about Zach and a preacher who stood over him speaking in tongues and foaming at the mouth.

Whatever the procedure may have been for boarding the bus to Goa, Lorrie Ann and Arman were unable to determine what it was. They stood in a mob of anxious people with suitcases late at night, where they repeatedly asked others if they were in the right place. They were told that they were, but neither Lorrie Ann nor Arman felt at all sure that they would make it onto a bus, which was why when a man beckoned them to board, they simply got on, even though the bus he put them on was not the first-class, air-conditioned bus with sleeping bunks they had been promised and had paid for, but a stifling tour bus where the AC was broken and the seats did not recline. As soon as they ascertained from their neighbors that the bus was indeed going to Goa, they decided it was worth it to just stay on and not make a fuss.

The drive, they soon discovered, was through a series of switchbacks in the mountains that the bus took at far above what seemed a safe speed. In fact, the bus was so loaded down that the brakes were not actually fully functioning, or at least this was Arman's interpretation of the frantic way the bus driver would punch the horn as he headed into each curve, warning all other cars to get out of the way. Traffic lanes in India were also more of a suggestion than a mandate, and so the bus driver handled the wild fishtailing of his vehicle with aplomb by making use of both his own lanes and the lanes reserved for oncoming traffic. It was hot inside the bus and it smelled strongly of exhaust. They had boarded at ten at night and were expected to arrive at their destination in Goa at seven in the morning.

For about the first two hours, Lorrie Ann felt she was having an adventure. By two in the morning, she felt trapped in a nightmare. She was unable to sleep, yet unable to stay awake. The floor of the bus was burning hot from the engines, and so she couldn't let her sandaled feet touch the floor without the skin of her feet starting to blister. She actually started crying at one point, silent tears just slipping down her face, both because she was uncomfortable and because she was ashamed that being uncomfortable was proving to be too much for her. At a rest stop she peed and then managed to beg two Valium off some British tourists, young men who agreed that this bus ride was one of the worst things that had ever happened to them.

The Valium helped, but it still seemed to be an eternity before they arrived in Goa and the bus ride came to an end. Lor realized that the fact that she was in such psychological distress from a simple nine hours of discomfort—not even pain, just discomfort—was a sign of how radically different she was from the Indians around her, who accepted this trial as nothing more than an ordinary part of life. All of the Indians were laughing and excited as they exited the bus, stretching their limbs joyfully, ready for a day of touristing in sunny Goa. Arman, even, had taken it a bit better than she had, and it made her understand more fully how much one is changed by war. Lor, of course, had never fought in a war. She had never even run an obstacle course. The most that she had done, really, was birth a child—even that she had done with an epidural and, in the end, while unconscious.

It made her think that all of Arman's talk about fat-fuck Americans being somehow unworthy of their status as world megapower was more justified than she had at first thought.

Despite the hellish ambiance of the journey, Goa was all they had been promised and more. Their hotel was located in a tiny and little-touristed village called Mandrem and was a large two-story circular green building like a beautifully frosted layer cake. She and Arman took a room on the ground floor that contained a platform bed, a small bathroom where the water that came out of the tap was a deep umber brown, and a small niche in the wall that housed a pure white statue of Ganesh, the plaster never having been painted. Their room smelled faintly of incense. The walls were painted purple and green. The tile floor was a mosaic of different colors of marble.

The other guests of the hotel were largely British or Australian. Most were families, the parents in their thirties or so, their children naked and brown with suntan, running around the terraced gardens like some kind of hippie fantasy. If it was taboo to bare your shoulders in Bombay, white women in Goa worried about no such thing, and wandered about in shocking states of undress, naked under thin silk dresses, or else topless at the beach. No one ever worried about anything, not even about what time it was, and businesses had no set hours of operation. If a business was closed, you could just continue to knock at the door and someone might come who could help you. If not, you would try again later, or else you wouldn't. You could rent a motorcycle on the strength of your word and a promise to bring it back sometime in the next week. You could pay a young man in a music shop to teach you how to build a guitar. You could get vegetable fritters by the fistful for ten cents American. You could spend all afternoon drinking beer and roasting on the sand, not being bothered by anyone except, at one point, a curious little calf the color of coffee with lovely black eyes as shiny as lacquered boxes.

And yet, reality here proved not to be any more lucid than reality in Bombay. In fact, with each passing day, Lorrie Ann felt she was falling deeper and deeper into some sort of terrible, unending dream.

CHAPTER THIRTEEN

A Kinder Sea

Part of the problem was that they had no plan. When they had first decided to go to India, it was "for a few months" and "to bum around." They assumed they would have some kind of enlightening experience that would allow them to discover what the next part of their lives should be. They were counting on India to be the mystical experience that would save them from their secular, Western nightmare, allow them to find their true selves, etc., etc. And yet, it turned out, India was a real place. It wasn't just a fantasy. And they had a set amount of money and a set amount of drugs, both of which were slowly running out.

What would they do when they ran out of pills? They had been in India only a month and already the pills were more than half gone. "We should start conserving," Arman said when Lorrie Ann pointed this out, and yet neither of them did anything to begin cutting back. They continued budgeting three pills a day each, but almost always having four. Lor wondered if she would get sick when they ran out. In a way, she was looking forward to it: a few cleansing days of fever and then a fresh start, sober, clear eyed. Perhaps then India would do its work on her. Perhaps India was failing to affect her because she was too high.

Obviously she did not think these things consciously; one does not think such stupid things consciously. Only assumptions, which are by nature unexamined, are allowed to be this stupid. Lor assumed these things as they lay naked on the sand or naked under their mosquito netting, as they ate Starbursts filled with drugs and drank lukewarm soda, as they befriended a dog outside a restaurant, or watched a man carrying a giant bag full of eggs on his head: perhaps two hundred eggs, balanced there atop his head in the bulging see-through garbage bag, magically not breaking.

Running out of drugs was not as worrisome to Lor as what would happen when they ran out of money. They had started the trip with roughly six thousand dollars. Three thousand had been eaten up by airfare, vaccines, and visas. (They had not exactly gotten all of the vaccines, but they had gotten some of them and they had bought the malaria medication. It was just that hepatitis B vaccine—you had to get it over the span of six months!) Luckily, India was incredibly cheap, and so they had spent only a thousand dollars in their first month. But eventually they would have to do something to generate money; eventually they would have to stop being tourists and start living lives. It was the slowly depleting tally of her bank account that made Lor know this.

In a way, it would have been better if they had had less money. There would have been a distinct call to action, an end in sight. It was worse to know they could go on this way, aimlessly vacationing, for months.

She sent her mother a postcard of the Taj Mahal, even though they hadn't been to see it. The card read, "Dear Mom, I miss you and Zach every day. I still don't understand how you could let them take him like that. It must mean that you think I'm some kind of monster. It must make it worse that I ran off to India. Perhaps it will make you hate me even more, but I am happy here. Much love, Monster."

But she wasn't happy. Not at all.

And then, one day, they met a woman.

They had been living for two weeks in the pretty green hotel that looked like a layer cake, where every morning they would sit on the veranda and play with the pug dog, Rosa, who had a lame back leg but who did not seem to mind, and where they would drink a pot of delicious French press coffee and eat a bowl of mango, coconut, papaya, and strawberries. The veranda overlooked a river that led out to the ocean, and Arman and Lorrie Ann would watch passively as it emptied itself unceasingly before them, a scintillating python of coppery brown-blue. The proprietor of the hotel was a small Afghani man named Rinoo, who never wore any shoes and who also never frowned. He was always smiling, calling Lorrie Ann Princess of the West and calling Arman Baba G, both in seeming sincerity. If they wanted to do something, it was Rinoo they asked where they ought to go or how it could be arranged.

But lately they had been running out of things to do. They had spent many days on the beach, punctuating their hours of sunbathing with beer and fiery hot fish curry. They had spent many days renting a moped (Arman could pilot one even without legs, whereas he was nervous of the motorcycles) and going to the neighboring town of Arambol to shop and eat in the different restaurants there. They had rented a Jet Ski. Lor had taken a yoga class. They had eaten every place it was advisable to eat. They had visited the spice farm. They had ridden an elephant. Rinoo was out of ideas, except, he said, if they didn't mind paying for a taxi, there was always the nightclub in Anjuna, the Paradiso.

It was a sign of how desperate Arman was for any kind of entertainment that he agreed to go, since he despised dancing even before losing his legs, and despised it more afterward. On the other hand, as Lorrie Ann well knew, he found Indian women intoxicating. Their beauty was a subject he never tired of pontificating about. And the chance to watch many young Indian women dance in a disco was certainly better than staying in the room getting moderately drunk on vodka and pineapple juice with Lorrie Ann. Besides, they had been to Anjuna only once and in the daytime for the flea market (where Lor had bought a beautiful labradorite necklace that shimmered as though enchanted).

And so, when night fell, Lorrie Ann and Arman dressed themselves up and took a cab the sixteen kilometers to Anjuna. (More appropriately, *the* cab—for the cabdriver, Dillip, waited for them outside their hotel day and night, having discovered, probably, that Arman was a good tipper and deciding that his luck was better as their twenty-four-hour driver than as a free agent trolling the town.) In Anjuna, Dillip dropped them off and assured them he would be there waiting for them no matter what time they finished at the disco.

Lor and Arman had to walk down the dirt paths of the town in order to get to the Paradiso, and it was as they were walking that men, almost invisible in the darkness, offered them drugs. Softly, as they passed, voices would mutter: hashish, coca, MDMA. Hashish, coca, MDMA. Because she and Arman were nervous, they kept walking, both saying, "No thank you," in the same embarrassed way they did to the beggar children who followed them everywhere. But after they had passed through, Arman turned to her and said, "Do you want some?"

"Some what?" she asked. Despite being, by this time, very fully addicted to painkillers, Lorrie Ann had tried no other drugs besides marijuana. She wasn't entirely sure what they all did.

"I don't know. Some E?"

"Would I like it?" she asked.

"Oh, you'd love it," Arman said.

"Do you think they're cops?" Lorrie Ann asked.

"Even if they are, don't you think we could just pay them off?"

"Probably."

"Let's try it," Arman said, and so they went back to the whispering men in the dark and told them that they would like some ecstasy please. The man they were speaking to was wearing a white-and-blue-checked shirt and he smiled wide so his teeth glowed in the darkness as he waggled his head. "Very good, sir," he said. "Please wait."

And so they stood there awkwardly for almost ten minutes. Several times they tried to go, but the man in the checked shirt assured them it would be just a few minutes longer. Eventually, a man on a moped came. "Hop on," he said.

"What?"

"Hop on!" they were told. And so both Arman and Lorrie Ann clambered onto the moped, hugging tight to its driver and to each other. The driver laughed with excitement at the difficult driving as he navigated the back roads of the town weighed down with Arman and Lorrie Ann, and even Lorrie Ann found herself grinning at how stupid and ridiculous this was. Finally they reached the end of a dark alley, and the man on the moped stopped the bike and gestured for them to disembark. He got off the bike too and beckoned for them to follow him into a small shack.

Inside the shack, which was perhaps ten feet square, were three sleeping children in a pile and one snoring woman. The man held a finger over his lips to indicate that they should be quiet. He located a flashlight and then began to root around in a cardboard box of buckets and dishes where he eventually found a ziplock bag filled with ecstasy tablets.

"MDMA, no?" he asked.

Arman and Lorrie Ann nodded.

"How many?" the man whispered. Lorrie Ann could not stop staring at one of the sleeping children who had a runny nose. When Zach had been that age, about three, he had seemed almost normal. Not yet emaciated, not yet skeletally distorted.

Arman shrugged. "Four?"

And so the man named the price, which was preposterously low, and he and Arman exchanged money for drugs, shook hands, and the three exited the shack in the moonlight.

"Wait here," the man said and dashed down the alley.

"Should we stay?" Lorrie Ann asked. "Maybe now is when he goes and gets the cop?"

"Do you know how to get out of here?" Arman asked. "Because I have no fucking idea."

Lorrie Ann admitted she didn't. "Here," Arman said, and handed her two pills. "Let's destroy the evidence."

"Both of them?"

Arman nodded as he dry swallowed his own. Lorrie Ann copied him. The man spontaneously reappeared from the shadows.

"Can I?" he asked, and held up a Polaroid camera.

"I think he wants your picture," Arman said.

"Oh," Lor said. But the man took this for consent and eagerly approached her, put his arm around her, and took a photo of himself with her. The flash was blinding, and the silence of the night was broken by the mechanical whir of the Polaroid ejecting the film.

"Thank you very very much!" the man cried, and ran back to wherever he had come from.

Lorrie Ann and Arman stared at each other.

"So," Lorrie Ann said, "do you want to just start walking toward the sound of the waves?"

"Sure," he said, and together they walked off arm in arm.

By the time they reached the disco, having been lost for almost an hour, Arman admitted that the pills were very strong. It would have been smarter to take one and see if they needed the other one. "But they were so cheap," he explained, "I thought they'd be shitty!"

Lor's teeth were chattering uncontrollably. The warm wind on her skin was intoxicating, and she found herself playing with the silk of her dress, rubbing it against her skin.

"I feel like my skin is warm sparkles," she said through her clenched teeth.

"I know," Arman said.

They both stood awkwardly on the edge of the dance floor, watching the flashing lights and the writhing dancers. The Paradiso was a beautiful club of many different terraced levels overlooking the sea. All of the structures were white stucco, and so the lights made the rooms glow soft purple and blue and pulsating pink. The architecture was a series of curves and domes, organic shapes that made Lorrie Ann feel she was inside a magical nautilus shell.

"There's no way I can dance," Arman said. "I'm sorry."

"I can't dance either," she said.

Together they floated toward a low wall and sat on it, still facing the dance floor.

"Humans are so pretty when they dance," Arman said.

"Humans are pretty all the time."

"No," Arman said. "They aren't pretty when they are killing each other."

"You're probably right," Lorrie Ann said.

"I'm definitely right. I've seen it."

"Oh yeah," Lor said, "I forgot."

They were silent for a little while.

"Do you want a drink?" Arman asked.

"God no. Do you?"

"No. I just thought I'd offer."

"No."

More silence. Unknown spans of time went by.

"Do you think it's wrong that I thought Zach was beautiful? I know he must have been ugly to other people. Could you ever see it? How beautiful he was?"

"Yes," Arman said. "There were times he was beautiful."

"I miss the way he would raise his eyebrows, like he was in on the joke. Like it was all one big joke," Lorrie Ann said.

"I know."

And just then a woman sat down right in between them. She was wearing a neon orange triangle bikini underneath a pair of baggy overalls. On her feet she wore bright red galoshes. "I have a favor to ask you," the woman said in a heavy Italian accent. "You do speak English?"

Lorrie Ann assured her that they did.

"Light and dark together," the woman said, shrugging, "can only mean that you are American."

Lor was still trying to figure out what she meant by light and dark when the woman asked Arman if she could borrow his fake legs.

"No," Lorrie Ann said immediately.

"What do you want with my legs?" Arman asked, amused.

"We want to play a trick on a girl named Cara," the woman said. She reached out her arms and put one around Lorrie Ann and one around

Arman. The skin of her arms was burning, as though it had retained the heat of the sun, and her perfume was spicy and sharp. Lorrie Ann began to feel very confused. Were they friends with this woman? How long had they been talking to her?

The trick that was to be played on poor Cara seemed to be to use the fake legs as stilts so that someone could videotape her having sex in the bathroom of the club and then live-project the image onto the dance floor.

"Why not just use a stool or a chair to look over the wall?" Lorrie Ann asked.

"It is a bathroom stall—we must sneak up on her!" the woman explained.

Arman was laughing, clearly tickled by the idea. "I would totally lend you my legs, but no one could balance on them using their feet—see, they have sockets that fit my stumps." He pulled up his Dickies shorts so she could see where prosthesis met flesh.

"No?" she asked. "What a boomer!"

It took Lorrie Ann a moment to translate "boomer" as "bummer." Arman was giggling like a little boy, and the woman leaned over and kissed him on the cheek. "Thank you anyway, darling," she said. "My name is Portia, by the way."

Lorrie Ann felt distantly the tolling bells of jealousy. God, she was tired of being jealous over Arman.

"And you," she said, turning to Lorrie Ann. "You are truly a beauty."

And then she kissed Lorrie Ann full on the mouth.

"I can't explain," Lorrie Ann said, "unless, have you ever done E?"

"No," I said.

"Well, kissing feels just amazing. Just heavenly."

"Oh," I said.

"You think I'm gross. You think I'm some kind of lesbian."

"No," I said, "I don't." There had been a time, when we were thirteen or so, when I had fantasized almost nonstop about kissing Lorrie

Ann. Fortunately for our friendship, those fantasies had stopped as soon as I started kissing boys and had failed to ever return. But I certainly didn't think it was unnatural.

"It was like being in a dream."

"I understand," I said.

"We wound up taking her back to our hotel," Lorrie Ann said, with a breezy casual tone that could only signify shame. I nodded, as though it were the only possible outcome: Of course! What was there to do with a stranger who kissed you but take her back to your hotel?

Perhaps if Arman had played a more active role, it could have been called a threesome. As it was, the three of them lounged around on the platform bed, nuzzling one another and drinking vast quantities of 7UP. Lor had never been so thirsty in her life and 7UP had never tasted so good. They had found the little man in the blue-and-white-checked shirt again and bought more E, so Portia was rolling with them. None of them had the energy or sustained attention for something as athletic as actual sex. There was a stained-glass lantern that hung from the ceiling on a chain and the panes of it were brown and yellow and red, so the resulting light was warm and made everything feel like a seventies home video. The statue of Ganesh cast huge shadows in his niche. Lor often did not know who was touching her or whom she was kissing. Everything just felt good. Arman kept laughing and saying, "Incredible," as though he had just been given the Venus de Milo as his personal possession, and it made Lorrie Ann embarrassed: how bald his pleasure was, how paltry and sweaty his desire. He was just altogether too grateful. It made him seem pathetic.

But then, wasn't there always something slightly embarrassing in male desire? Maybe it was just that every woman has had the experience, usually quite early, of being with a man who is entirely turned on when she is not turned on at all, which was, frankly, a lot like being sober in a room full of drunks.

And so there was also a subtle bond between Lorrie Ann and Portia that consisted of a very quiet and unspoken disdain for Arman. When he said "You're so beautiful" to Portia, which could have hurt Lorrie Ann's feelings (though Portia was indeed quite beautiful, had been a model and not just as a pretension but as an honest-to-God profession—she was nearly six feet tall), Portia cut her eyes to Lor, as if to say, "What an idiot," and so Lorrie Ann was able to grin and remain lighthearted.

Eventually, the three of them drifted into a dreamy slumber, from which Lor was roused only by Portia's tugging on her shoulder. "It's morning," Portia whispered. "Let's go outside."

Lor sat up in bed. She was in her bra and panties. Arman had fallen asleep fully clothed and with his legs still attached. Portia was standing beside the bed, wearing that orange string bikini, barefoot. "Let's go," she whispered again.

Lorrie Ann threw on a silk dress she had bought in Arambol and followed Portia out onto the beach, where the sun was just rising.

"So how did he lose his legs?" Portia asked, taking her arm and clinging to Lorrie Ann. They walked in their bare feet on the wet and hard packed sand right at the edge of the water, and, when a wave caught her foot, Lor was shocked by how warm the water was. The Indian Ocean was magic. She was so used to the cold Pacific.

"Fighting in Iraq."

"A soldier, then," Portia said lightly and, Lor couldn't help feeling, a little dismissively.

"Is that a bad thing?" she asked.

"No." Portia laughed. "I am not political. I think what your country does is disgusting mainly because it is fashionable to think so. I am really very shallow and think only about myself."

Lorrie Ann looked over at Portia, studied her face in the dawn light, unsure how to take her words. It was impossible not to look at Portia, really. Her hair was a mess of rich, brown curls, but her eyes were a light, watery jade and slightly too wide set, making her look at all times like a questing woodland creature.

"I can't tell whether or not you are serious," Lorrie Ann said.

"I'm very serious," Portia said. "People are so afraid of their own flaws, but I'm not. I am also very lazy, I have a poor memory, I don't want to be a mother, I don't like animals, and I am materialistic to a fault. But I know all of these things, and this is power, no? I am not running from myself."

"I'm running from myself," Lor said. They were walking toward a clump of sleeping cows. Lor had never seen so many cows in her life before she came to India. She had never realized before how beautiful they were. Should she stop eating them? She hadn't eaten any beef since coming to India, obviously. But maybe she would continue this, consciously.

"Why?" Portia asked.

"I tried my whole life to be a good person and nothing ever worked out for me."

"Oh, so do you want to cry about it?" Portia asked.

"No, I don't want to cry about it," Lor said, stiffening.

"You can cry on me," Portia said, and held out her arms in a strange pose, like Jesus on the cross. "Cry on me!"

Lor just stared at her.

Portia burst out laughing. "Oh, you are so serious! You get your feelings hurt so easily! It must be horrible to be you, like being covered in open sores! The lightest touch of a lover must feel like a torture!"

"I should go back," Lor said, and started to turn.

"No!" Portia shouted, grabbing her by the hands. "Come on! Get in the water with me!"

"You want to go swimming?"

Portia dropped her hands and quickly tugged her bikini bottom down. With a whoop, she pulled off her top.

"Take off!" she said, reaching to pull up the hem of Lorrie Ann's dress.

Lorrie Ann raised her arms, obedient as a child, so Portia could strip the dress off her, but she blanched when Portia began to tug at her panties.

"Look at this," Portia said, touching with her red painted fingernail the long scar from Lorrie Ann's emergency cesarean.

"I always hoped it would fade more," Lorrie Ann said. But this was a lie. Secretly, she believed that she was part of some sort of rapidly growing cult of women marked by the same scar: women who had been cut open by men for their own good.

Portia started to pull Lor's panties down.

"No!" Lor said. "I'll go in like this."

Portia shook her head. "No, you won't."

Lor grabbed the waistband of her panties with both hands and tried to look fierce.

Portia leaned in and kissed her then, and while Lorrie Ann was distracted, she unhitched Lor's bra, tugged it off, and then reached down and pulled Lor's panties down around her knees. Lor scrambled to cover her breasts and her pubis with just her two hands.

"Come on, you sad, sad girl!" Portia called, and ran like a crazy thing straight into the sea.

Even as Lorrie Ann recounted her titillating, quasi-scandalous adventures for me at my kitchen table, I was plagued with impatience. Clearly, this Portia character was no good, and no amount of Lor's admiring description could make me feel otherwise. She was some kind of Eurotrash whore who enjoyed meaningless partying and was living her life according to dice theory like it was a fucking Joan Didion novel. That was all fine and well for ex-models, but not for Lorrie Ann.

Besides which, even I, having heard only the bare bones of the story, could have told you everything that was to come: Lorrie Ann would wind up leaving Arman and traveling with this woman, they would have wild parties and Lorrie Ann would experiment with her nihilistic side before eventually deciding Portia was nuts and leaving her, only to be found, barefoot and bleeding, by me in Istanbul. Wasn't that what she had said? That she was traveling with a friend, but that the friend turned out to be crazy? How long had it taken Lorrie Ann to figure that one out? Anyone who left an Indian discoteque with a legless Armenian and a blond American girl so stoned they can barely talk was not exactly high on my list.

I also, of course, wondered when Franklin would come home. With every word Lorrie Ann spoke, my muscles became tighter, the nerves of my spinal column practically prickling as I strained to hear Franklin coming up the stairs and down the hall to our home, where he would discover me harboring Lorrie Ann.

Franklin had spent so many hours listening to stories of Lorrie Ann that he had confessed to me he was terrified of meeting her. I had stressed to him all that was incredible, almost godlike, about Lorrie Ann: her ethics, which were mysteriously sourceless and possibly a true example of spontaneous generation, her incredible swimming ability and adorable nose, her saintly love for her child, her unending cheerfulness in the face of horrible sacrifice, her Vermeer sensuality, her wasted intellect, her bravery, above all: her bravery. Here was the goddess I had so championed, right there at my kitchen table.

And she was a junkie.

I wanted to hide her from his eyes as though she were my own rotten self.

CHAPTER FOURTEEN

The Price of Pain

After their swim, Lorrie Ann loaded Portia into Dillip's cab, and then returned to the room where Arman was still slumbering. Something about his heavy sleep and his mouth breathing made her faintly disgusted with him, and so after snorting a whole pill to herself, she went out on the veranda and had breakfast alone with Rinoo. They talked about the possibility of a trip to the ruins at Hampi.

"It is a magic place," Rinoo said. "Real magic."

Lorrie Ann wanted to go, but she knew that it would be a lot to request of Arman because the trip would be hard on him. He was best when he could sit at regular intervals, and she had found he was most agreeable in situations where these intervals came up naturally so that he didn't feel he was being pandered to. As though he could read her mind, Rinoo said, "Maybe Baba G can stay here and Princess of the West can go alone?"

"Maybe," Lorrie Ann said, reaching down and picking up the little pug dog that was begging to be lifted into her lap. "Good morning, Rosa," she said.

"Very bad dog, that one," Rinoo said. "She got into the refrigerator during the night and ate almost a half kilo of butter."

"No!" Lorrie Ann exclaimed, turning the happily panting Rosa to face her. "Did you eat butter? Did you eat a lot of butter?"

"You think it's cute, but now I am going to have to put boxes in front of the refrigerator every night!"

"She really gets it open?" Lorrie Ann asked.

"She does! I don't know how, but she does it!" Rinoo smiled, his eyes crinkling, as though he were secretly proud of the little pug with her lame back leg and her fierce love of butter. He was glad that the little dog was a little dog, and that included being glad that she was difficult and got into the butter.

"How did you end up in India?" she asked.

"I was a hippie," Rinoo said, crinkling his eyes again. "I was bumming all around and then I found Mandrem and I said, Here is pretty good!" He gestured wide with his arms at the river and the palm trees all around them.

"It is pretty good here," she agreed.

There was a silence then. Lor felt sick. She was in paradise and all she did was take drugs so that she wouldn't have to feel anything.

"She's going to have puppies," Rinoo said suddenly.

Lorrie Ann looked wonderingly at Rosa, who was still in her lap. "You are?" she asked the little dog.

"Yes," Rinoo said. "In maybe . . . one month. You will still be here?"

"Maybe," Lor said, but she prayed she wouldn't be.

Lorrie Ann did not realize she was considering taking a trip to Hampi until she mentioned it to Arman a few days later.

"You could just stay here, if you wanted. Have some adult fun or whatever. Go to Anjuna again." She was surprised at herself for offering this. Always, Arman had maintained that an open relationship was necessary, not just for his own sex drive, which was frankly not difficult to satisfy, but because it was the only rational arrangement between a man and a woman who were not intending to bear children together. Lor could understand and even agree with the logic of his argument, and she tolerated his dalliances with other girls, even though they always hurt her. Now, she realized, the thought of Arman with someone else didn't bother her at all. She experimented, forcing herself to graphically imagine it, but she couldn't bring herself to care.

"What do you want in Hampi?" Arman asked.

"Rinoo said the ruins were really amazing. That it's just this very special, ancient place."

"Ruins of what?"

"I don't know," Lorrie Ann said, turning over on the sand. They had bought new towels from a persistent child that morning and the dye had not been properly set in the fabric, so now the whole front of her body was dyed red and blue swirls. "Do you think this will come off in the water?" she asked, rubbing at her thighs.

But Arman said nothing, just stared at the horizon without changing his expression and then took a sip of his beer.

Later that night Arman became horribly drunk. They had eaten at what was supposed to be a Chinese restaurant, but where the food had tasted suspiciously like Indian food fried in a wok, and then they had bought a bottle of vodka and drank it sitting out on the beach. Lor did not understand how hard Arman had been hitting the bottle until he spontaneously threw it into the sea.

"What?" he said. "It was empty."

Lor sighed. Arman had a hard time walking on sand anyway, but he was much worse at it when he was hammered. It was going to be a long walk back to their room, and she was tired.

"Let's start back," she suggested.

"No," he said. "It's nice here."

"Baby, I'm tired," she said. "Let's go back and we can get a candy bar or something if the store's still open." Lorrie Ann did not particularly like sweets, but Arman loved them. He never seemed to be aware of how often she used rewards of chocolate or candy to get him to do things. It always struck her as bizarre that he didn't notice. But it worked again, and he clambered up and, leaning on her, made his way back to the path that led to the store.

She bought him too much candy at the store, but she couldn't help it.

He got so excited by trying the new ones and because they couldn't read any of the Hindi packaging they had a relatively high fail rate at finding things he liked. "Just get one of everything," she suggested. Arman grinned, a little sheepish, but happy. He was so much like a little boy sometimes that it made her heart ache, a strange mixture of pity and love. She thought of the way Portia had announced all her flaws. I like people with problems worse than my own, Lorrie Ann thought. She was amazed that she felt better after allowing herself to form the words in her own mind. She felt like she could actually breathe. I use them to feel better about myself, she continued, astounded by the sudden lightness in her heart.

In the room, Arman curled up, his legs off, around his pile of candy. He kept trying to make her taste the ones he liked, but she wouldn't.

"I don't really want any more," she said.

He stared at her, and his eyes filled with tears. "Why?" he wailed. "Why won't you try it?"

Lorrie Ann was alarmed. Arman was not prone to crying. "What's wrong?"

"You don't love me anymore," he sobbed.

"Don't be ridiculous, of course I love you."

"You're going to go to Hampi and leave me! Please don't leave me!" Arman was sobbing hard now, nearly choking. "You were going to go and just not come back, and I knew it, I knew I'd just wait and wait here and you'd never come back!"

"Don't be silly," Lorrie Ann said, reaching out a hand and smoothing the fabric of his T-shirt over his back in circles. She kissed the top of his head. "I would never do that."

But the idea of doing so slowly blossomed in her like a rose.

"You weren't thinking that?" Arman panted.

"I wasn't!" Lorrie Ann said. "I promise! I would never ever do that to you." She kissed him again and his crying slowed. She scooted closer to him, nudging the pile of candy out of the way.

"I feel sick," he confessed.

"I know," she said.

And a little while later she held the tiny trash can of their room for him as he threw up all the chocolate he had eaten.

Lor was worried that he would die in his sleep, but he didn't. She knew that it was very dangerous to mix painkillers and alcohol. It was Arman himself who had taught her that. They drank beer all the time, or had drinks, but he had always stressed to her the importance of not getting hammered, though he did not actually follow this rule himself. Perhaps a part of her was hoping he would die. She didn't know. She only knew that when she woke up and discovered that he was still breathing steadily, she felt an overwhelming desire to get out of that room. She packed a purse for herself with cigarettes, loaded Starbursts, and her sunglasses, scribbled him a note on the back of a brochure, and left him sleeping in the room. She didn't even stop to have breakfast with Rinoo. She just went out on the main road and rented a moped and drove herself to Arambol.

She parked on a side street near the beach, and, after waiting for a group of chickens to get out of her way, made her way out onto the main drag, where she bought a chai from a chai-wallah on a bicycle and began to browse the stores. The moment she saw the STD ISD shop, a uniquely Indian institution that was an entire store full of international pay phones, she knew she had come to Arambol to call her mother. She hadn't used an STD ISD shop before except once to call her bank and tell them to take the hold off her debit card, so she was nervous when she walked in, but the boy at the counter just motioned her to a phone.

"How much?" she asked.

"You pay after," he said. "You pay after."

"Do you know the country code for the United States?" she asked him.

"Zero one one."

"Thank you."

The shop smelled of warm plastic and black licorice and sweaty bodies. There was a pile of pineapples in the corner and a cat sitting on top of them, licking its paws. She dialed 011, then a 1, and then her mother's cell phone, and it rang for what seemed like an impossibly long time. Lorrie Ann decided that what she was calling her mother to announce was that she was coming home. It was over. It had been stupid, and now it was over. This decision brought her almost unspeakable relief.

When Dana's voice mail picked up, she listened attentively to her mother's voice, fully intending to leave a message, but then, when the beep came, she found that she couldn't. She opened her mouth, but nothing would come out. She was frozen for a moment, then found herself slamming the receiver down in its holster, as though she were angry.

A little embarrassed, she edged out of the booth and got out her money to pay the boy.

"No, no," the boy said, waving her off. "You come back and try again later. Not pay now."

He waggled his head at her and smiled.

"Okay," Lorrie Ann said numbly, then stumbled out of the shop and into the bright sun of the boulevard, where she promptly ran smack into Portia.

"My friend," Portia cried, "I was hoping to see you again! Are you hungry?"

"I don't know," Lorrie Ann said. "Maybe."

"You don't know?" Portia laughed, and she dragged Lorrie Ann down the street and into a café where she ordered them dosas, huge thin curls of some kind of dough with a consistency between a fortune cookie and a pancake.

"Where is the gimp?" Portia asked, breaking off a piece of dosa and dunking it in a little dish of tomato chutney.

"At the hotel sleeping it off," Lorrie Ann said.

"You say this like he does it too much."

"Maybe he does," Lorrie Ann said, but it wasn't really true. Arman didn't often sleep in. He didn't often get too drunk. She was only experimenting with her own disloyalty.

"I was thinking," Portia said, "that I wanted to invite you on a trip. Some of my friends are going to Dubai. Do you want to go?"

"What are you going to do in Dubai?" Lorrie Ann asked. "I had been thinking about asking you to go to Hampi."

"Where is this?" Portia asked.

"Some famous ruins. East of here."

"I would go," she said, "but only if then you go to Dubai with me."

Lor flagged down the waiter and asked for a lime soda. "I'll have to ask Arman," she said.

"Oh," Portia said. "I can only bring you. I should have said that. My friends have this incredible apartment in Dubai. If I bring a girlfriend who shares a bed with me, this is okay. But not to bring a strange American couple. No one would understand this."

"Hmm . . . ," Lorrie Ann said.

"Please come!" Portia cried. "It will be so much more fun if you are there! They are all models and they never eat. Won't you eat with me?"

"Let me think about it," Lorrie Ann said.

"This means you want to come but you are trying to figure out how to get rid of him?"

Lorrie Ann sputtered as she took a sip of her lime soda.

Portia laughed. "It's okay. I will help you. We will make a plan!"

The plan was, roughly, that Lorrie Ann would go to the bank and get Arman a cashier's check for a thousand dollars, which was half of what they had left. She would write him a letter. Then she would go home, spend the rest of the day with him, and sneak out in the middle of the night, leaving the letter and the cashier's check, but taking half the pills, and go to meet Portia in her hotel in Arambol. Dillip would drive her. She would pay him extra not to tell Baba G where she had gone. The next morning, she and Portia would be on a bus bound for Hampi.

After Hampi, they went to Dubai. There they partied with an entire circus, a literal circus, and Lorrie Ann made out with an acrobat while

Portia had sex with a dwarf. After that, they went to Bangkok, then Barcelona and Ibiza. They ran into Leonardo DiCaprio in Tel Aviv, where they partied with all of Portia's model friends. They were briefly incarcerated in Berlin, but only for a night, and it was some kind of misunderstanding.

Of course Lorrie Ann's own money had run out soon enough, but Portia was loaded and Portia was generous. Further, the two ladies almost never paid for drinks or for dinner or for the hotel suites. Often, they flew on private jets chartered by whatever group they were traveling with. Lorrie Ann discovered that she had, without realizing it, lost a lot of weight, and was easily able to fit into all Portia's size 2 couture clothes. The only thing she couldn't borrow was shoes, and she bought a pair of black sandals that could be worn with almost anything. Portia was green with envy over Lorrie Ann's tiny feet, but Lorrie Ann pointed out that Portia was almost six feet tall and that if her feet were any smaller she would become structurally unsound. "You should see my mother's feet," Lorrie Ann said. "She's the one with really perfect feet."

In Hvar, a count, also a multimillionaire, had asked Lorrie Ann to marry him one night and she had even said yes, but then in the morning he didn't seem to remember it and she didn't bring it up, in part because a sloth, which had been rented from the zoo for the party, had somehow died during the night and the entire morning was like an extended game of Clue, all of them trying to piece together how the sloth had ended up floating in the pool with the side of its head bashed in. One of the girls, a former Playboy bunny, had had some kind of emotional breakdown over the sloth and did nothing but sit on a deck chair, cradling its wet, dead body all morning as she wept into its fur. Finally, it had to be taken from her.

"I'm sorry," I said. "I just can't listen to any more of this."

Lorrie Ann stopped short. She had been enjoying telling me all this. She glowed as she mentioned Leonardo DiCaprio and counts and the names of exotic cities. These were her adventures and I was telling her to stop.

"Is something wrong?" she asked.

Her hands were folded on the table in front of her, as though she were a child at school. What did she think? How on earth was she justifying it to herself?

"Say it," she said.

"Nothing," I said. I did not want to say things to Lorrie Ann that I couldn't take back. I wanted to think it through.

"I know you're thinking it—just say it. Say it."

"He's all alone!" I cried. "He's alone in a nursing home and you're fucking doing blow in nightclubs throughout Europe!"

Lorrie Ann smiled as though I had said exactly what she expected. "And it makes you sick," she said. "It makes you sick to think of him suffering while I have a good time."

"Yes," I said. "I'm sorry, but it does."

"Tell me, how much of my life would be enough? How much am I supposed to be willing to give up? All of it?"

"No, obviously—I'm not talking about that," I said, unsure what I really was asking of her.

"You want me to be a martyr? Is that the idea? Motherhood equals martyrdom. There isn't supposed to be any limit to the amount of suffering you can voluntarily endure?"

I felt that she was twisting things, making this about something else. "No, but you can't be partying in this frivolous, gross way while he's suffering. Doesn't his suffering matter to you at all?"

"How is it any different than you enjoying your life with Franklin here in Istanbul, having the gall to do something as useless as translate an old fucking poem, when there are women being raped and dying every fucking day in the Congo, men slaughtering one another, children becoming soldiers. They rape the women with guns. Did you know that? After they are done raping her themselves, they sometimes put a gun up her and pull the trigger. So tell me, how is it different?"

"He's your son!" I said.

Lor sighed, as though I were offering her the most pedestrian and boring of arguments.

"We're all brothers and sisters, Mia. Every ounce of human suffering is equal to every other. Zach's suffering is not more than a child's in the Congo just because we are genetically related. That's just . . . obviously fallacious."

When had Lorrie Ann started using words like "fallacious"? Was it Arman and his collection of strange books that was responsible? When had she begun living according to general principles so abstracted from reality? It was almost as though Zach were an idea and not a person. But then, I realized, she had approached the decision about whether or not to have him in the exact same abstract way. I sensed dimly that all of Lor's life had been this same kind of grueling march back to the Chevron to return that wilted ten-dollar bill. It was a mathematical goodness, without spontaneity or heart.

She covered her face with her hands for a moment, then sighed and resettled herself at the table. She spoke as though earnestly trying to explain to me the simplest of factual things: "If the general idea is to decrease human suffering, then it is unethical for me to seek suffering. If I thought I could make Zach's suffering less, I would do it, because then it would balance out. But my choice was that either both of us should suffer unspeakably or only he should suffer unspeakably. If I were making the choice regarding someone other than myself, the answer would be clear. If I had to decide: either Mia and Zach can both suffer unspeakably or only Zach can suffer unspeakably, obviously, the right thing would be to choose that only he suffer. But somehow when I make the same decision regarding myself, it is considered selfish instead of sane."

It was just a math problem to her. I thought about the way Zach looked at her, with wonder, with such awestruck love.

"But obviously," I said, "seeing you would make his suffering less! You know that. You know he loves you and he's scared and he's all by himself in a strange place."

Lorrie Ann sighed. "I have come to believe," she said, as though she were finally confessing the truth, a truth she had wanted to shield me from, but now had no choice but to reveal, "that what they are doing is morally wrong."

"They?"

"The doctors. The hospitals. The social workers."

"In what way?"

"They keep him alive—that's the only definition of goodness they know, so they don't care what the cost of life is, they want life and only life at any cost. They discount his suffering, they discount his misery. They even refuse to give him painkillers because they want him to live longer. It is beginning to seem to me like Mengele. Like science without any human feeling. It is the way robots would run things, creatures without any feelings."

"But—"

"They do it for dogs, Mia. For dogs. For dogs, we believe in kindness over life. Put them out of their misery. Once their lives become agony, we end it."

"But who has the power to decide that for another human being? Zach can't decide. You can't decide."

"I should be allowed to decide. I love him more than anyone else. I should be allowed to decide. Now it is a doctor who decides. A doctor who doesn't care about him at all."

Honestly, I could understand her outrage. I knew exactly how much medicine had betrayed Lorrie Ann: the My Little Pony eye shadow nurse, the doctors who used ulcer medicine on her without worrying. She didn't trust these people and why should she?

"In your particular case," I said, "I agree. I would want you and not some doctor to have control over whether Zach lives or dies. But would you really want every mother to have that right?"

"Yes," Lorrie Ann said quickly. She'd clearly already thought about it. "I think mothers should be allowed to kill their children."

"Across the board?"

"Across the board. From in utero until, I don't know, until they are eighteen?"

"Eighteen!"

"All right, maybe twelve. Until they can decide for themselves. If they can decide for themselves. If the child is mentally incompetent, it is the mother's job to decide."

"What about the father?"

"Fuck the father," Lor said.

"Are you serious?" I was completely stunned. And yet, to be completely honest, I was enjoying the argument. I loved to argue; I loved the activity itself, of forming arguments and then rebutting them, finding holes in the logic.

"Jim never had the same kind of connection to Zach that I had. I could feel what Zach needed in my gut. I knew when he had a dirty diaper, when he was hungry, when he was just overtired. Jim loved him, but he didn't feel Zach inside his own mind—he didn't have that intuitive connection."

I put on the kettle for more tea, but then it occurred to me that what we really needed to do was clean up Lorrie Ann's bloody feet. I kept the kettle on, but got down a big plastic bin from on top of the fridge and filled it with hot soapy water. "But," I said, "I would never, ever have wanted my mother to have the right to kill my brothers. I feel like I should have had that right—but not her! Can you imagine?"

"Your mother was bad," Lor said, "but she wouldn't have killed your brothers."

"But what if she did?"

"She wouldn't have. You have to trust women. We rarely kill unless we have to. We are very reasonable."

"You say 'we' as though women were some kind of unified body."

"We are," she said. I put down the tray of soapy water in front of her and knelt down. I had used dish soap, so it smelled like lemons. Lor hissed with pain as each foot went in.

"People are people. Some of them are insane, most of them aren't. But women aren't all one way, and men aren't all another way."

"Sure they are," Lor said. "Women have vaginas and men have

penises. I'm sick to death of people who claim to be feminists arguing that women are the same as men. They aren't. They should be equal to men in our esteem, but they are not the same as men. And as history shows, men are prone to kill people for almost no reason at all. Women hardly ever do that."

I felt we had gotten off track. This didn't need to be an argument about the difference between men and women. This was about Zach. This was about the grossness of Playboy bunnies holding dead sloths and marriage proposals you forgot about in the morning. I used a washcloth gently on the bottoms of her feet.

"I think there's a piece of glass in there," Lor said.

"Do you want me to get the tweezers?"

She nodded, biting her lip, and I ran to the bathroom to get some tweezers. When I got back, the kettle was singing and I flicked off the burner. "Do you even want any more tea?" I asked.

"No."

I left the kettle steaming on the stove and knelt in front of Lor again. "Which one?"

She held up her left foot. "In the heel."

I smoothed the side of my finger up and down the skin of her heel until I found the lump and the sharp point of the shard of glass. "What I'm saying," I said, "is that I think the current system works most of the time. It doesn't work for you, but for most people it's the best thing. So it's imperfect, but it's the best we can do."

"Well," Lor said, "it's not good enough. And I'm sorry, but I don't think it's the best we can do at all! I don't think anyone is even trying to make it better. That's like saying a canoe is the best we can do!"

I got the little sliver of glass with the tweezers—I could hear that I had it by the scraping glass and metal sound, but it kept slipping as I tried to pull it out.

Lor went on, "Why not strive for perfect justice on earth? Why not try to find something that works absolutely perfectly all of the time? I mean, it's like we've just given up on justice. No one's even trying anymore. We just have all these shitty stupid laws, and people always say, 'Well, it's the best we've got!' Fuck that. Fuck them. Oh, ow, that hurts!"

"It's out," I said, holding out for her inspection the sliver of green glass I had extracted from her heel.

"Listen," Lor said, as she plucked the glass from me to see it closer, "we all know that the current justification for abortion is just bullshit. It's not yet a life? Come *on*! That's not the point! That's semantics! It would become a life if you left it alone, and everyone, everyone knows that. Women who get abortions, they don't feel light and easy about it—but they know, they know deep in their blood that it is their right to kill their children."

Her argument made me uncomfortable. When I had had my abortion, I had not considered it a "collection of cells." I had thought of it as a baby, and I had decided it was my right to kill it.

"That is not the point. That is not the point," I said. "The point is, even if what they are doing is morally wrong, that doesn't mean Zach deserves to be all alone."

"You want me to be party to actions I believe are unethical, and I just can't. You want me to sit there and watch while they torture my boy. Well, I'm not that brave. Sorry to disappoint you."

"I'm not asking you to be brave," I said, flustered.

"But you would rather I was sober," she said. "And it takes being brave to be sober. Part of the reason I do drugs is because I can't handle any of this, and you want me to be able to handle it because you would feel better about that. But, Mia, I don't make decisions in my life based on how it makes you feel."

I stammered because of course it sounded absurd, the idea that she would make major life decisions according to my feelings, and yet that was exactly what I wanted her to do. "But you know this is gross. You know it is."

"Exactly," Lor said, "which is why I choose to be high all the time."

"I think I might be pregnant," I blurted. It was almost as if her honesty had pulled it out of me the way a metal filing is drawn to a magnet.

Lor looked up at me as though I had rung a gong. "That's so exciting," she said.

Just then, Franklin walked in the door with Bensu on his shoulders.

CHAPTER FIFTEEN

Yes or No

Franklin stood there for a moment, his hands on Bensu's ankles, taking in the scene. Bensu was wearing little black patent-leather dress shoes. I remembered suddenly the tea set I had bought her. I wasn't entirely sure how much Franklin had heard. He could read me as easily as he could read Inanna, and he knew he had walked in on something, but had he heard the word "pregnant"? Had he heard that it was my voice saying it?

"Hey, baby," I said. I caught his eye, but his face was a mask of friendliness.

"Look who I found out in the hall," Franklin said.

"I refuse to betray my country," Bensu said. "Do whatever you want to me."

"She's a spy," Franklin explained. "And you must be ... ?" He reached out a hand to shake with Lorrie Ann, and Bensu had to cling to his hair in order to keep her balance as he leaned. If it hurt him, the way she grabbed his hair, he gave no sign of it. My pulse began to regulate as more and more it seemed that Franklin hadn't heard anything.

"Lorrie Ann," she said.

The change in Franklin was instantaneous and so genuine it almost broke my heart. "Oh my God!" he cried. "Why didn't you call me and tell me?" he asked, turning to me. "We're so, so happy to have you here. I'm so glad to meet you!"

Behind him I mimed to Lorrie Ann a zipper across my lips. I mouthed: "He doesn't know."

Lorrie Ann was clearly flustered, trying to greet Franklin and take in my frantic sign language. "It was a surprise," she said, smiling winningly at him. I noted that she did not say: "I called Mia for help when I was barefoot and bleeding in the Grand Bazaar."

"How crazy!" Franklin exclaimed. "Still, you should have called me, Mia. I would have picked up something special."

"I'm making chicken," I said.

"Chicken will be fine," Lorrie Ann said. "More than fine."

She flicked her eyes at me, and I knew she was saying: "He didn't hear. It's okay." Once more, we were co-conspirators, the way we had been as girls. That was how easy it was to regain: one secret, and suddenly we were a team.

"You should see how she cooks the chicken," Franklin said. "She rubs it with cinnamon and all these crazy spices—unbelievable."

"If you are going to kill me," Bensu said from above him, "please have mercy and do it quickly."

"Oh, okay," Franklin said and swung her down from his shoulders. "Where would you like me to kill you?"

"In the living room," Bensu said.

"Come this way then," Franklin said. "I'll be right back," he assured us, but Lorrie Ann and I were both too curious to see how he was going to kill Bensu in the living room, and we followed them.

"Now you have to stand bravely against the wall," he said, "and close your eyes and then I'm going to shoot you with this gun"—he gestured with his fingers, making the shape of a handgun—"and then you have to die, all right?"

Bensu nodded gravely and readied herself against the wall.

"Any last words, spy?" Franklin asked.

"I only want to say," Bensu said, "that I have chosen to die instead of to betray my country. And also that I am very jealous that she got to meet Leonardo DiCaprio." Bensu tried to point at Lorrie Ann, but her eyes were closed and so she wound up pointing at the ottoman beside the red chair. So that was why I had kept hearing someone out in the hall; Bensu had been spying. Had she heard me say I might be pregnant?

"I see," Franklin said and raised his eyebrows at me and Lorrie Ann. "Prepare to die!"

Bensu smoothed her brow, her eyes still closed, and waited bravely for death.

"Pow pow pow!" Franklin said, shooting her with his fingers. "Pow pow!"

Bensu's eyes flew open, those emerald eyes, with a look of pure betrayal. She clutched at her chest as she slowly slid down the wall, her legs buckling beneath her. "Shame on you," she said. "I'm just a child!"

Franklin just shrugged, still smiling, as Bensu went through her death throes. She moaned and spasmed for a very long time. When it seemed she was finally done, he went over and offered her a hand. "Very good dying," he said.

"Thank you," she said.

"Hey Bensu," I said, "I have a present for you."

"What is it?" Bensu asked skeptically.

"Why don't you come in the kitchen and see?"

Franklin and Lorrie Ann watched from the doorway as I presented the tea set to Bensu. I was dimly aware that I was being slightly theatrical, trying to show Lorrie Ann what a good person I was, trying to show Franklin how good with children I was. My mind flashed briefly to the Yes or No test right there in the kitchen drawer, tucked alongside the place mats. Was I auditioning somehow?

"Isn't it pretty?" I asked, pointing at the pattern of golden triangles along the edges of the teacups.

Bensu could smell the falseness a mile away. "Why were you yelling at her?" she asked me, still not taking the tea set from my hands.

"At who?" I asked.

"That one," Bensu said, indicating Lorrie Ann with a nod of her head.

"It was just a misunderstanding," I said.

"You shouldn't yell," Bensu said. "It isn't proper for a lady to yell."

"Take it," I said, trying to hand her the tea set. Had I been yelling at

Lorrie Ann? Was that how it seemed? It had seemed to me only that we were arguing.

"I should get home to my mother," Bensu said, and backed off a few paces, walking backward until she bumped into Franklin's legs.

"You don't want your tea set?" I asked.

"I already have one," Bensu said.

"No, you don't," I said. "You're always pretending to drink out of doll shoes!"

"Are you going to have a baby?" she asked, and it felt exactly like she had stabbed me in the stomach with a metal barbecue skewer.

"No." I laughed. "What gave you that idea?"

"Then is she?" she asked.

"Nope," I said, trying to act confused and baffled by her questions. Kids! They say the strangest things! I was smiling, but my cheeks were numb, as though they were shot full of Novocain.

"That is a very nice tea set," Bensu said, trying to make it up to me. "Too bad that I already have one."

"Too bad," I said.

"I'll take you downstairs," Franklin said, and Bensu nodded, holding up her tiny hand to be taken in his big one and placidly following him out the door.

"Well, that was fucking weird," Lorrie Ann said once they were gone and out of earshot.

"I know," I hissed.

"So do you know for sure yet?"

"No, I haven't even taken the test—I just, it just feels like I am."

Lorrie Ann nodded, eagerly. "Are you done being mad at me?" she asked.

"Of course," I said, even though I was in no way done being mad at her. It was more that, in the end, my love for her trumped everything.

"Thank God," Lorrie Ann said. "It's the worst feeling in the world when you're mad at me." She took the tea set out of my hands and hugged me, long and hard.

Her hair smelled of lavender covering over something greasy and unclean, like rancid cooking oil.

One of Franklin's most profound gifts was social ease. I didn't consider myself socially awkward, exactly, but there was an unbendingness in me as well as a propensity to say cruel, but mostly true, things that seemed to make other people uncomfortable, whereas everyone, absolutely everyone, loved Franklin. I wasn't jealous of him about it; I was extremely grateful.

When he returned, sans Bensu, he brought with him an air of bonhomie so great that the moment he set foot in the apartment I could feel the muscles in my shoulders sag with relief. He opened a bottle of wine and began asking Lorrie Ann questions about herself almost as soon as he was through the door. He had retained every detail of her life, and he asked after Dana and Zach by name.

He asked her if she still worked at The Cellar.

He asked after Arman.

He even asked about the cat.

I was shocked and amazed by how much he knew about her, and Lorrie Ann was very obviously both flattered and alarmed, since she couldn't remember the first thing about him and could ask him nothing in return. But even more than Franklin's encyclopedic knowledge of her life, I found myself amazed by the answers his questions elicited.

About Zach, Lorrie Ann said simply, "His disease had progressed to the point that in-home care was no longer an option. He's in an inpatient care facility and I miss him every single day. Every day."

About The Cellar, she said, "Maybe I had just gotten too old to be a waitress anymore. I was struggling with my mom in the hospital and with Zach, and even though I had worked there four years, they wouldn't cut me any slack. They treated me like I was a teenager, late for work because I'd overslept. The whole experience kind of stunned me, to be honest."

About Arman and the trip to India, she said, "We had both always wanted to see the world, and for the first time in my life, I was free to. So we traveled around India. Ultimately, I wound up traveling with another girl I met along the way and he went back to the States. He owns a smoke shop there and he has this whole life, whereas I didn't have anything to return to, so it just made sense for me to keep traveling."

All the while as they spoke I quartered the chicken, rubbed the skin with spices, set the pieces in the baking dish, and put them in the oven. I made a salad of radishes, onions, and parsley as I waited for the water for couscous to boil. Obviously I could not call her a liar. Everything she said was perfectly true, even as it was deeply misleading. And even if she had lied outright, social propriety would have kept me quiet. I did, however, slice those radishes so thin they were nearly translucent.

Eventually, of course, Lorrie Ann excused herself to go use the bathroom. I was fairly sure she was going to shoot up in there. The moment she was out of the room, Franklin was behind me at the stove, nuzzling me and taking in deep whiffs of my neck and hair. He always liked to smell me. It gave him some kind of knowledge of me, of whether or not I was okay. He rubbed his face back and forth in the crook of my neck, just inhaling and inhaling.

"She's not like I thought," he said softly. "Are you okay?"

"I'm fine," I said. "She's on drugs. She's addicted to heroin."

"Ah," Franklin said.

"I'm so upset," I said. "I don't know how to help her. I don't know how to fix it." As I spoke, my voice got smaller and smaller and tighter and tighter, until by the end I was like a cartoon mouse. I had my eyes tightly shut but I was still stirring the couscous, fluffing sliced olives and dates into the webby grains. Franklin said nothing, but went on breathing into my neck, inhaling my smell and exhaling hot breath right against my skin.

"I think I may have offered to let her stay here," I said.

"That's okay," Franklin said. "We'll figure it out. It will all be okay."

"It feels like I just found out she has cancer and she's going to die. I just keep thinking that, every time I look at her: You're going to die, you're going to die, you're going to die." This was true, even though I had not allowed myself to become conscious of it until that moment. The entire afternoon, from the moment I first saw her and she pointed the copy of Proust at the sky, a certain despair had been flickering in the corners of my vision. Lorrie Ann had entered the land of the dead and I had no idea how we would retrieve her.

"Shh . . . ," Franklin said.

"She won't be out of the bathroom for a while," I said. "She's shooting up in there."

"Oh," Franklin said, and I could feel him relax a bit as he hugged me tighter to the front of him. "Do you want to try and get her into some kind of rehab or something?"

"Maybe," I said. But I suspected Lor would refuse to go. My uterus felt different: swollen, tender, alive. There were some things you could not undo, some places you could not return from.

"It will all be okay," Franklin said. And even though I felt he was far too optimistic, I also suspected that there was wisdom in his optimism; Franklin's scale for "okay" spanned thousands of years. He didn't worry about someone being unhappy for a few hours or days. He didn't really worry about unhappiness at all. I think he worried about animals and sunlight and possibly grain. He worried about the furtherance of human knowledge as a grand cooperative endeavor that made him coworkers with everyone from Proust to Einstein to the author of Inanna.

"Did you know," he asked me, "that you're the most beautiful woman in the world?"

"No," I said. My eyes were still closed, but my spoon had stopped its mechanical stirring of the couscous.

"It's true," he said, and I smiled. I had never thought of myself as the pretty one.

When Lorrie Ann returned, Franklin was still holding me from behind as I pretended to cook.

"Aw," she said. "Look at you two."

"Dinner's ready," I said.

"I'll set the table," Franklin said, and turned from me.

There must have been three or four seconds before he opened the drawer when I could have processed what he said and stopped him, but it seemed to take that long for his words to filter into my mind. When I finally heard what he said and realized that if he opened the drawer, he would find the pregnancy test, I turned around, my mouth open to speak. He was standing there, completely silent, the Yes or No test box in his hand. Lorrie Ann was sitting at the table, watching us as though we were a play.

"I—" But there was no way for me to finish the sentence.

"Probably," Franklin said, turning to me, his eyebrows upraised as though he were begging, "I did a bad thing. Probably you wanted to wait and take this without us watching you, and I should have just pretended not to see it. But now I just can't do that."

Lorrie Ann suddenly beat her hands in a drumroll on the kitchen table, and both Franklin and I startled and looked over at her. "Sorry," she said, "but this is so exciting! So are you going to take it?" She had definitely shot up in the bathroom. Her pupils were tiny as a snake's.

"Right now?" I asked.

"Why not?" she said.

I looked over at Franklin but he was just holding the test, looking at me. "You don't have to," he said.

"Go! Go, do it!" Lorrie Ann pounded on the table again in her excitement.

I kept looking back and forth between them, my mouth open like a fish gasping at the sudden change from sea to air.

Franklin reached out and pulled me to him, pressing me into his chest. "I love you," he said into my hair. When he pulled away, I realized he had somehow put the box in my hand.

"Just go take it," he said.

How had they managed to do this? How had I let this happen? I gave Franklin a pleading look.

"I'm sorry, baby," he said. "Do you want me to go in with you?"

"No," I said. To have Franklin watch me pee on the stick would be even worse. At the very least I wanted the privacy of the bathroom, the time alone to read the results before having to come out and announce them.

"How long have you guys been trying?" Lorrie Ann asked.

"I love you," Franklin said again, ignoring her question and giving me a gentle push down the hall to the bathroom.

In the bathroom, I sat on the edge of the tub, trying to breathe. I was, in truth, almost entirely certain I was pregnant. My period was three weeks late, and I was on the pill. I had actually been in the process of switching brands since my usual kind wasn't available here in Turkey. I started the new pack, and then when I came to the pretty pink pills that signified I was supposed to start bleeding, nothing happened. I took all seven, and still nothing. I started on the next month's gleaming row of white pills, but after a week of those I decided to stop taking them.

But why? Why stop taking them?

(Because, I worried, they might hurt the baby!)

But wasn't I planning to kill the baby?

(. . .)

And so I knew that if I took the test, it would come out positive, and then I would have to go out there and tell them, and then . . . what would happen?

I knew obviously that whatever happened, Franklin would be decent. It would be impossible for him not to be. In fact, it was his rigidly "good guy" status that made me worry most. I knew from everything he had said about Elizabeth that he did not want children, at least not now. I didn't think he would leave me or something like that—he was too good a guy. If I wanted an abortion, he would support me. And if I wanted to keep it, he would support me. But what if he felt forced to do the right thing and marry me, even though he didn't want me or the child?

It seemed to me that the danger of this kind of false pretense was even higher with an audience, with the dead goddess Lorrie Ann looking on, judging us mere mortals.

Even worse, part of what Franklin would want and need to know was whether I wanted the child, and I did not know the answer. I could not even bring myself to fully consider the question. I couldn't allow myself to start wanting the child in case I would then have to kill it.

What I wanted most was to not lose Franklin, and I worried that either way, yes or no, I would still wind up losing him. If we kept the baby and he felt trapped, then slowly, over years or months, I would lose him. I couldn't even really think what having a baby would mean for us financially or career-wise. It was too terrifying.

And if we didn't keep the baby, I was not sure I would ever be able to forget that we had made such a decision together. I knew that if Franklin consented to kill our baby it would extinguish some of my feelings for him. Which was why, if I was going to kill the baby, I would rather Franklin not know about it at all. I could handle being Medea, being a monster, but I could not handle asking Franklin to help, to consent, to agree.

It was uncomfortable sitting on the lip of the tub because it was so narrow, part of a hyper-modern tub/shower combo that looked like it could be launched into space, so I stood up and began, absently, to water the plants. Besides the wonderfully mismatched living room furniture, it was the strange excess of plants in the bathroom that I loved most about that apartment. There were several jade plants, a dracaena, some African violets, a hanging spider plant, and two ferns. I loved to take a bath in the morning in there. It was like being in a greenhouse. Part of me was toying with simply not taking the test at all. If I didn't take the test, it would be less of a lie to go out there and say I wasn't pregnant, because I wouldn't know I was, and then I could have a few more days to figure out what the best thing to do was.

There was a knock, and I turned when I heard the door open, sure that it was Franklin who had dared intrude on me, but it was Lorrie Ann.

How many hours upon hours had Lorrie Ann and I spent shut up in bathrooms together? Time itself seemed to shift and resettle as she closed the door behind her, the past and the future fanning out from the present moment with the clicking riffle of playing cards.

"I'm pregnant," I said. "I'm sure I am."

Lorrie Ann was already nodding, her lips pressed together, as she closed the small distance between us and took the test box out of my hand. "Why don't you take the test anyway?" she suggested, almost at a whisper.

"I'm trying to decide what to do," I said. "How do you decide what to do?"

"Take the test," she said again, slipping her fingernail underneath the cardboard seam at the end of the box.

"What possible criterion does one even use to make life decisions?" I asked, but Lorrie Ann did not respond. I realized, in part because the faint metallic hum of the lightbulb seemed overpoweringly loud, and also because Lorrie Ann was not responding to me, that I was somehow estranged from the moment. I was failing to react appropriately to the task at hand.

Lorrie Ann handed me the plastic stick. "Pee on this," she said.

Obediently, I pulled down my jeans and panties and settled on the toilet. "I hate peeing on these," I said. "They always splash."

"Just wait—if you are pregnant, you're going to have to pee in about a thousand tiny cups and by that time your belly will be so huge that visibility will be pretty much nil. Every single time I peed all over my own hands."

"I don't think I'm—if I'm pregnant, I don't think I'll be keeping it," I said. I was holding the test stick under me, but I couldn't make myself pee.

"Sure," she said, "but you can think about all that later."

"No, I need to decide now." I still couldn't pee.

"Why?" she asked, kneeling so she could look me in the eye. Her breath smelled like fruity gum or candy.

"Because I have to decide what to do about Franklin."

"What do you have to do about him?"

"I need to figure out how to . . ." I didn't know exactly how to phrase this next part. I needed to figure out how to control his reaction. I needed to figure out what I wanted so that I could give him cues so that he could not hurt me. I could come out breezily talking of abortion appointments, or I could come out with a shy smile, or I could pretend to be embarrassed as a way of drawing him out to see what his feelings were. All of these game plans were playing out in a simultaneous jumble in my mind.

"Why don't you let Franklin worry about how Franklin reacts?" Lorrie Ann said. She reached over and turned on the sink faucet.

"Who are you," I asked, "Dr. Phil?"

"Pee," she instructed.

"Do you think the chicken is burning?"

"Pee!" she said.

And I did.

I remember when Lorrie Ann took her pregnancy test, back in the summer after graduation, back when Zach was just the promise of a baby and not an actual baby, back before Jim was a soldier and then, later, a corpse, back before Lor was a junkie, back before Arman lost his legs even. It was the weekend and her parents were home and my parents were home and so, logically, we went to the mall.

We had bought a two pack of tests from the Rite Aid on the walk to Fashion Island. We had also bought a box of Red Vines and two Dr Peppers. It was excellent to bite off the top and bottom of a Red Vine and use it as a straw for the Dr Pepper. The walk to the mall involved a long uphill stretch on Avocado Avenue that was in full sun, and the sugar from the sodas together with the scalded white pavement and shimmering heat gave us both a kind of giggly delirium we couldn't shake. By the time we made it to the bathroom of the Barnes & Noble (the nicest, most luxurious bathroom we knew of at the mall), we were in helpless, senseless hysterics.

I wish badly that I could remember what we were laughing about. Were we making fun of a teacher? Another girl? What had been so funny? But you can never remember what you were laughing about, and even if you could, it seems doubtful that it would still be funny.

We couldn't stop laughing even when the first test came back positive. I pushed her back into the stall with the second test. Both of us were laughing so hard we were almost choking. Lorrie Ann was snorting and then laughing at herself for snorting. "I can't believe you're pregnant," I kept saying.

"This is terrible!" Lorrie Ann kept saying, even as her diaphragm went on pumping laughter out of her like some manic organ grinder.

An old lady came in at one point (old lady—the woman was probably in her forties!) and gave us disdainful looks, but it didn't matter: we couldn't stop.

After the second test came out positive, Lorrie Ann was bent over the sink, laughing so hard it was a kind of sobbing. "Do you want to keep these?" I asked, brandishing the tests. Lorrie Ann stood up, grabbed them from my hands, and held them up to her ears like earrings. "I suppose so," she said. "What do you think? Do you think Jim will like them?"

"Omigod," I said, in a high sibilant voice, "are those designer? Are those fucking e.p.t?"

Lorrie Ann shrieked, snorted: "e.p.t!"

When I took the pregnancy test after Ryan Almquist, Lorrie Ann had not been with me. I had been alone, babysitting my little brothers. I took the test, found out I was pregnant, then hid the test stick in an empty box of Alpha-Bits in the kitchen trash and went to watch *The NeverEnding Story* with my brothers. I snuggled Alex close to me, breathing in his sweet biscuit scent, as I tried to get my heart rate to return to normal. We all stayed up too late that night, our bare legs sticking to the black leather sofas, creaking as we adjusted our positions, watching *The NeverEnding Story* and then *Teenage Mutant Ninja Turtles* and then *The NeverEnding Story* once more. I don't think I even told Lorrie Ann I was pregnant until after I had scheduled the abortion.

Did it matter? For me, the past had stitched us together so that parts of me were simply connected to parts of Lorrie Ann. But as I waited with her in the bathroom for the pee to absorb, for the stick to change colors, I felt a snag and then a sudden freedom, as though we had finally ripped free of each other and the past no longer mattered. She was just another female animal mouth-breathing with me in the bathroom.

We both watched the test on the lip of the bathroom sink. Slowly the plus sign formed. Lorrie Ann held up the back of the box helplessly: plus is for yes, minus is for no.

She grinned, shrugged. "Exciting!" she said, reaching out to rub my arm.

"No," I said, swatting her away. "Not exciting."

"I don't get it," Lorrie Ann said. "You're twenty-nine. You and Franklin clearly love each other. What is the big problem?"

"He broke up with his last girlfriend because she wanted kids."

Lor made a pucker, sour face. "Ew, that's not good."

"I know. She wanted to get married. He felt he wasn't at the point in his career where he could make that kind of commitment."

"Is he at that point in his career now?" Lor asked.

"No. It's a two-body problem," I hissed. "Both of us are looking for tenure-track positions and it would be almost impossible for both of us to ever find jobs in the same place. It's a very common academic problem: the two-body problem."

"But surely there's some university somewhere in the world that needs a cuneiform person and a Latin person?"

There was a pounding on the bathroom door and both Lorrie Ann and I startled. "How's it going in there?" Franklin yelled through the wood.

"Good," I called. "Just a minute."

Lorrie Ann waited a moment, then whispered, "But have you talked to him about it?"

"It's one of those things we completely avoid ever talking about. Classics is kind of a dying discipline. These departments aren't growing. Even if we did manage to find a place trying to fill two positions at once, it wouldn't be a top-notch place and we are both really, really top notch. Both of us would be taking a hit. The two years of this grant have been—like this magical time outside reality."

"How do you guys really not talk about this?" Lorrie Ann was gently tapping the pregnancy test against the lip of the sink.

"Because," I said, "if we publish this book and it's a big enough deal, which I think it could be, the two-body problem might just go away. We'd have bargaining power. We could say, 'We work as a team, you can't get one without the other.'"

"I see," Lorrie Ann said.

"Can we just—obviously I'll tell him, but this is going to involve some really intense conversations. It's not just a simple 'yippee, I'm pregnant' thing. So can we just tell him this one came back negative?"

"And then what?" Lorrie Ann asked.

"Then next week, or whenever you're gone, I'll tell him my period still hasn't come and take another one and that one will come back positive and then we'll take it from there."

Franklin moaned through the door, "I'm dying out here. What does it say?"

"Please," I whispered.

I knew from the look of pained hesitation on her face that I had already won. I was wrapping up the test in toilet paper, making of it a miniature mummy that I stuffed back in the box and stuck in the trash.

"I don't like it," Lorrie Ann said.

Franklin began knocking again, this time more quietly and rhythmically, and I realized he was knocking the tune of "Pop Goes the Weasel."

I pulled the door open. "False alarm," I said.

"Really?" Franklin said, his hand still frozen and upraised from knocking. "So that's a negative?"

I nodded. "What a relief, right?"

He backed up to let us out of the bathroom and I moved past him briskly toward the kitchen. If he saw anything amiss in Lorrie Ann's face, he did not mention it. Both of them simply trailed behind the small amount of wind I made in our hallway by rushing to save my scorched chicken, even as inside me that plus sign finally began to detonate, unfurling inside me a huge mushroom cloud.

CHAPTER SIXTEEN

The Galla Who Accept No Gifts

"I confess," Lorrie Ann said. "I have no idea when or where Sumer was, and I can't let this conversation go on any fucking longer without asking."

Franklin laughed, showing her the wide Cheshire arc of his teeth, which were so white they had an almost bluish cast. His dentist always complained that the teeth of redheads were impossible to match crowns to: a different kind of white than regular people's teeth. "Sumer is what Iraq was before Iraq was Babylon," he said.

"Iraq was Babylon? How did I not know this?"

"Because U.S. education is shit," I said. I had become filled with scorn for the U.S. educational system since I had begun teaching in grad school. My students came to me weirdly unformed, gluey as under-baked rolls.

"Is it really worse than other places?"

"Yes," Franklin and I answered in unison.

"I asked my kids how long English had been a language. The answers go from two thousand to ten thousand years," I said.

"I take it English hasn't been spoken for that long," Lorrie Ann said. I had lit candles on the table and she leaned forward to press the pad of her finger into a spilled puddle of wax. She had eschewed her cardigan and the golden skin of her shoulders was exposed.

"Oh, you know that," Franklin said. "You know Jesus was two thousand years ago and he wasn't speaking English. You know that."

"I'm just saying," Lorrie Ann continued, "no one ever asked me a question like that before, so it would be hard to know what to answer. I don't blame the kids for saying dumb things. You can say dumb things without actually being dumb, you know."

"I don't blame the kids either," I said, though I wondered if this were strictly true. I did blame them—for how little they seemed to want, for not demanding more. They were all seemingly half asleep. This was a common conversational topic among academics: what was wrong with the youth, what was causing it, what could be done. We never tired of talking about it and could become passionate even while repeating arguments we'd said a hundred times. "I blame the educational system. Tell me this, how on earth do they manage to avoid teaching them anything meaningful and then turn around and orchestrate complicated sex scandals? Did you see that latest one in California where the kids were all blindfolded and made to drink the teacher's semen?"

"No, I must have missed that one," Lorrie Ann said.

"There were pictures—the guy was taking pictures of them blindfolded," Franklin crowed. "For *years*! For fucking years!" He reached out for the bottle and refilled his glass. I realized that Franklin was on the road to getting tanked. I held out my glass and Franklin filled it, but Lorrie Ann shot daggers at me with her eyes. I brought the glass to my lips, as though to defy her, but then found myself only pretending to take a sip, like Bensu sipping at a doll shoe. I could not resist resting my hand on the small pudge of my belly. It would only look like I was full, like I had eaten too much, but it comforted me, putting my hand there.

Death was terrifying, but so was life. Life had come for me, was, even as we spoke, even as we pretended that we had directed the course of our lives via conscious decision making and the colossal power of our human forebrains, even as we made puns and repartee in our human language, layering symbols upon symbols, life was directing the forking network of veins in my abdomen and fashioning out of nothingness a creature in the dark.

I did understand that it was I who had insisted on keeping from Franklin the plus sign that was even now continuing to detonate inside me, but the fact that I had chosen all of this did not make it any easier. I felt like I was trying to hide the fact that I was gut-shot. What was worse was how successful my deception was: Franklin did not even notice that there was anything wrong with me. The blood continued to ooze and ooze from me, invisible. Only Lorrie Ann could see it: my fake sip from the doll shoe of my wineglass, my hand resting over the tender tangle of my womb.

"But back to Babylon," Lorrie Ann insisted.

"Right," Franklin said. "So first it was Sumer. Then the Akkadian Empire. Then Babylonia. Then Assyria. Then you're in classical Iraq—a whole bunch of periods, before you're in medieval Iraq, and that's where you have the Ottoman Empire, and then pretty much modern Iraq after that."

"I recognize like all of those names," Lorrie Ann said, "but I had no idea they were all the same place."

"Time is long," I said.

"Well, and," Franklin pointed out, "each of those empires was larger than just Iraq, they just happened to include Iraq."

"So explain Sumer to me in like three sentences or less."

Lorrie Ann's request made me roll my eyes. She had before her one of the best cuneiform scholars in the world and she wanted the tourist version, as though Franklin's specialty ought to be tailored to her brief attention span.

"Three sentences? Gosh, that's tough!" Franklin said, putting his head in his hands and taking the challenge as some kind of fun game. "Okay," he said, "Sumer is what happens when you have a fertile delta, two rivers, and the ability to import metal and timber from Asia, the invention of bronze so you could make better tools, the invention of the potter's wheel, and the domestication of the ox. And when you put all those things together, you get the invention of cities, the invention of writing, the flourishing of art and religion, beneficent kings—everything you could ever want. The first major civilization of the world. Was that three sentences?"

"Depends on how you punctuate it," I said, but they ignored me. I began to stack the plates and ferry them back over to the sink. Lorrie Ann had hardly touched her food.

"So Sumer was before Greece and Rome and all that?" Lorrie Ann asked. I scraped her dinner into the trash.

"Way before. We're talking 3000 BC as the start of proto-literate Sumer."

"So this stuff you translate is the first writing ever?"

"Pretty much," Franklin said.

"Older even than hieroglyphics?" She was examining her own finger, which was now coated in melted wax from the candle she had been playing with. "I thought Egyptians invented writing."

"No, cuneiform was first. Not by a whole lot, but it came first."

"That's crazy cool!" Lorrie Ann said. "So you guys translate like the oldest stuff there is!"

I wanted to slap her. It was almost as though she were playing dumb, exaggerating her own California valley-girl cadences. I had explained ancient Sumer to Lorrie Ann several times on the phone over the past few years. Since Arman, she had been becoming better and better read. And so her protestations of ignorance rang false with me, and I could only assume they were designed either to flatter Franklin or to injure me in some way, to lure me into being some kind of pretentious pedant as an obscure punishment for making her lie for me.

I did not want to think about Sumer. I did not want to talk about Sumer with Lorrie Ann, about all that Sumer had come to be for me, a kingdom of my imagination, a place I could wander in my mind, a way of understanding my own earthy feelings for Franklin. Lorrie Ann did not deserve to know about Sumer. I especially did not want her and Franklin talking about Sumer together for some reason.

There was an ancient Sumerian proverb: Whatever it is that hurts you, don't talk to anyone about it. That was the kind of hard advice Sumer had to offer. There in the delta, among the oxen and the first poetry ever to be written down, there where men were lettuce planted by the water and goddesses begged to have their holy urns filled with honey cheese, there where civilization had begun. What would they think of us now?

I looked out the window at the glowing lights of Istanbul. I thought they would be amazed. I thought they would be proud. Even including the Holocaust, even including the genocide of the Native Americans and slavery, even including Hiroshima and Nagasaki. I looked at Franklin with his healthy white teeth, his unscarred skin, his long, strong bones, and inside him: the architecture of his mind, the vaulted ceilings of his knowledge. Human beings knew so much more now than they ever had. They understood the laws of physics, the rotation of the earth, evolution. Sometimes when I thought about what we were becoming, I couldn't breathe, so badly did I hope, did I wish that human beings would become all that we could be. Yes, I thought the people of ancient Sumer would be blown the fuck away if they could see my lover Franklin.

"So Jim died in Sumer," Lorrie Ann said wonderingly.

I realized that what she said was true, and I felt ashamed that I had wanted to keep Sumer from her.

"Jim died in Sumer," I agreed, and for a moment we all looked at the tablecloth, as though Jim could be discerned in the weft of the fabric. As if that was where he had disappeared to.

"I'm going," Lorrie Ann said suddenly, "to be going through withdrawal soon."

Franklin and I both sat up slightly straighter. "Oh?" This was the first time Lorrie Ann had mentioned her drug addiction in front of Franklin and I noted with interest that she was canny enough to understand that I had squealed on her while she was in the bathroom.

"I was wondering if I could do that here."

"Of course," Franklin said, then caught my eye. "Right?"

"Of course," I said. "Does that—I mean, what exactly does that entail?"

"It will be like I have the flu for about three days. Maybe less. No raving. No hallucinating. Just lots of diarrhea and fever."

Franklin laughed, a little nervous at her honesty, or else delighted—it was hard to say.

"You're welcome to stay here," he said.

"Thank you," she said, beaming at him, and then looked over at me and reached out to take my hand. She squeezed it and looked into my eyes. "I am very lucky that you agreed to meet me today," she said.

"Don't be silly," I said.

"But," she said, "is there like a corner store where I could buy some provisions?"

"Provisions?"

"Whatever the equivalent of Imodium A-D is? And some candy bars, maybe? And some juice?"

"There's a corner store maybe three blocks away," Franklin offered.

"Perfect. I'll go. Can I just borrow some shoes from you, Mia?" she asked.

"You don't like the slippers with the pom-poms?" I asked, laughing.

"I just thought—"

"No, I know, I have no idea why I bought them. But I don't think any of my shoes will fit you—they'll all be way too big."

"Don't you have any sandals or anything?" Lor asked, slipping her cardigan on and getting up from the table. "Flip-flops?"

I didn't know what to say for a moment. "You know I don't wear sandals," I said. My little toe had never become something remotely resembling a toe again. It was just a wad of flesh like chewing gum appended to my foot. Even the little nail had come off and refused to grow back.

"Oh God, I forgot—your toe."

Franklin was standing and surveying the sink full of dishes, stretching his arms above his head. "Yeah, I'll never forgive Paddy for that one."

"Paddy?" Lorrie Ann asked.

And suddenly I knew everything that was going to happen.

"For running over her toe like that. I mean," Franklin said, "I know it was an accident, but still. The guy's a lush."

Lorrie Ann stared at me hard. "You told him that Paddy ran over your toe?"

"I'll go with you to the store," I said, reaching a hand for her elbow, trying my best to psychically impel her to just let it alone.

"No," Lorrie Ann said, swatting me away with her hands. "What, Mia, do you lie to him about everything?"

"Lie to me?" Franklin asked, turning fully from the sink now. Because I was facing Lorrie Ann, my back was to him, but I could feel him come up behind me and place a hand on my waist. That was his first instinct: to protect me from her.

"Honestly, Mia, I thought maybe you knew what you were doing," Lorrie Ann said, "but then, all night we've been talking and—he's great! He's fucking fantastic! He's one of the best guys I've ever met in my entire life and you are fucking this up."

"I don't know what this is about," Franklin said, making a circular motion with his hand in the air between me and Lorrie Ann on the word "this," "but she isn't fucking anything up."

I couldn't speak. Lorrie Ann's hair was shining like gold in the candlelight. She was so beautiful.

"She broke her own toe with a hammer. She had an abortion in high school and she couldn't get it scheduled except for the day before we had a championship game in softball, so she broke her own toe to get out of playing in the game."

I closed my eyes.

"I know about the abortion," Franklin said. He squeezed my waist.

We both waited to see if he would say anything more, but he didn't. Outside, I could hear a gaggle of teenagers laughing and talking together in Turkish. It was Saturday night. It came back to me in a flash: what it was like to be young and going out to a party on a Saturday night, your pulse quickening with the desire that something, anything happen.

"She's pregnant. The test came back positive. But she didn't want to tell you," Lorrie Ann said.

I felt Franklin's hand drop from my waist and I turned to him. "I'm sorry, baby. I'm sorry," I said. "I just needed time to think about it."

"You're pregnant?" he asked, and his voice almost cracked. He looked confused, like a dog that has been hit for no reason.

But I couldn't stop. It was a kind of logorrhea, the words that kept spilling from my mouth: "And we've joked about the two-body problem before, but I just thought if this could happen after the book comes out then it would be a different story, and I don't mind giving up my career, but how could I ask you to give up yours?"

"You're going way too fast for me," Franklin said. "Are you pregnant?"

I nodded.

His face crumpled, and he hid behind his hands. After a moment, he rubbed his face as though to wipe the expression off it. His eyes were wide and staring. He was furious.

"I'm sorry," I said.

"So you really did lie to me?"

"She was going to take another test next week and tell you the truth," Lorrie Ann offered.

"Shut up, Lolola," I said.

"I'm going for a walk," Franklin said, and snapped the dish towel that was in his hands so that it landed in the sink.

I held my face still as best I could and looked at the floor.

And then he was gone.

Yes or No, plus or minus, life or death. We were supposed to decide these things by what? Having conversations? Slamming doors?

I had taken Space's body to be cremated at the vet, but then, by some sort of voodoo or spell, I found myself unable to pick up her ashes. I don't know what they do with the unclaimed ashes of the bodies of dogs. I suppose they throw them in the garbage.

When they sent Jim back there were only pieces of him, and Lorrie Ann was not allowed to see them. They could have been pieces of anybody. Jim had in fact described for her the process by which locals were often hired to rove the city streets with trash bags, looking for human pieces. Sometimes there would be a piece big enough that you could tell which part of the body it had come from: a piece of scalp, an ear, a portion of a hand. But often they were simply chunks of meat like the stew beef you could buy at the supermarket. Iraqi men would wander around, their right hands protected by plastic grocery bags, their left hands clutching garbage bags held open to collect the pieces, bent over to scan the ground like chickens searching for grain.

They gathered whatever could be found and then divided it by the number of soldiers that were known to have died. They sent the small clumps of stew meat back to the States in metal coffins, as though the stew meat could be equated with the human form in any satisfying math.

How tiny was the being inside me? The size of a pea? Of a kidney bean?

How could something that small feel so much to me like something that had a will? Like something that wanted to live?

"I'm sorry," Lorrie Ann said, in the reverberating silence that followed the slamming of the front door and the exit of the love of my life.

"You are the most selfish person I've ever known," I said.

"Mia."

"Get the fuck out of my house."

She just stood there, primly holding the back of her chair as though waiting for the maître d' to pull it from the table for her. "Get the fuck out," I said again.

"Maybe in a minute, when you're less mad, it might be better if I were here."

I walked over to the table, poured the last of the wine into my already full glass, brought it to my lips, and gulped.

"Maybe you need a friend," she said, eyeing me.

"You aren't my friend," I said. "We haven't lived in the same state, let alone the same city, since we were eighteen years old. The fact that I thought we were friends was delusional. I don't understand you. I can't make peace with your decisions. I can't make you my friend again just by telling you a secret, okay? Because you're just going to fucking betray me by blurting it all out!"

"There is some way," Lorrie Ann said, carefully, as though she were stepping around a mine, "in which we are friends. We've known each other for an awfully long time. That counts for something. And maybe I told Franklin because I *am* your friend."

"It doesn't count for enough," I said, and tossed back the rest of the wine in my glass. "You told Franklin because you're high enough to think that you know best about someone else's life, when you don't know anything. But you know what, you've always thought you were better than everybody. Hell, I thought you were better than everybody! I had this whole mythology about you and how fucking perfect you were. But how did that help you? It didn't do a fucking thing. It didn't matter how much I loved you—my love was just this sort of selfish indulgence, this thing I was doing for myself. When I came back to try to help when Zach was born, I was in the way. I've always just been in the way for you. That's why you don't think it's any big deal to betray me."

Outside I could still hear the sounds of laughing groups of girls and guys, wandering from bar to bar. Istanbul had become a happening place to be. A destination. A party city. That was how Lorrie Ann had wound up here, after all.

"I know it doesn't seem like it right now," Lorrie Ann said into the silence of the kitchen, for it had been some time since either of us spoke, "but it's a happy thing when a child is conceived. No matter what. It's a joyful thing."

I just stared at her. She tucked some loose strands of hair behind her ears. "Maybe you could let me celebrate with you."

"I've just lost the love of my life," I said.

"Don't be melodramatic," Lorrie Ann said. "He went for a walk. He'll be back. And when he comes back, he'll love you just as much as he did when he left."

"God, you're so sane—it's awful!" I said, and slumped down in a chair. Lorrie Ann just laughed. "Honestly, though," I said, "if there is a time in my life that I get to be melodramatic, isn't this it?"

"No," Lorrie Ann said, coming to sit with me, "you never get to be melodramatic ever again."

"Why is that?"

"Because," she said, and reached out a hand, pressed her palm against my tummy, "you're gonna have a baby."

"You don't know that," I said.

"You're pregnant, Mia," she repeated, smiling at me.

"He didn't smile. Even for a second. I know it's too much to expect, but I thought maybe he would be happy."

"He didn't have much of a chance," Lorrie Ann pointed out.

"I know," I said. "I just wanted so badly for him to be happy."

The way Jim had been happy.

The way Dumuzi had been happy.

I wanted, more than anything, I realized, for Franklin to look at me with wonder, startled, the way the first man who ever bit into a peach must have looked: alarmed to realize that life was so good, so sweet, so abundant. I wanted to be that magic for Franklin.

We had never talked about having children of our own, though. I had made a joke once that if we had children we should raise them speaking Latin like Montaigne and I felt that something about it had made him uncomfortable: maybe he had laughed too much, or not enough, but either way I got the feeling that he felt I was proposing having children, when of course I had not been, I wouldn't have dared. Not knowing that the idea of children had been what drove a wedge between him and Elizabeth, Elizabeth who had an abundance of dark hair, which she kept tied back like a prairie woman and who had an unnaturally large and perfect mouth like Julia Roberts.

Whatever it is that hurts you, don't talk to anyone about it.

I looked at Lorrie Ann in the candlelight, which was now low and guttering, and in her face I could almost see the ghost of Zach's features. That had been the worst thing about Zach really: how much he looked like her. A distorted, howling *galla* made of Lorrie Ann's own beautiful face. Where was he now? What hands smoothed his brow? It was too terrible to even think about, let alone speak of.

I felt then that I would kill to protect the tiny bean inside of me, the plus sign, the zygote. I didn't know why—it wasn't so much that I wanted to become a mother or to have a child. It wasn't anything to do with the Gerber baby or with the way an infant's head smelled or with tiny shoes. It wasn't anything I could name.

"I just get the feeling," I croaked to Lorrie Ann, "that it wants to live."

She nodded quickly as though she knew exactly what I was talking about, and suddenly I found that I was howling like an animal that has been mortally wounded, and Lorrie Ann's arms were around me, and I was fifteen again, and she was my friend.

CHAPTER SEVENTEEN

Amor Fati

Some time after that, Lorrie Ann journeyed to the corner store to obtain her provisions. In addition to her Imodium A-D, candies, and juice, she also brought back a small plastic tub of baklava that she claimed was for the baby and a pack of cigarettes that she promised to smoke only on the balcony. Together we sat on the oversize red chenille sofa, our legs folded tailor style, facing each other with the plastic tray of baklava between us.

"Even the idea of Mother's Day just made me cringe," Lorrie Ann said. "It felt like I might actually be becoming less of a person, less valid, less interesting."

"There is something powerfully uncool about motherhood in the cultural Geist," I agreed.

"But then what it actually was? Being a mom? Well, it seemed not just like the most important thing I'd ever done, but the most important thing anybody could do. What is more important? Buying and selling imaginary money? Making cars? Everything people make in this world is for people, and women are the only ones who make people."

"Men are sort of essential to the process," I pointed out. Lorrie Ann stuffed another baklava into her mouth. She seemed ravenous. I was beginning to understand that something about the drugs made only sweet things taste good to her. It was strange how normal and manageable Lor being on heroin was rapidly becoming.

"Sure, and fatherhood is super important too. I'm not trying to make this a women-only club by any means. Just that even men rarely view their role in child rearing as the most important thing they do, when in fact it is clearly the most important thing that anybody does."

"I don't know about that," I said.

"What's more important?" Lorrie Ann asked.

"Scholarship? Art? Politics?" I took a bite of one of the baklava and suddenly understood why Lor was unable to stop eating them—they were dense with butter and honey. I had to fight not to shove the whole thing in my mouth at once.

"Politics?! Politics is the most useless thing I've ever even heard of!" Lorrie Ann crowed. "You know what Arman had to show for his life? He killed a few people. Well, five people, one of whom was a child. He did that for George W. Bush. Do you know how much time women spent making those five people he killed? And all for what? Ideas, worldview, politics. It's women who encode children with values and worldviews to begin with!"

There was something about Lorrie Ann's fanaticism that I found tiring. "Women are undervalued," I said. "I get it."

"No," Lorrie Ann said, "I'm not saying I want women to be valued more highly. That would be terrible. Then people would start paying attention to what we were doing."

"What do you mean: to what we were doing? What are we doing?"

"I'm just saying, when a woman is a maiden, she's in the spotlight. Everybody cares what a pretty, young girl does and says. And she's got some pretty strict archetypes to adhere to: Sleeping Beauty or Cinderella or Britney Spears. Pick your poison. But when you become a young mother? People don't give a fuck what you're doing. Their eyes glaze over before they even finish asking you. Once a woman starts doing the most important work of her life, all of a sudden, nobody wants to know a thing about it."

"That's kind of true," I said. Even I had a hard time retaining interest in my grad school friends once they had become mothers. "People should care more about motherhood."

"God no! Please! I'm saying that this shroud of uncoolness around motherhood provides a tremendous amount of freedom."

I sucked the honey off my fingers. "But freedom to do what?"

"Freedom to be," Lorrie Ann said.

There was something lofty about the phrase that I both immediately loved and felt suspicious of.

Lorrie Ann went on, pressing flakes of puff pastry onto her fingertip and then nibbling them off. "Plus the experience of actually having children is so much more than anyone prepares you for, is so much realer than you thought reality could be—the experience itself blows the clichés of motherhood out of the fucking water."

"Really?" I said. "I just never got that sense from you." I had seen Lor mother Zach, and I had even marveled over what a good mother she was, but I had always assumed that if she could somehow switch places with me, she would have.

"Women who have babies don't talk about these kinds of things to women who haven't had babies." She shrugged.

"Some kind of secret club?" I asked.

"I think it's a protective instinct. The same way a religious person wouldn't talk about his relationship with God to an atheist." I felt at once that Lorrie Ann was somehow my ethical or spiritual superior, having gained access years ago to some secret world of motherhood while I chased the false idols of cultural elitism, and at the very same moment I thought: She's a fucking junkie! These insights of hers are delusions of grandeur and nothing more. Let her have her delusions. Let her believe she is part of some secret cult of motherhood.

"I can't even think about the motherhood part right now, honestly," I said. I kept straining to hear Franklin in the hall, his foot on the stair, but there was nothing, not even the little sounds of Bensu spying.

"Sure." Lor nodded.

"I'm in love with Franklin. Like really in love," I said.

She nodded.

"And this whole time I've been, like, straining to be perfect, to not move, to not break the spell, because this is the best thing that has ever happened to me and I know that I don't deserve him, but—"

Lorrie Ann made a snorting noise. "Deserve him? Who deserves anything?"

"You know what I mean," I said.

"No," she said, "tell me, do we deserve the spring? Does the sun come out each day because we were tidy and good? What the fuck are you thinking?"

I was struck dumb.

"He loves you," she said. "He loves you."

After a few hours, I wanted badly to go to bed. I wanted to go to bed in part because Lorrie Ann was like an air fern: how she was continuing to stay awake and alert was entirely mysterious to me. It seemed possible that she could stay awake forever. But I also wanted to go to bed because when Franklin came home I wanted to be in the bedroom where we could whisper in private, where he could, perhaps, shuck off his clothes, stinking of beer and cigarettes from whatever dive bar he had hunkered down in, and, in the vulnerability of his nakedness, find me under the covers by the dim light of the moon. This softened, possibly even non-verbal meeting seemed preferable to me than having him walk in on Lorrie Ann and me stuffing our faces with baklava and bitching about our lives, emitting that witchy stink of women gabbing without men.

And so I made up the couch for Lorrie Ann and lent her one of my sleep shirts. It was when she peeled off her sundress and her impossibly tiny blue silk bra (she was so skinny now that she was even smaller breasted than me) that I saw the tattoo across her shoulder blade: *Amor Fati*.

It could be translated "love of fate" or "love of one's fate." Nietzsche was obsessed with the idea, though he got it from the Stoics. He wrote in *Ecce Homo:* "My formula for greatness in a human being is amor fati: that one wants nothing to be different, not forward, not backward, not in all eternity. Not merely bear what is necessary, still less conceal it— all idealism is mendaciousness in the face of what is necessary—but love it."

In all, it was nothing more than a fancier version of "embrace the suck."

"I didn't take you for a Nietzsche fan," I said.

"Portia," Lorrie Ann said, as though that explained everything.

"Are you going to go back to her?" I asked. It seemed appropriate that Portia would love Nietzsche; I actually held Nietzsche himself in slightly higher esteem than I did his fans, which is only to say that I did not actively hate Nietzsche for being himself.

Lorrie Ann slipped my old blue-and-white-striped sleep shirt over her head and tugged it down. It looked huge and billowing on her. "I lied to you," she said.

I almost wanted to laugh. How could there possibly be more lies? And yet, of course there were more. There were always more. I rubbed the heel of my hand into my forehead.

"Portia didn't throw all of our shoes off the balcony. I threw all of our shoes off our balcony. She's not the one who went crazy—I'm the one who went crazy. We got into a fight."

"A fight over what?"

Lorrie Ann pursed her lips, sighed, sat down on the made up couch. She looked so much like the little girl who had slept over at my house so many times. "There was a girl. She was young. She had been party-ing with us for a few nights in a row, and one night she was crying in the bathroom of our hotel suite. She had had some bad sex. I mean, she had started off really liking this guy and she'd gone home with him, but then he was rough with her and she tried to leave. She had these huge handprint bruises and a split lip. I said it was rape. Portia said it was the girl failing to be realistic."

"Oh, God," I said.

"She said, 'Men are men, dogs are dogs, a dog will bite you if you take a bone from his mouth. Why are you surprised?' "

"How disgusting."

"No, it's weird—with Portia, she says these things and it doesn't reg-ister as awful right away. She was telling these things to the girl to be *nice*. She was mentoring her. 'You made a miscalculation,' she told the girl, 'and the best thing to do when you have done that is cut your losses and go limp. If you had just done what he wanted, he wouldn't have had to beat you so badly.' "

"Gross," I said.

"But can you see how, if you've lost everything beautiful in your life, that might seem true?" Lor asked. She looked at me with an earnestness that I had not seen in her since she was fifteen.

"Yes." I nodded.

"The worst thing is that I didn't even get mad at her in the moment. It was days later. I kept thinking about that girl. She looked like you. I mean, not really, but there was something about her that reminded me of you, and I couldn't get her out of my mind, and then Portia said something about me being lucky for having such pretty feet, and— I mean, I don't have to tell you that lucky is something I have never been, not once, not ever—I just lost it. We got into this bizarre scream-ing match, where I kept saying, 'Lucky is not feet!' and she kept say-ing, 'Luck is nothing but feet! Everything else is what you make it!' And then I threw all of our shoes off the balcony and into the river, and stormed out."

There was silence for a moment as both of us pictured all of those fancy shoes: some scattered on the pavement, some floating on the Bos-porus like fantastical, miniature boats.

"You need to go home," I said. I hadn't even been planning to say it, but it slipped out. Without fanfare or dramatics, it just came out—that's how badly it needed to be said.

Lor nodded slowly, and her face twitched as she looked at me.

"You need to go home to your boy," I repeated.

"I know," she said. "But there's like . . . a wall."

"A wall?"

"Some kind of huge, towering wall in between me and America."

"You'll be okay," I said. "I promise."

"I know," she said, "but how to get over the wall?"

"Is the wall your fear?" I asked.

"No," she said, with an eerie matter-of-factness. "The wall is how

I've been not thinking about him. I built it, but if I'm going to go back, I'll need to take it down."

I sat beside her on the couch. The baklava tray was empty.

"Can I help?" I asked.

"I don't think so," she said. "But thank you for telling me to go home. It's true. That's the only thing left to do."

There was a ring to those words: the only thing left to do. Suddenly, I worried Lor might kill herself. When I looked back over at her, she was crying into her clasped hands.

"I'm fucking terrified," she said. "I miss him so much."

I wrapped my arms around her. Crying, I understood. Crying, I knew what to do with. "I know," I said. "I know."

"I'm so sorry," she said, over and over again. "I'm so sorry."

"It's okay," I said, and in that moment, her anguish was more real to me than anything in the world. I rocked her back and forth until she stopped crying, and then I tucked her into the couch, expecting at any moment for Franklin to walk through the door.

I waited in the dark for hours. In my mind, I had imagined that I would hear the front door, then Franklin's steps as he made his way through the darkened living room back to our bedroom, and then, louder, crisp and suddenly near, the sound of our bedroom door unlatching, the sound of his sandals scuffing on the vinyl flooring, his keys being set down on the dresser. I did not count on the fact that Lorrie Ann would still be awake and that Franklin would stop to talk to her for almost half an hour, assuming as they both did that I was asleep.

"She asleep?" I heard him ask.

"I think so. Her light's been out for hours."

"Are those your cigarettes?"

"Yes."

"Can I bum one?"

"Do you want to go on the balcony?" she asked.

"Fuck that," he said, and I heard them both light cigarettes. Then I heard his heavy step as he stumbled to the kitchen and clattered around to find the ashtray that had come with the apartment: a curious little orange ceramic thing with black fleurs-de-lis crudely painted on it.

"That fucking tea set," Franklin said when he got back to the living room.

"What was that about?"

I could smell the cigarettes. They weren't even bothering to blow out the window. I felt somehow peeved that they were subjecting me, an innocent, sleeping, pregnant woman, to their secondhand smoke, and yet I knew this was entirely insane.

"She wanted to do something nice for Bensu. She just doesn't know how to be natural. It's a shame, you know? She tries so hard but it's always obvious she's trying so hard."

"You should have seen her try to date boys in high school." Lorrie Ann laughed. "She'd march up to them and tell them that she would like to date them. Or fuck them."

I felt like I was going to throw up. I could recognize that neither of them perceived themselves as saying anything mean about me. If anything, there was something loving about the tone of their voices. And it wasn't even that I was unaware of these flaws in myself—in fact, I was only too aware of them. It was that I had thought that Franklin and Lorrie Ann were somehow magically unaware of these flaws.

Franklin laughed. "She's so fucking fierce," he said. Then, in a different tone: "And insane! God, I keep thinking about it. Why did she lie to me?"

"Oh," Lor said, exhaling, "why does anybody lie? She was scared."

"I know. I know, she was scared. But that still fucking sucks for me."

"It's scary, finding out you're pregnant," Lor said.

"Yeah?"

"Fuck yeah. And it's not—I don't know, it's just not a clean choice. It's not something completely rational."

"I may be too drunk to talk about this," Franklin said.

"I'm just saying it's emotional. You can feel the baby inside of you."

"Already?"

"Already," she said. "Not like kicking and moving, but you're aware of it."

"But you decided not to have an abortion. Right?" Franklin said. "I mean, isn't that the whole dichotomy, you both got pregnant, and Mia had an abortion and you didn't."

"I've had an abortion," she said.

I froze. I was listening so hard that my spine was tensed, as though I could use my own vertebrae to amplify their voices.

Was she lying? She'd had her fucking uterus removed!

"I didn't realize," Franklin said. "I'm sorry."

"No. You don't need to be sorry. You've only just met me! I don't expect you to know every footnote of my life story."

There was a heavy silence then.

"But this doesn't need to be some debate about abortion," Franklin said. "I mean, does she even want an abortion?"

"I don't think so," Lorrie Ann said. "I don't think she wants to kill it, but I think she's terrified of having it too. Which is why she's so hung up on whether or not you want it. If you wanted it, she could handle having it, she could face the fear of it. But she thinks you don't want it."

"God, she's a retard!" he cried. "I'm in love with her! I wanted to marry her!"

"But isn't that why you broke up with your last girlfriend?" Lorrie Ann asked.

I heard the lighter flick again, and I knew Franklin was lighting another cigarette. He chain-smoked when he was hammered. He had wanted to marry me. A sudden switch to past tense. Did that mean he didn't want to anymore?

"Yeah, but that was because I didn't want to have babies with *Eliza-beth*. Not that I didn't ever want to have babies. And that was five years ago! Did she even tell you the context of that conversation?"

"No."

What had the context been? I couldn't remember.

"She had been explaining to me that after raising her brothers she wasn't sure if she ever wanted to have kids, that she wasn't prepared to be that unselfish again, to have that much responsibility, and she wanted to make sure I was okay with that."

Lorrie Ann laughed like a donkey. "I'm sorry," she said. "I know it's not funny, but that's kind of funny."

"Yeah, I know," he said. "I'm sure she meant it at the time too. But now, I mean, does she want it? Is that why she's being so weird? She wants it?"

"Do you want it?" Lorrie Ann asked.

Franklin didn't answer for a long time. "I don't know," he said. I heard the lighter flick again. Maybe his cigarette had gone out, or maybe Lorrie Ann was lighting up too. "It doesn't feel real. I need to talk to her about it."

"It won't feel real until the baby's born," Lor said.

"You know, I almost half guessed when Bensu asked her. I thought: Maybe she's pregnant. Maybe Bensu heard something. I was excited. God, I feel like an idiot."

"Don't feel like an idiot. She loves you. She just went about things in a stupid way. But that's Mia, right? You said it yourself—she can't act natural. Everything is a little bit forced. She overthinks it. Hard shell, squishy insides."

"Yeah, but like . . . can you really start a family and start a life with someone who goes about things like that? Can you trust someone who doesn't fucking trust you?"

I felt like I was falling an infinite distance, sitting there on our mattress in the dark, as Franklin's voice said things I never expected to hear, had no idea he thought.

"I don't know," Lorrie Ann said.

There was a long silence, and then Franklin said: "How do you do that? I've always wanted to be able to blow smoke rings. I even had people try to teach me, but it never worked out."

"You have to get some backspin on it by tucking in your lips right as you blow out," she said.

Silence.

"That was good!" she said.

How, *how* could they be blowing smoke rings right now?

"I've gotta take a piss," Franklin said.

"Can I borrow some money?" Lor asked.

My eyes snapped open in the darkness. There was something so pred-atory about it—asking Franklin instead of asking me. But of course she would need money to go back home, to leave the party circuit.

"How much?"

"I don't know," Lor said. "Like a grand?"

"And I'm guessing you don't want me to tell her," he said.

"No," she said reflectively, "you can tell her."

"Fine," he said. "I'll go to the bank in the morning."

"Just write me a check," she said.

"In the morning," he said. "I'm beat."

Then I heard him shuffle toward the bathroom and the creaking sound as he closed himself in with the plants to pee. Did we have a thousand dollars? Certainly there was money in the grant, but it was tightly controlled.

As I waited for Franklin to finish peeing and come into our room, I tried to calm my heartbeat. All of the pieces of conversation I had overheard were jangling around in my bloodstream: the money, Frank-lin's sudden past tense "I wanted to marry her!," Lor's weird lie about having had an abortion. He had been excited! When he first guessed, he had been excited! But then, the terrible question: Can you trust someone who doesn't trust you? A new, cold, and strong feeling entered me. The answer was no. You could not trust someone who was behaving the way I was behaving. I sat in our bed, waiting.

When he finally came in, I heard him set his keys down. I heard the shuffle of his feet, bare, on the vinyl flooring. Then I heard his pants hit-ting the floor, the clink of his belt left in the loops, and the brief cotton wrestling match with his button-down and undershirt. Then I felt him begin to crawl up the bed.

"Franklin," I said. "I need to talk to you."

I felt him pause on all fours.

"You don't have to say anything," he said. "I get it. I mean—it's your body. I can understand why you would want a few days to figure out how you feel before you have to figure out how I feel."

"I need to say this," I said, and patted the bed next to me. Franklin continued his crawl and scooted under the covers up next to me. He smelled overwhelmingly of cigarettes and booze. "I am so deeply sorry," I said. "I've been acting like a teenager trying to fool her mother. You are nothing but open and honest and kind with me, and in return I was trying to manipulate you like I was going to trick you into loving me. I'm so sorry. You deserve so much better. And if you'll let me, I would like to do better. I will be better."

The streetlight was coming across his face in slashes. "Thank you," he said.

I reached down and grabbed his knee, pull-rubbing the tendons that connected to his thigh.

"So what are you thinking?" he asked. "About the—pregnancy?"

I noticed he'd avoided using the word "baby."

"Well," I said, feeling the honesty bite in my lungs like winter air, "I feel very scared that having a baby would ruin our lives. I don't know how we would work out our careers, where we would get jobs in the same place. I don't know how we would afford it. But even more than that, I am scared that having the baby would force you to marry me because you wanted to do the right thing. I don't want you to be confined by doing the right thing. I want you to do what is really and truly best for you. And I know that with Elizabeth it wasn't right, and so I was worried it wouldn't be right with me."

Franklin grunted.

"And of course," I went on, "I've had an abortion before. So it's not that I'm against abortion. I'm not." I thought of Lorrie Ann saying women had a right to kill their children. "But I do feel like having an abortion at twenty-nine is a very different thing than having one at fifteen. And . . . if it is what you wanted, I would think about it, but I don't feel good about it. When I think about it I feel dread."

He grunted again.

"What do you feel?" I asked, my voice shaking.

"I don't know," he said. "I don't know how I feel. I have a headache and I'm still a little drunk, and I don't want to say the wrong thing."

My heart sank. I clenched my jaw and froze the muscles of my face. I didn't want to make him feel bad by crying. I wanted him to be perfectly free.

"I mean, I know that rationally everything you're saying about the jobs and about money—all of that is true. But I still . . . I don't know. Don't you think we could make it work?"

This was not at all what I was expecting him to say.

"And even," he went on, "worst-case scenario, we wind up teaching Latin at a liberal arts college or something? Still—what a life! I don't know. I just . . . I know you're scared, and I know we should think about it more, but I guess my most basic, gut reaction is that I'm fucking overjoyed."

"You are?" My eyes were stinging and I couldn't really breathe, that's how violent my happiness was.

"Yeah. Is that okay? I mean, is that okay with you?"

"That's more than okay," I choked out.

I could hear the smile in his voice. "Good," he said.

"I just—Franklin, I just feel so strongly that it wants to live."

"We made a baby," he said. "We made a person."

"I know," I said, but in my mind I was already frantically praying to God, a God I knew I did not truly believe in, to let me keep this, to let me keep all I had been given. I didn't know why I had been allowed to have so much. It didn't seem right that I could be allowed to have still more. But I would take it. Even if it was all pure accident, and I hadn't earned any of it, I would take it. What had Lorrie Ann said? Do we deserve the spring? No one, I thought, could ever deserve or not deserve the kind of happiness that was flooding me, lying there in that bed with Franklin, the bean of life twitchy in my womb, the streets of Istanbul finally quiet, the mists of the Bosporus rolling in.

"I heard Lorrie Ann ask you for money."

"You did? Yeah, I mean, I don't care, I'll give her the money. But I mean, isn't there a rule or something: don't give money to junkies?"

"No," I said. "She's going home. She's gonna make things right."

"That's wonderful," Franklin said. "Mia?"

"What?"

"Will you marry me? For real? Will that still be true in the morning?"

"It will be true every morning for the rest of time," I said, and I really felt, as an almost physical reality, that everything was going to be fine. Everything was going to be all right.

But of course, when we woke up in the morning, Lorrie Ann was gone, and, mysteriously, she had taken the tea set with her.

What Goes Up

Almost three years later, when I was back in California, I arranged to see Arman.

It had been a blessing, really, to have Lorrie Ann gone that morning. To wake up to the empty sublet, the garish colors of its un-matching furniture staring jauntily back at us in the gray light of the misty Istanbul morning. To be allowed to ignore her and everything that had happened in her life and make eggs and toast and coffee in our underwear and giggle over our good fortune: to love each other, to be getting married, to be having a baby. And in the kind of hypocrisy native to everyday living, I pretended that possibly Lorrie Ann might still go home. She had said she was going home. I wanted to believe that she still might, even though she had left without getting the money from Franklin, even though, as far as I knew, she didn't have a way of getting back to the States. The note she had left said only: "Don't fuck it up, you two. Franklin, you're the real deal and I love you. I wish I could stay, but I've gotta go. Don't be mad, Mia. We really were friends, you know. XOXO, Lolola."

At the time, I thought that it was her life, and that as much as I wanted to live it for her, she was going to have to do it on her own.

But as the weeks and then months passed, I realized I had no way of getting in touch with her. None of my old numbers for her worked. She didn't have a Facebook account. I had no idea what Portia's last name was and so could not have tracked her down that way, even if she had returned to Portia, which I found doubtful after the defenestration of shoes. I tried calling Dana, who was sweet, but who had not heard from Lor in over a year. When Franklin and I got married later that year, I sent the invitation via e-mail to her old Yahoo account. Surely she had an e-mail account she checked regularly, I just didn't know what it was, and I guessed it wasn't her deeply odd, teenage handle: MistressOCats Baby@yahoo.com.

When Grant was born, I sent his birth pictures and a letter of apology to the same e-mail account. She was right, I wrote: actually being a mother blew everything else out of the water. She was right: there was nothing more important.

I had, of course, been expecting to have a little girl, a treacherous little Inanna, a mimeograph of Lorrie Ann and myself. I did not know what it would be like to fall in love with a little boy. I did not know that his hair would be the color of applesauce with cinnamon and that in all his baby pictures he would look profoundly worried: his brow furrowed as he tiredly faced the camera, his chubby face as jowly as a seasoned politician's.

And so it came to pass that Franklin and Grant and I moved back to Southern California when Grant was two. We had published the Inanna cycle and it had gotten rave reviews. We'd even made money off it. We had also been offered a pair of positions at UCSD, which we took gratefully. It was easy to look up Arman, and if I'd truly thought he might have news of Lorrie Ann, I would have contacted him long before. But maybe because I was back in California again, he was newly on my mind. One day, I just looked up the number of his smoke shop, Pipe Dreams, called, and asked for Arman.

The man who had picked up did not answer me, but seemed to be waiting for me to say more.

"Arman?"

"Who is this?"

"It's Mia," I said, "Lorrie Ann's friend."

"What the fuck do you want?"

Apparently this was Arman. I was glad at least that his family had given him the smoke shop back.

"I don't know what I want," I said. "I haven't heard from Lorrie Ann in years, and I guess I just wondered if you knew what happened to her."

"No." Arman sighed, then said something to someone in the background.

"That's too bad," I said.

"I wish her the best," he said, "I really do. But I'm not surprised she hasn't called me. I mean, would you? You know she left me in India, right? Fucking broke off my ass and in a foreign country."

"She told me she left you a thousand dollars."

There was a beat of silence, then Arman said, "Yeah, as a check that I couldn't cash *anywhere*. I mean nowhere would take that fucking check. It was a nightmare."

"That sounds awful," I said. "I'm sorry that happened to you."

"Long time ago," he said. "But hey, you know, do you want to get coffee sometime and catch up?"

I was surprised that he wanted to see me. Later I would realize that by calling him on his lie that Lorrie Ann had left him penniless in India, I had revealed that I had spoken to her more lately than he. How could he resist trying to find out what I knew?

"Uh, sure," I said.

"There's a Starbucks right around the corner from the shop," he said. "Could you come by today?"

"Not today," I said. "I have Grant with me. My little boy."

"Oh Jeez, congratulations. Saturday then? Three o'clock?"

As I prepared to make the drive north that Saturday, I realized that somewhere along the line I had gotten old. Not in a bad way. I was putting on tinted moisturizer in the hall mirror and going over the plan for the day. My youngest brother, Alex, and his new boyfriend were in town. I wasn't wild about the boyfriend, who was a hipster with stylish dreadlocks and whose name was Rion, "with an 'i,' like 'lion,'" he had told me proudly. We were going to meet them and my mother at the mall by our old house in Corona del Mar, but I was heading up early to meet Arman beforehand.

"I don't like you going alone," Franklin said. He was eating flax pancakes and yogurt at the table while Grant sat in his booster seat, poking the yogurt with his plastic spoon.

"I'm meeting a man with no legs in a Starbucks. What do you actually think is going to happen?"

"I don't know, I just wish I could be there."

"Go to the park with Grant. Swing on the swings," I said, sliding the lever back of an earring through my ear. I looked in the mirror. I looked like a grown woman with a child. I looked educated. I looked taken care of. I looked soft.

"You look great," Franklin said, watching me appraise myself. "We'll meet you by that big fountain at the mall at five?"

"At five," I said.

Arman was sitting hunched over a table when I arrived. I waved at him and motioned that I was going to get a drink. It was startling seeing him—I had really only ever met him a few times, but I had heard so many stories about him and thought of him so often that a fictional Arman had begun to replace the real one in my mind. It was with a start that I recognized the curly broadness of his upper lip, the pug-dog roundness of his eyeballs. Mostly, seeing him made me viscerally remember Lorrie Ann in a way that was both exciting and painful.

When I came to the table with my chamomile tea, he smiled at me with a genuine openness and gratitude that surprised me. "Thanks so much for coming," he said.

"It's a trip to see you," I said.

"I know—it's like seeing her, almost."

"I know."

"I realized when you called the other day," he said, "that I've been slowly changing things in my mind. That I've been editing my memories of her. Like, I got used to telling people she left me broke in India because, you know, I wanted my family to give me the smoke shop back. I didn't want them to know I had any money, right? So that became the official version, and it was only when you mentioned the check that I even remembered that it had happened that way. I felt like I was losing her because my mind kept changing her, you know?"

"I know exactly what you mean," I said. "I've replayed the same memories so many times that they're practically threadbare."

"So when's the last time you talked to her?" he asked. His hair was down and loose all around his shoulders, and he tucked it behind his ears as he asked me. It made him look earnest and young.

I told him about meeting up with Lorrie Ann in Istanbul, about her stories of Portia and her life as a party girl, about her sudden departure during the middle of the night, her vaguely enigmatic note—that shift to the past tense: we really were friends.

"Yeah, she fucking loves to do that," Arman said. "Leave in the middle of the night and leave a note."

I hadn't realized until he said it that she'd done that to both of us.

"I don't get it," I said. "Sometimes I think she was the best person I ever knew in my entire life. And other times, she seems just like a shithead."

"Well, she was fucked up," he said.

"I don't like that—I don't like just making it about the drugs."

"No, I don't mean like she was wasted, I mean she was one of the most profoundly damaged people I've ever met," Arman said, bobbing his head like a chicken in a succession of quick nods.

"Was she?" I asked. She had come from such a happy family; she had always been so beautiful, so effortlessly suited to the world, such an adept swimmer, even in the cold Pacific. I had not really considered her as damaged.

"I always wondered," Arman said, "if maybe her dad didn't, like, mess with her."

"Terry? No," I said.

"Somebody messed with her," Arman insisted.

"Nobody messed with her! I was there—I knew Terry. He wasn't like that. Her family was incredibly happy. Tight-knit."

"Nobody knows anybody when it comes to shit like that," Arman said.

"Why do you even think this?"

"Stuff she said, ways she was. She always got really bad bladder infections. Had just tons of problems with her vagina. Sometimes she was so tensed up she couldn't have sex at all."

"That could have just been from the bad birth with Zach, though, right?"

"But he wasn't even born vaginally, so why would that make her vagina, like, hysterically sensitive?"

"Hysterically sensitive?"

"She couldn't even wear tampons. Said it hurt her like crazy."

"Maybe she was just really tiny," I said.

"No, it was like an emotional thing. It came and went depending on how she felt. That's why I think maybe Terry messed with her."

"But she never said anything to you, right?"

Arman shook his head, his black hair glistening in the overhead track lighting. "But, like," he went on, "she always used to talk about how guilty she felt over Terry's death because she had been wishing for him to die and then he got in that accident."

Why would Lor have been wishing for Terry to die? Suddenly the peculiar clarity with which I could see each particular strand as part of the shimmering whole of Arman's hair gave me the impression that I might be dreaming.

"But I was there!" I said. "She wasn't wishing that Terry would die. I mean, maybe she had like a fleeting thought because he'd grounded her or something. But she didn't say anything at all to me about this." I fussed with the crackly wrapping of the pack of madeleines I had bought. I remembered the way Lor had become withdrawn after Terry's death. The sudden vegetarianism, the refusal to make fun of Brittany Slane.

"I know, I know," Arman said. "And who knows. Maybe I'm wrong. But I'd bet everything I've got that somebody messed with her, even if it wasn't Terry."

Against my will, Arman's words were causing massive tectonic shifts in my understanding of the past. That family that had been so secretive, so aloof, so together—I had thought they were bound together by their love for one another. I had thought Terry was cool! Suddenly his insistence on wearing top hats and big gold earrings well into his forties seemed stranger, almost sinisterly adolescent. I wondered whether Dana was embarrassed when he dressed like that for parent-teacher night. What if he *had* been messing with Lor?

"This never happened," I said.

"Well, how else do you explain the fact that her uterus just busted open when she was in labor?"

"The Misoprostol—" I began.

"Come on," he said, "really? You think just the Misoprostol?"

It was true that most of the women with uterine ruptures resulting from Misoprostol had had previous cesareans. It had been one of the details about Zach's birth story that always bothered me. "So what, you think she was so emotionally scarred by her father that it actually affected the tissues of her uterus?"

"No," Arman said, jerking his head back and giving me a stern stare, nostrils flared. "I think she must have had a bad D and C sometime when she was a kid. He wouldn't have been able to take her to a real abortion clinic."

"This is crazy," I said and hid my face by taking a sip of my tea. Was that why she had told Franklin she'd had an abortion? Was she talking about something that had happened before Zach?

Even though the lights in the Starbucks were bright, I had the impression that I couldn't see, but also that I could see too much. Whenever I looked at Arman's face, I could see all his pores and I had to look away. I had always thought that Lorrie Ann was a victim of God. The idea that she was a victim of man was somehow much worse.

"This is nuts," I said.

"It happens every day."

"But I was there!"

"How else do you explain it then?"

"Explain the uterine rupture?"

"No," he said, "explain how incredibly fucked up she was."

I just stared at him. There was that past tense again.

"Yeah." I swallowed. "She was pretty fucked up, I guess."

The whole night with my family, my mind was like a seagull flying against the wind in a storm. There was such a forceful logic to Arman's theory—it explained all the tiny details of Lor's life that just didn't make sense: the uterine rupture, the weird lie about having an abortion, the fact, even, that she had chosen partners as safe and yet loser-ish as both Jim and Arman. And yet it seemed impossible that anything of the kind had happened. How often had I spent the night at her house? How often had she spent the night at mine? We told each other everything.

Still, there wasn't time to think about it. I was at a restaurant that sold twenty-dollar sandwiches toasting Alex for his new job, and watching my mother, who had blossomed into her role as grandmother in a way that I could never have expected, teach Grant how to scrunch up a straw wrapper and make it grow like a worm with drops of water. I was holding hands with Franklin under the table, I was laughing, I was asking Rion where he had gone to undergrad, I was insisting that we order dessert and conning my mother into sharing the cheesecake with me as she told me that my other brother, Max, had a new girlfriend who sold Kirby vacuum cleaners and was Wiccan. We all agreed this was a good thing: Maxie was simply too serious. After law school he had gotten a job with a big firm in New York and started working ninety hours a week and never coming home. We hoped his whacky girlfriend would lighten him up.

After dinner, we all decided to walk around the mall, which was open air, a vaulted terra-cotta place, dotted with planters and palm trees. There was a koi pond, and so we took Grant there and sat around on metal chairs as he dashed along the edges of the pond, following the biggest koi, a thick, fat, red-orange fish with dull, silver eyes.

"You're a good mother," my mom said. Franklin and Alex and Rion were talking boisterously about some new superhero movie that was going to come out.

"Thank you," I said. "That means the world to me, that you would say that. I want so badly to be a good mother."

"And Franklin is the best dad I've ever seen."

"I know," I said. I was thinking about how scared my mother must have been to lose my father. She had been so young when I was born, only twenty, and my father had been a salesman, made lots of money. Right away, he had bought them a big house, gave her a BMW, a Rolex. It was a dream, like a fairy tale. When she found out he was cheating, when I was two, she had confronted him and he had immediately suggested he move out, but it took years before he would give her a divorce. He was canny, and he knew that if he could show the court that for four years they had been separated but still married and my mother had been supporting herself, he wouldn't have to pay any alimony, and so that was exactly what he did. I could still remember those years, when it was just my mother and me, eating pancakes for dinner. No wonder she had leaped at Paddy once the divorce came through. No wonder she had wanted a glass of wine at the end of the night.

"You were a good mother too," I said.

"I wish I had been better," she said, not looking at me but at Grant, who was on his stomach flat on the concrete beside the pond with his hand in the water, trying to pet the fish.

"I don't think I could have done any better," I said. "If I had been in your situation."

My mother shrugged. "You play the hand you're dealt."

Had Lor gotten clean or had she stayed addicted? Was she, even now, jamming some dull needle into a vein in a Paris bathroom as the next woman in line beat on the door? Girls didn't come from perfectly happy families and then just become self-loathing heroin addicts. Did they?

What was most alarming, in the end, was the vertiginous sense that I did not know Lorrie Ann, and, in fact, had never known her. I could not sort out who she might be in my head. "We really were friends," she had written me.

How, I kept thinking, how had she possibly left Zach? Having had a baby of my own now, I found it newly unfathomable. I reached over and squeezed my mother's hand.

"MOMMY!" Grant cried. "I touched it! I touched its EYEBALL!"

That night, when Franklin and I were in bed, I turned to him. "Do you think someone molested Lorrie Ann?" I asked. "When we were girls?"

"I didn't know Lor," Franklin said. "So I can't say. Is this something Arman said?"

"Yeah. It's what he thinks." The darkness outside our bedroom window seemed vast. There were rats that lived in the palm trees, I knew, that could jump like miniature kangaroos. I pictured hundreds of rats leaping about in the darkness in multiple chaotic directions. "What if I didn't really know her? What if all those years I just saw what I expected to see, what I wanted to see?"

"You did," he said. "You knew her."

"Can anyone know anyone? Do you know me?"

"If I don't," Franklin said, rolling on top of me, "then I will devote the rest of my life to trying to know you."

"And what if you never succeed?" I said.

"I still won't ever stop trying," Franklin said, looking down into my face, close up.

"What if I give you to the demons? The way Inanna betrayed Dumuzi?"

"I'll come back."

"Even from death?"

Franklin nodded, dragged a kiss across my cheek. "Even from death."

The next morning, bleary eyed and putting coffee on to brew, with Grant clinging to my pajamaed leg, I discovered that every apple in the bag of apples had a single bite taken out of it. I held up the bag.

"Grant, did you do this?"

"Oh yeah!" he said happily.

When, how had he done this? I had just bought the apples the day before, and somehow, during the course of the afternoon, he had snuck in here, most likely multiple times, without being seen, taken a bite of each apple, and then replaced it neatly in the bag. He had even retied the twist tie.

"Why?" I asked.

"I don't know," he said, giggling.

It occurred to me that I knew Grant as little as I knew anyone and that this did not bother me at all. No, instead I found the unendingness of his strangeness to be a great comfort. There would always be more Grant to get to know. It was the greatest joy on earth, getting to know him.

Later I wrote to Lorrie Ann at MistressOCatsBaby@yahoo.com:

Lolola,

Probably you don't even get these e-mails I send, but I can't seem to stop. I had coffee with Arman. He thinks your father was raping you. Is that why your brother slept on the balcony? Is that why everything turned out so shitty? Is that why your mother filled the house with watchful, silent gnomes? Was everything secretly part of a nightmare and I just didn't know it?

Every time I think about you, you seem different. You're like some goddamn infinite prism. Lots of times it seems like the tragedy of your life was Jim or being so broke, or, according to Arman, your getting raped by your father. But today it seems to me that the real tragedy must have been loving Zach.

You must have loved him so much, and he could never talk back to you. He could never tell you what it was to be Zach. He could never tell you he loved you too. He could only look at you through the mask of his face, his eyes dulled with pain. How much did he understand? I think about you feeding him through that horrifying feeding tube. I think about the endless surgeries, the recoveries on nothing but Tylenol. I think about the years and years you spent holding him, trying to ease his pain with just your touch. Trying to make him know that he was loved and safe, though you couldn't keep him safe no matter how much you loved him. As a mother myself now, I cannot imagine the agony you went through. It seems to me this morning to be as large a human achievement as Christ on the cross. They say he paid for our sins. Isn't that a funny idea? A spiritual line of credit.

I used to think that somehow there was a set amount of shitty-ness that just had to happen to people, and that normally it got fairly equally distributed, but somehow you rigged things so that you got my share. Horrible things you didn't deserve kept happening to you, and good things that I didn't deserve in a million years kept happening to me. I wished I could switch places with you, or else teach you the endless mental rituals I did to keep bad luck at bay. I think on some level that I really believed that obsessively thinking I didn't deserve my good fortune was what kept the good luck coming.

How insane! You were right: we don't deserve the spring, and we don't deserve the winter either. They just exist. I wish I could have been a better friend to you. The idea that even when we were girls I couldn't see you for who you were, but was blinded by the idea of you, so that I didn't notice what was happening to you, if indeed Terry was messing with you—this idea breaks my fucking heart.

I'm so sorry.

Where are you?

Your friend,

Mia

CHAPTER NINETEEN

Must Come Down

A month later, she wrote back:

> Mia,
>   *I hardly ever check this account, and now I'm sorry I did. You seem to still believe that my life is all about you. You wonder about my bad luck? Is it punishment for some sin I committed? Or is God testing me? Does he deal me the shitty hand because he knows I can take it? Or even, unfathomably, is it somehow your fault that I have bad luck? You ask: Was your father raping you? But you ask this because you believe it will tell you something about yourself.*
>   *As you know, my life is my own.*
>   *Sincerely,*
>   *Lolola*

I was so stung by this that I did not know how to respond. I had thought that my last letter to her had been full of love. I wasn't expecting her to be angry with me. I quickly went back and reread my letter. There had been a careless presumptuousness in the tone, it was true, that was caused by the fact I didn't actually think she would ever receive it. My letter had suffered from the same self-conscious readerlessness of a diary entry, that performed quality.

Still, it didn't seem like there was really anything in the letter itself that was so terrible. "My life is my own," she had said. Did she think I was trying to make her life my life? Had I? Was I really this horrible, life-sucking little gremlin that went around using other people as reflecting ponds so that I could admire myself? To think so was like the fulfillment of all my worst fears.

And yet, I could also imagine a reality in which Lor was forced to build the same kind of wall against me that she had built against Zach. Wasn't that why she really hated me? Because I had dared to say it? You need to go home.

You need to go home and see your boy.

And she hadn't. Instead, she had stolen my tea set and disappeared.

She was obviously telling me to mind my own business, and yet, I found I couldn't.

Dana was surprised, but not unhappy, to hear from me. One Sunday, we arranged to meet at the Coco's that had miraculously survived the changes in Corona del Mar, right on the corner of Narcissus and PCH. I remembered being a kid and going with my mom and Paddy and Max and Alex to that Coco's. I always ordered the spaghetti. The inside had been completely redone, and very large murals of baked goods together with the obviously oversize booths and dinner chairs, which made the patrons look like children sitting in adult furniture, gave the inside a vaguely hallucinatory feel. Dana was already seated at a table toward the back and she waved to me across the room.

As soon as I saw her, I realized I had been thinking of her all wrong. When Lor had told me the stories of her life, about Zach and the Native Americans and Dunny, I had been picturing the Dana I had known when we were young: the navy blue eyeliner, the frizzy brown hair, the premature wrinkles. But something miraculous had happened to Dana.

Gone was the blue eyeliner. In fact, I don't think she was wearing any makeup at all, and yet her face glowed with health and her skin was bright and soft looking. As she had aged, her cheekbones, which had always been high, became even more exaggerated, as had the heavy hoods of her eyelids. Her hair had turned entirely white, and she wore it down and loose around her shoulders. She was wearing a simple cream-colored tunic sweater, and, I saw when she stood up to greet me, tan leggings and beaded moccasins. She wore no earrings, no wedding ring, no jewelry of any kind. As we sat again, she beamed at me with a smile bordering on the beatific.

"So good to see you, Mia," she said, in a voice much softer than I remembered. "You look beautiful!"

Had Dana become some kind of saint? Or was this the relaxed serenity of the truly insane? "Thank you," I said. "So do you—your hair! I love it."

She reached up shyly to touch her hair, then leaned in and half whispered, "I love it too! My mother's was white. I never thought mine would turn, but then it did." She shrugged, smiled.

We ordered. Both of us got the spinach omelet, and for quite a while Dana kept me busy answering questions about myself: my career, Franklin, Grant. I didn't know how to ask about Lor. I guess I assumed that probably Dana had heard as little from Lor as I had. Instead, I asked about Dana's life. As it turned out, she had continued to be friends with Dunny and together the two of them had started a support group for parents of severely disabled children. She also volunteered two days a week at the library and had started a children's program called Native World where they learned about the native peoples, plants, and animals of California. She and Dunny both visited Zach in the nursing home, usually twice a week.

She certainly did not seem psychotic. Could she possibly still be receiving disability from the state? It was not the kind of thing I felt comfortable asking about, and so I didn't, though I did feel better that at least someone had been visiting Zach. At least he hadn't been all alone. Dana transitioned to talking about Lor so breezily that I didn't hear her for a moment and then suddenly came up short.

"And Lor's doing well," she said, "with that band of hers. I'm sure she sent you their first album. Joachim is doing good too. I think she's finally really and truly happy, you know, which she deserves."

"What?" I sputtered.

"After all those years," Dana said, "although Jim was a saint, and I always thought Arman was a good boy too."

"She has a band?"

"Yes," Dana said, clearly confused. "You didn't know?"

"No. No, I haven't heard from her except one e-mail in the last three years. And she didn't say anything about a band."

"Well"—Dana laughed—"it's not like you would hear them on the radio or anything."

"Is she clean?" I asked.

"Oh, she's been clean for ages now. That was just a phase." Dana waved her hand dismissively, as though Lor had never even had a serious problem with drugs.

"Where is she living?" I asked.

"Iceland. She and Joachim travel around Europe with the band, but Iceland is their home base."

"Joachim?"

"Her boyfriend," she said. "A really wonderful man. Very tall."

"Did you fly to see them?" I asked. "Did you visit them in Iceland?"

"No, not yet!" Dana said. "Though I keep threatening to."

But she had said he was tall. Why would it occur to her to say that unless she had met him in person? Which meant that they must have come here, come back to California.

"When's the last time they were out here?" I asked.

"Christmas," Dana said. "They came out for a couple weeks. I guess they are doing quite well, so they came and visited and then took me and Dunny to Hawaii!"

"That's wonderful!" I said, eyeing the glistening painting of a giant croissant behind her. It must have been nearly five feet tall. A painting of a croissant nearly as tall as myself. I felt dizzy. So Lor had come home after all. "I'm so glad she's doing so well," I said. "So she's singing?"

"Yeah, she's singing. Terry would have been so proud. Just so proud. I wish he were alive to see her."

It suddenly seemed improbable that Terry had molested Lor. In fact, I was mortified that I had even written her with the question. And yet, what else explained it?

"I had no idea," I said, trying to find something to say. "I talked to Arman a few months ago, but I guess he hadn't heard from her either."

"That boy is such a sweetheart," she said, which I found to be a deeply odd characterization of Arman.

"What's the name of the band?" I asked.

"Amor Fati," she said. "Which means—well, I forget what it means. She explained it all to me, but I can't remember it. I'm sure you can look it up or she'll explain it or whatever."

Amor Fati. Iceland. Joachim. Suddenly, Lor was thrust right back into her old role in my life: the goddess, impossibly, untouchably beautiful and perfect. She was a fucking musician in fucking Iceland. Her hardships had been revealed, in the end, to be an illusion, a mistake, just a phase that added to her allure. There had never been any danger, just as Cinderella had never been in danger of remaining a maid forever.

"I know what it means," I said, though there was a frog in my throat and the words were muddled.

"What?"

"I know what *amor fati* means," I said.

Do we deserve the spring? Lor had asked. And I had thought that maybe I had finally caught up to Lor, understood her insight. But I didn't. I still wanted there to be some connection between what we did and what we got. Just as I didn't believe she deserved the horrors of Zach's birth, or the hardships of Jim's death, I did not believe that she now deserved to be a successful musician in Iceland with a boyfriend named Joachim. I did not believe she deserved to go on vacation in Hawaii while Zach languished in a nursing home. Was he nothing to her? Could it really be okay to walk away from that kind of love, from that kind of belonging? Was there no punishing God to call bullshit?

It also suddenly seemed clear that Lorrie Ann had never loved me the way that I loved her. I had assumed that she had stayed away from me out of shame: she knew that I disapproved of the drugs, of the lifestyle, and so she stayed away. The idea that she was clean, that she was happy, that she was in love, that she was singing, and she did not want to talk to me, did not want to tell me her good news, did not want me to hear her music—well, it made me feel like an idiot for loving her. For thinking of her. For allowing her life to live inside my own like a ghost. She had come to California and she hadn't even called me.

I replayed over and over again in my mind the moment we met at the Grand Bazaar in Istanbul. I had thought she called me at the time because she wanted to see me, needed me in her distress, but now I wondered if she hadn't called me because she simply had no other choice. Perhaps she dreaded seeing me. Perhaps all night she had been planning only to borrow money and then disappear.

And then to take the tea set! Why take the fucking tea set?!

It wasn't even clear, I realized, that Lorrie Ann was actually as happy as Dana said she was. Dana insisted that Jim was a saint, that Arman was a sweetheart. Maybe she had a permanent case of rose-colored glasses. How would Dana know if Lor was clean anyway?

And how big a deal was this band? Had they just made a CD on a four-track in their apartment, or were they actually signed by a real record label? And even if they were signed by a label, how hard could it be to get signed in a country the size of Iceland? It could easily be that Lor and her junkie boyfriend Joachim played once a week at a dive bar in Reykjavík and just made a big deal of it to Dana to make her feel better.

What wouldn't we say to make our mothers feel better at this late date?

By the time Franklin came home that afternoon with Grant, I had downloaded and listened to both of Amor Fati's albums. They were available on iTunes. The second album was better than the first, but they were both pretty good. I felt frantic and angry and sad, all at once. The records were by a real label. Amor Fati even had a website, a good one. They had tour dates posted. She was legit.

"Lorrie Ann's a rock star," I said, once Franklin had gotten himself a beer and settled down to watch football.

"Oh dear," he said.

"I mean—a rock star! Really? A rock star?"

"She's not a rock star," Franklin said. "Right? I mean, she's in a band or something?"

"Look at this," I said, and I loaded one of their videos on YouTube and played it for him. It was a live performance in a huge, rolling field in Iceland. Lor was wearing a cream-colored, raw-silk dress, and was balanced on a stool with her guitar, which seemed giant, big as a boat compared to her, hugged to her chest. She sang with her eyes closed. The whole song, her eyes were closed. In one of the close-ups, I could see she still bit her nails. There were thousands of fans. They filled the entire valley, swaying, rapt, as she sang.

"Yeah," Franklin said. "Okay, so she's a rock star."

"I know that I should just be happy for her." Grant could sense my restlessness and kept trying to give me Clown Puppy, a horrifying dog-doll in blackface makeup, or what I argued was blackface, who lit up and told the names of red, blue, and yellow in three languages.

"I don't want Clown Puppy," I said.

"So, is Zach still alive?" Franklin asked.

"Yeah, and Dana and Dunny visit him."

"Well, that's good."

"I agree," I said, "but she's coming back here. She's visiting California! She took Dana and Dunny to Hawaii! What happened to the wall she built that was keeping her from thinking about Zach and making it impossible for her to ever return to the land of our girlhood or whatever that line of bullshit was?"

"I don't know. I don't know how she's justifying it." Franklin shrugged. "But I will say this, however it's working, however she's doing it, I doubt it's good. Like spiritually, internally good."

"So . . . ?"

"So what?"

"What do I do?" I asked.

"Here, Daddy," Grant said, handing him a little plastic truck. Franklin accepted it wordlessly.

"Well," Franklin said to me, "what can you do? You can't make her be what she doesn't want to be. She wants to be a musician. Fine, she's a musician. In fact, it seems like a kind of best-case scenario, really. Now all her tortured-ness has a purpose. She can be all weird and emo onstage."

"This isn't a joke," I said.

"I know—I know," Franklin said. "But, in all seriousness, how do you think people get to be musicians in the first place? Maybe that's how it works—they make an increasingly devastating series of life decisions, and then some kind of crystallization process takes place, and they wind up suited to it."

It actually wasn't a bad hypothesis. "I don't know," I said. "I don't want to keep thinking about it. Let's just have a good Sunday."

Dana was happy to give me the name and the address of the nursing home where Zach wound up. "He loves visitors," she said.

She didn't ask me why I was going. She didn't act like it was surprising at all. I had worried she would ask, and I couldn't imagine what I would say. The best articulation I could give, really, was what Lor herself had said: it was the only thing left to do.

I found a washed-up looking man with shoulder-length hair in a very worn gray suit, kneeling and praying softly by Zach's bedside. He startled when he noticed I had entered the room and wrapped up his prayers quickly.

"Please God," he said softly, "expel the devil from his body. Untwist his limbs from the evil demons that strangle them. Let him be filled with light and peace. Amen." His voice was throaty and hoarse.

He looked at me furtively as he left the room, and his eyes were a startling and possibly drunken turquoise against the red of his sun-burned face. He looked insane. Was he possibly homeless? Some sort of wandering, homeless preacher? And yet he seemed harmless. How could his strange prayers harm anyone?

I stepped up to Zach's bed. I had calculated in my mind: he was almost thirteen. He was still painfully thin, and he seemed scrunched down in his bed so it was difficult to get a sense of his full height. His eyes were open and he was looking at me. It was not difficult to imagine that demons were the ones who had done this to him. But really, I thought, remembering Lor, it was doctors who had done this.

"Hi. I don't know if you remember me," I said. "I was a friend of your mother's."

He looked so much like Lorrie Ann that it took my breath away. He even had that light dusting of halftone freckles across his upturned nose, the narrow jaw that turned his face into a heart. The expression in his eyes changed, as though he recognized me or had heard what I said.

"Your mom?" I said.

He turned his face away from me.

"Your mom misses you so much," I said, though I did not know why I was saying this to him or whether it was the truth.

He gave a garbled yell and kept his face rigidly turned toward the wall.

"You don't want to talk about her?" I asked. I felt like I had been kicked in the gut. All this time and I had never once wondered what Zach thought of Lor. If she had returned, it would have been to a son who hated her, who would possibly never forgive her.

"I won't talk about her," I said. "I promise."

He turned back to me, appraising, perhaps curious why I was there if not to torture him with memories of his mother.

"I would like to be your friend," I said.

Silence as he regarded me.

"I would like to come here and sit with you and get to know you. Maybe once a week. Would that be okay?"

Suddenly, his face broke open into what was unmistakably a grin, a wild, asymmetrical grin. He gave a happy sound that I instantly translated as a giggle.

"Do you still like dancing?" I asked.

Zach and I cobbled together some moments of communication that morning, and I danced shamelessly to some early Michael Jackson that I played off the tiny speaker on my iPhone. I also read him a Babar book that was sitting by the side of his bed. I wondered, then, might Zach find Babar a little boring by now?

I asked him this and he shouted something I interpreted as a yes. I told him that I would bring him a book for bigger boys called *The Hobbit*. He looked at me with weird concentration, like he was trying to poop, and suddenly I realized that he was slowly, meticulously nodding. It took everything he had to repeat such a small motion, but he was trying in order to show me he liked the idea. "It's a really good book," I gushed. "You'll like it."

At one point a nurse came in, who was quite bright and cheery, and invited me to step into the hall while she changed Zach, and I did, in case Zach had modesty about his privates, but I spied on her from the door. She treated him gently and with respect. There was no rash on Zach's narrow buttocks. I was unable to understand what about this place was so terrible that Lor had been forced to flee.

Mostly we just sat together, sharing the morning sunlight that fell into his room and spilled across the floor as though to show off its abundance. Outside we could see a single palm tree that had been bent slightly by some storm or other. There was a blurry, human Zen to spending time with Zach, an honesty built from his inability to speak at all.

"I think you're brave," I said to him after a long silence.

Zach made a motion that was very much like a shrug.

Suddenly, I saw, behind a picture frame on Zach's dresser, a little yellow teapot. I stood up, and approached it slowly, as though it were a rabbit that would run from me. It was from the very same set that I had bought Bensu: I recognized the cunning little golden triangles against the bright yellow ceramic. Why would she give the tea set to Zach?

The moment I picked it up, he started screaming. A nurse ran in. "Oh," she said, "please put it down. That is a special gift from his mother. She sent it in the mail. So sad. He broke all the other pieces so we keep that one piece for him and do not let him hold it."

I set it down and Zach stopped yelling. He was panting, breathless, glaring at me. At first I thought he didn't want me to touch it, this special relic from his mother. "Please don't touch," the nurse said, before leaving us alone again. Zach did not stop staring at me, did not even blink. I picked up the teapot, and he watched me.

I slowly walked it over to him and set it in his open hand. His fingers clenched around it so hard he almost dropped it, but I pushed it back into his hand. His movements were both clumsy and weirdly precise, and it reminded me of the frustration of playing one of those claw games where you try to grab the toy. I watched as he pulled the little teapot behind his head, then jerked his elbow down, hurling it at the wall, where it broke into shards of yellow, scattered on the floor.

"Whoops," I said, and I swear to God he laughed.

I wanted badly to ask him about his mother, to try to understand her through his eyes, to achieve some kind of parallax, but I had promised him, I had said that I wouldn't talk about her.

And really, I thought, there wasn't anything left to say.

As I drove home that day, I felt excited. A new part of my life was beginning, here, nestled in the coves of the Pacific. If I had been so blinded by the idea of Lorrie Ann that I failed to see who she actually was, I had been just as blinded by who I thought I was. I didn't need any longer to be the bad one, the sexy one, the wicked one. Or even the smart one, the good one, the pretty one. Instead, I was a young mother, and hardly anyone gave two shits what I did or who I was. I was absolutely free. Free to make friends with a boy who could not speak. Free to drive along PCH thinking nothing at all. Free to cut my hair off. Free to love my husband, who was lettuce planted by the water. Free to collect gnomes. Free to encode my children with whatever values and worldviews I chose. Free to say whatever I was thinking. Free to be happy without reason. Free to trust I would be loved. But mostly, free to love.

When Zach died that winter of pneumonia, Lor did not come to the funeral. Dana tried lamely to excuse her, saying, "They're on tour and they just can't cancel the Berlin dates. They can't. She was so sad she couldn't come."

"Um hmm," I said, nodding.

"So sad," Dana repeated.

I smiled at her, touched her shoulder through the thick, black cable-knit of her sweater. "But we're here," I said. "It's a good funeral, Dana. You did such a nice job planning it out."

"Thank you," she said, nodding, tucking that gleaming white hair behind her pink little ears. Zach had been cremated, and Dana had hired a boat to take a small group of us out far enough from shore that we would be allowed to dump the remains. On board were myself, Franklin, and Grant; Dunny and Dunny's girlfriend, a horsey-faced, good-natured woman, tall and built like a string bean; then Dana and Bobby.

As we rode out past the waves, our little yacht, sweetly called *The Quiet Place,* jogged up and down with the swells. It was cold, but Franklin and Grant stayed on the aft deck with me, while most of the group huddled inside the main cabin with its long, cream leather couches. I felt happy for Zach that he had died and gotten free of his body. I did not worry about him at all, but I did get weird prickles of sadness that we hadn't gotten to finish the whole trilogy, but had stopped halfway through *The Two Towers.* He had loved the books so much, it seemed a shame that he didn't get to find out how they ended.

As we rode, our faces pressed into the wind, I mostly thought of Lorrie Ann. Against my will, I missed her. I hoped she had let go of trying to be the good one, the untouchable one, the goddess, just as much as I had stopped trying to make her be that. I hoped she could feel my love, somehow, just as Grant and Franklin and I could feel the sun on our faces, despite the wind.

A Note About Inanna

While Mia and Lorrie Ann are entirely fictional, the Sumerian poetry about the goddess Inanna is very real. To find out more about the true story of how Inanna was translated and to read the full version of the poems quoted in this book, please refer to *Inanna, Queen of Heaven and Earth: Her Stories and Hymns from Sumer* by Diane Wolkstein and Samuel Noah Kramer. It is an incredible volume, and I would not have written this book if not for that translation, which ensnared my mind and made me fall in love with Inanna in all her ancient strangeness.

Acknowledgments

Thank you to the brilliant Molly Friedrich, for being crazy enough to agree to read my novel in the first place and for making this book what it is today, teaching me about novel writing, motherhood, and friendship in the process. Thank you too to my editor, Jennifer Jackson, who always knows better than me, but never forces me to be aware of this, and whose grace, strength, and insight are an inspiration. Thank you to my readers: Lucy Carson, Matthew Ducker, Simone Gorrindo, David Isaak, Joe Kertes, Nichole LeFebvre, and Molly Schulman. Thanks to Erinn Hartman and to all the people at Knopf who have made this process like a dream. Thank you to my husband, Sam, who is my lettuce planted by the water, my reader when the ink on the pages isn't even dry, my best friend and co-creator of weird kitchen dance moves, the love of my life, my lion, my Dumuzi. But the biggest thank-you of all these goes to my mother, Kimberly, who bought me the chance to be a writer with her blood and sweat, who believed in me so much she tricked me into believing too. You taught me what love was and how to live a life that honored truth and beauty. You taught me tenacity and laughter. When I was a little girl, I believed you were the most beautiful woman who had ever lived, and I still think that today. Thank you for all of this, for everything you gave me.

A Note About the Author

Rufi Thorpe received her MFA from the University of Virginia in 2009. Currently, she lives in Washington, D.C., with her husband and son. *The Girls from Corona del Mar* is her first novel.

A NOTE ON THE TYPE

The type used in this book was designed by Pierre Simon Fournier *le jeune* (1712–1768). In his *Manuel typographique,* Fournier introduced the point system by which type is still measured.

Composed by North Market Street Graphics,
Lancaster, Pennsylvania

Designed by M. Kristen Bearse